THE CRIMSON BLIND

and Other Stories

D1585682

THE CRIMSON BLIND

and Other Stories

H. D. Everett

WORDSWORTH EDITIONS

In loving memory of
MICHAEL TRAYLER
the founder of Wordsworth Editions

1

Readers who are interested in other titles from
Wordsworth Editions are invited to visit our website at
www.wordsworth-editions.com

For our latest list and a full mail-order service contact
Bibliophile Books, 5 Thomas Road, London E14 7BN
Tel: +44 0207 515 9222 Fax: +44 0207 538 4115
e-mail: orders@bibliophilebooks.com

This edition published 2006 by
Wordsworth Editions Limited
8B East Street, Ware, Hertfordshire SG12 9HJ

ISBN 1 84022 538 6

Typeset in Great Britain by Antony Gray
Printed by Clays Ltd, St Ives plc

CONTENTS

THE CRIMSON BLIND
and Other Stories

The Death Mask

'Yes, that is a portrait of my wife. It is considered to be a good likeness. But of course she was older-looking towards the last.'

Enderby and I were on our way to the smoking-room after dinner, and the picture hung on the staircase. We had been chums at school a quarter of a century ago, and later on, at college; but I had spent the last decade out of England. I returned to find my friend a widower of four years' standing. And a good job too, I thought to myself when I heard of it, for I had no great liking for the late Gloriana. Probably the sentiment, or want of sentiment, had been mutual: she did not smile on me, but I doubt if she smiled on any of poor Tom Enderby's bachelor cronies. The picture was certainly like her. She was a fine woman, with aquiline features and a cold eye. The artist had done the features justice – and the eye, which seemed to keep a steely watch on all the comings and goings of the house out of which she had died.

We made only a brief pause before the portrait, and then went on. The smoking-room was an apartment built out at the back of the house by a former owner, and shut off by double doors to serve as a nursery. Mrs Enderby had no family, and she disliked the smell of tobacco. So the big room was made over to Tom's pipes and cigars; and if Tom's friends wanted to smoke, they must smoke there or not at all. I remembered the room and the rule, but I was not prepared to find it still existing. I had expected to light my after dinner cigar over the dessert dishes, now there was no presiding lady to consider.

We were soon installed in a couple of deep-cushioned chairs before a good fire. I thought Enderby breathed more freely when he closed the double doors behind us, shutting off the dull formal house, and the staircase and the picture. But he was not looking well; there hung about him an unmistakable air of depression. Could he be fretting after Gloriana? Perhaps during their married years, he had fallen into the way of depending on a woman to care for him. It is pleasant enough when the woman is the right sort; but I shouldn't myself have fancied being cared for by the late Mrs Enderby. And, if the fretting was a fact, it would be easy to find a remedy. Evelyn has a couple of pretty sisters, and we would have him over to stay at our place.

'You must run down and see us,' I said presently, pursuing this idea. 'I want to introduce you to my wife. Can you come next week?'

His face lit up with real pleasure.

'I should like it of all things,' he said heartily. But a qualification came after. The cloud settled back over him and he sighed. 'That is, if I can get away.'

'Why, what is to hinder you?'

'It may not seem much to stay for, but I – I have got in the way of stopping here – to keep things together.' He did not look at me, but leaned over to the fender to knock the ash off his cigar.

'Tell you what, Tom, you are getting hipped living by yourself. Why don't you sell the house, or let it off just as it is, and try a complete change?'

'I can't sell it. I'm only the tenant for life. It was my wife's.'

'Well, I suppose there is nothing to prevent you letting it? Or if you can't let it, you might shut it up.'

'There is nothing *legal* to prevent me – !' The emphasis was too fine to attract notice, but I remembered it after.

'Then, my dear fellow, why not? Knock about a bit, and see the world. But, to my thinking, the best thing you could do would be to marry again.'

He shook his head drearily.

'Of course it is a delicate matter to urge upon a widower. But you have paid the utmost ceremonial respect. Four years, you know. The greatest stickler for propriety would deem it ample.'

'It isn't that. Dick, I – I've a great mind to tell you rather a queer story.' He puffed hard at his smoke, and stared into the red coals in the pauses. 'But I don't know what you'd think of it. Or think of me.'

'Try me,' I said. 'I'll give you my opinion after. And you know I'm safe to confide in.'

'I sometimes think I should feel better if I told it. It's – it's queer enough to be laughable. But it hasn't been any laughing-matter to me.'

He threw the stump of his cigar into the fire, and turned to me. And then I saw how pale he was, and that a dew of perspiration was breaking out on his white face.

'I was very much of your opinion, Dick: I thought I should be happier if I married again. And I went so far as to get engaged. But the engagement was broken off, and I am going to tell you why.

'My wife was some time ailing before she died, and the doctors were in consultation. But I did not know how serious her complaint was till the last. Then they told me there was no hope, as coma had set in. But it was possible, even probable, that there would be a revival of consciousness before death, and for this I was to hold myself ready.

'I dare say you will write me down a coward, but I dreaded the revival: I was ready to pray that she might pass away in her sleep. I knew she held exalted views about the marriage tie, and I felt sure if there were any last words she would exact a pledge.

'I could not at such a moment refuse to promise, and I did not want to be tied. You will recollect that she was my senior. I was about to be left a widower in middle life, and in the natural course of things I had a good many years before me. You see?'

'My dear fellow, I don't think a promise so extorted ought to bind you. It isn't fair!'

'Wait and hear me. I was sitting here, miserable enough, as you may suppose, when the doctor came to fetch me to her room. Mrs Enderby was conscious and had asked for me, but he particularly begged me not to agitate her in any way, lest pain should return. She was lying stretched out in the bed, looking already like a corpse.

' "Tom," she said, "they tell me I am dying, and there is something I want you to – promise."

'I groaned in spirit. It was all up with me, I thought. But she went on. "When I am dead and in my coffin, I want you to cover my face with your own hands. Promise me this."

'It was not in the very least what I expected. Of course I promised.

' "I want you to cover my face with a particular handkerchief on which I set a value. When the time comes, open the cabinet to the right of the window, and you will find it in the third drawer from the top. You cannot mistake it, for it is the only thing in the drawer."

'That was every word she said, if you believe me, Dick. She just sighed and shut her eyes as if she was going to sleep, and she never spoke again. Three or four days later they came again to ask me if I wished to take a last look, as the undertaker's men were about to close the coffin.

'I felt a great reluctance, but it was necessary I should go. She looked as if made of wax, and was colder than ice to touch. I opened the cabinet, and there, just as she said, was a large handkerchief of very fine cambric, lying by itself. It was embroidered with a mono-gram device in all four corners, and was not of a sort I had ever seen her use. I spread it out and laid it over the dead face; and then what happened was rather curious. It seemed to draw down over the features and cling to them, to nose and mouth and forehead and the shut eyes, till it became a perfect mask. My nerves were shaken, I suppose; I was seized with horror, and flung back the covering sheet, hastily quitting the room. And the coffin was closed that night.

'Well, she was buried, and I put up a monument which the neigh-bourhood considered handsome. As you see, I was bound by no pledge to abstain from marriage; and, though I knew what would have been her wish, I saw no reason why I should regard it. And, some months after, a family of the name of Ashcroft came to live at The Leasowes, and they had a pretty daughter.

'I took a fancy to Lucy Ashcroft the first time I saw her, and it was soon apparent that she was well inclined to me. She was a gentle, yielding little thing; not the superior style of woman. Not at all like – '

(I made no comment, but I could well understand that in his new matrimonial venture Tom would prefer a contrast.)

' – but I thought I had a very good chance of happiness with her; and I grew fond of her: very fond of her indeed. Her people were of the hospitable sort, and they encouraged me to go to The Leasowes, dropping in when I felt inclined: it did not seem as if they would be likely to put obstacles in our way. Matters progressed, and I made up my mind one evening to walk over there and declare myself. I had been up to town the day before, and came back with a ring in my pocket: rather a fanciful design of double hearts, but I thought Lucy would think it pretty, and would let me put it on her finger. I went up to change into dinner things, making myself as spruce as possible, and coming to the conclusion before the glass that I was not such a bad figure of a man after all, and that there was not much grey in my hair. Ay, Dick, you may smile: it is a good bit greyer now.

'I had taken out a clean handkerchief, and thrown the one carried through the day crumpled on the floor. I don't know what made me turn to look there, but, once it caught my eye, I stood staring at it as if spellbound. The handkerchief was moving – Dick, I swear it – rapidly altering in shape, puffing up here and there as if blown by wind, spreading and moulding itself into the features of a face. And what face should it be but the death-mask of Gloriana, which I had covered in the coffin eleven months before!

'To say I was horror-stricken conveys little of the feeling that possessed me. I snatched up the rag of cambric and flung it on the fire, and it was nothing but a rag in my hand, and in another moment no more than blackened tinder on the bar of the grate. There was no face below.'

'Of course not,' I said. 'It was a mere hallucination. You were cheated by an excited fancy.'

'You may be sure I told myself all that, and more; and I went downstairs and tried to pull myself together with a dram. But I was curiously upset, and, for that night at least, I found it impossible to play the wooer. The recollection of the death-mask was too vivid; it would have come between me and Lucy's lips.

'The effect wore off, however. In a day or two I was bold again, and as much disposed to smile at my folly as you are at this moment. I proposed, and Lucy accepted me; and I put on the ring. Ashcroft *père* was graciously pleased to approve of the settlements I offered, and Ashcroft *mère* promised to regard me as a son. And during the first forty-eight hours of our engagement, there was not a cloud to mar the blue.

'I proposed on a Monday, and on Wednesday I went again to dine and spend the evening with just their family party. Lucy and I found our way afterwards into the back drawing-room, which seemed to be made over to us by tacit understanding. Anyway, we had it to ourselves; and as Lucy sat on the settee, busy with her work, I was privileged to sit beside her, close enough to watch the careful stitches she was setting, under which the pattern grew.

'She was embroidering a square of fine linen to serve as a tea-cloth, and it was intended for a present to a friend; she was anxious, she told me, to finish it in the next few days, ready for despatch. But I was somewhat impatient of her engrossment in the work; I wanted her to look at me while we talked, and to be permitted to hold her hand. I was making plans for a tour we would take together after Easter; arguing that eight weeks spent in preparation was enough for any reasonable bride. Lucy was easily entreated; she laid aside the linen square on the table at her elbow. I held her fingers captive, but her eyes wandered from my face, as she was still deliciously shy.

'All at once she exclaimed. Her work was moving, there was growing to be a face in it: did I not see?

'I saw, indeed. It was the Gloriana death-mask, forming there as it had formed in my handkerchief at home: the marked nose and chin, the severe mouth, the mould of forehead, almost complete. I snatched it up and dropped it over the back of the couch. "It did look like a face," I allowed. "But never mind it, darling; I want you to attend to me." Something of this sort I said, I hardly know what, for my blood was running cold. Lucy pouted; she wanted to dwell on the marvel, and my impatient action had displeased her. I went on talking wildly, being afraid of pauses, but the psychological moment had gone by. I felt I did not carry her with me as before: she hesitated over my persuasions; the forecast of a Sicilian honeymoon had ceased to charm. By-and-by she suggested that Mrs Ashcroft would expect us to rejoin the circle in the other room. And perhaps I would pick up her work for her – still with a slight air of offence.

'I walked round the settee to recover the luckless piece of linen; but she turned also, looking over the back, so at the same instant we both saw.

'There again was the Face, rigid and severe; and now the corners of the cloth were tucked under, completing the form of the head. And that was not all. Some white drapery had been improvised and extended beyond it on the floor, presenting the complete figure laid out straight and stiff, ready for the grave. Lucy's alarm was excusable. She shrieked aloud, shriek upon shriek, and immediately an indignant family of Ashcrofts rushed in through the half-drawn *portières* which divided the two rooms, demanding the cause of her distress.

'Meanwhile I had fallen upon the puffed-out form, and destroyed it. Lucy's embroidery composed the head; the figure was ingeniously contrived out of a large Turkish bath-sheet, brought in from one of the bedrooms, no-one knew how or when. I held up the things protesting their innocence, while the family were stabbing me through and through with looks of indignation, and Lucy was sobbing in her mother's arms. She might have been foolish, she allowed; it did seem ridiculous now she saw what it was. But at the moment it was too dreadful: it looked so like – so like! And here a fresh sob choked her into silence.

'Peace was restored at last, but plainly the Ashcrofts doubted me. The genial father stiffened, and Mrs Ashcroft administered indirect reproofs. She hated practical joking, so she informed me; she might be wrong, and no doubt she was old-fashioned, but she had been brought up to consider it in the highest degree ill-bred. And perhaps I had not considered how sensitive Lucy was, and how easily alarmed. She hoped I would take warning for the future, and that nothing of this kind would occur again.

'Practical joking – oh, ye gods! As if it was likely that I, alone with
the girl of my heart, would waste the precious hour in building up
effigies of sham corpses on the floor! And Lucy ought to have known
that the accusation was absurd, as I had never for a moment left her
side. She did take my part when more composed; but the mystery
remained, beyond explanation of hers or mine.

'As for the future, I could not think of that without a failing heart.
If the Power arrayed against us were in truth what superstition
feared, I might as well give up hope at once, for I knew there would
be no relenting. I could see the whole absurdity of the thing as well as
you do now; but, if you put yourself in my place, Dick, you will be
forced to confess that it was tragic too.

'I did not see Lucy the next day, as I was bound to go again to
town; but we had planned to meet and ride together on the Friday
morning. I was to be at The Leasowes at a certain hour, and you may
be sure I was punctual. Her horse had already been brought round,
and the groom was leading it up and down. I had hardly dismounted
when she came down the steps of the porch; and I noticed at once a
new look on her face, a harder set about that red mouth of hers which
was so soft and kissable. But she let me put her up on the saddle and
settle her foot in the stirrup, and she was the bearer of a gracious
message from her mother. I was expected to return to lunch, and Mrs
Ashcroft begged us to be punctual, as a friend who had stayed the
night with them, would be leaving immediately after.

' "You will be pleased to meet her, I think," said Lucy, leaning
forward to pat her horse. "I find she knows you very well. It is Miss
Kingsworthy."

'Now Miss Kingsworthy was a school friend of Gloriana's, who
used now and then to visit us here. I was not aware that she and the
Ashcrofts were acquainted; but, as I have said, they had only recently
come into the neighbourhood as tenants of The Leasowes. I had no
opportunity to express pleasure or the reverse, for Lucy was riding
on; and putting her horse to a brisk pace. It was some time before she
drew rein, and again admitted conversation. We were descending a
steep hill, and the groom was following at a discreet distance behind,
far enough to be out of earshot.

'Lucy looked very pretty on horseback; but this is by the way.
The mannish hat suited her, and so did the habit fitting closely to
her shape.

' "Tom," she said; and again I noticed that new hardness in her
face. "Tom, Miss Kingsworthy tells me your wife did not wish you to

marry again, and she made you promise her that you would not. Miss Kingsworthy was quite astonished to hear that you and I were engaged. Is this true?"

'I was able to tell her it was not: that my wife had never asked, and I had never given her, any such pledge. I allowed she disliked second marriages – in certain cases, and perhaps she had made some remark to that effect to Miss Kingsworthy; it was not unlikely. And then I appealed to her. Surely she would not let a mischief-maker's tittle-tattle come between her and me?

'I thought her profile looked less obdurate, but she would not let her eyes meet mine as she answered: "Of course not, if that was all. And I doubt if I would have heeded it, only that it seemed to fit in with – something else. Tom, it was very horrible, what we saw on Wednesday evening. And – and – don't be angry, but I asked Miss Kingsworthy what your wife was like. I did not tell her why I wanted to know."

' "What has that to do with it?" I demanded – stoutly enough; but, alas! I was too well aware.

' "She told me Mrs Enderby was handsome, but she had very marked features, and was severe-looking when she did not smile. A high forehead, a Roman nose, and a decided chin. Tom, the face in the cloth was just like that. Did you not see?"

'Of course I protested. "My darling, what nonsense! I saw it looked a little like a face, but I pulled it to pieces at once because you were frightened. Why, Lucy, I shall have you turning into a spiritualist if you take up these fancies."

' "No," she said, "I do not want to be anything foolish. I have thought it over, and if it happens only once I have made up my mind to believe it a mistake and to forget. But if it comes again – if it goes on coming!" Here she shuddered and turned white. "Oh Tom, I could not – I could not!"

'That was the ultimatum. She liked me as much as ever; she even owned to a warmer feeling; but she was not going to marry a haunted man. Well, I suppose I cannot blame her. I might have given the same advice in another fellow's case, though in my own I felt it hard.

'I am close to the end now, so I shall need to tax your patience very little longer. A single chance remained. Gloriana's power, whatever its nature and however derived, might have been so spent in the previous efforts that she could effect no more. I clung to this shred of hope, and did my best to play the part of the light-hearted lover, the sort of companion Lucy expected, who would shape himself to her mood; but I was conscious that I played it ill.

'The ride was a lengthy business. Lucy's horse cast a shoe, and it was impossible to change the saddle on to the groom's hack or my own mare, as neither of them had been trained to the habit. We were bound to return at a foot-pace, and did not reach The Leasowes until two o'clock. Lunch was over: Mrs Ashcroft had set out for the station driving Miss Kingsworthy; but some cutlets were keeping hot for us, so we were informed, and could be served immediately.

'We went at once into the dining-room, as Lucy was hungry; and she took off her hat and laid it on a side-table: she said the close fit of it made her head ache. The cutlets had been misrepresented: they were lukewarm; but Lucy made a good meal off them and the fruit-tart which followed, very much at her leisure. Heaven knows I would not have grudged her so much as a mouthful; but that luncheon was an ordeal I cannot readily forget.

'The servant absented himself, having seen us served; and then my troubles began. The tablecloth seemed alive at the corner which was between us; it rose in waves as if puffed up by wind, though the window was fast shut against any wandering airs. I tried to seem unconscious; tried to talk as if no horror of apprehension was filling all my mind, while I was flattening out the bewitched damask with a grasp I hardly dared relax. Lucy rose at last, saying she must change her dress. Occupied with the cloth, it had not occurred to me to look round, or keep watch on what might be going on in another part of the room. The hat on the side-table had been tilted over sideways, and in that position it was made to crown another presentation of the Face. What it was made of this time I cannot say; probably a serviette, as several lay about. The linen material, of whatever sort, was again moulded into the perfect form; but this time the mouth showed humour, and appeared to relax in a grim smile.

'Lucy shrieked, and dropped into my arms in a swoon: a real genuine fainting-fit, out of which she was brought round with difficulty, after I had summoned the help of doctors.

'I hung about miserably till her safety was assured, and then went as miserably home. Next morning I received a cutting little note from my mother-in-law elect, in which she returned the ring, and informed me the engagement must be considered at an end.

'Well, Dick, you know now why I do not marry. And what have you to say?'

Parson Clench

Stoke-St Edith is a small and deeply rural parish, a complete back-water; at least it was so fifteen years ago, and changes move so slowly within its boundaries that I should doubt its being greatly altered, even now. It has been said about the Stoke-St Edith people that they just begin to realise they are born when it is time for them to die, and that it takes at least as long to convince them they are dead. And by the latter proposition hangs a tale.

As sometimes happens, though the case is rare, this retired and unimportant parish has a fatly endowed living, such as was reckoned in former times a suitable provision for younger sons. And some two-and-sixty years before the period of this story, the Albury younger son of that date not being of an age to take orders, the Reverend Augustus Clench was put in to keep the benefice warm for him.

But when the time came for Mr Clench to surrender his cure, the younger son had developed other views, and the warmer was undisturbed. And so the long procession of years went on, and the old gentleman – whom none of us could picture as ever having been young – became more and more autocratic, more deeply conservative, more blind to all advantage in change, even when change was plainly for the better. It seemed to us juniors that he must have been born in a black gown and bands, bald-headed and wearing spectacles – (no doubt the bald head was fact) – and that of all things at Stoke-St Edith he was the least mutable. So it came as a shock to us all, then scattered far and wide, when among the newspaper announcements we read that the Reverend Augustus Clench was no more.

I was not a resident in the parish when the following events took place, but I heard of them from a faithful correspondent, and later supplemented her account by personal enquiry on the spot.

The next presentation to the living was in the gift of the widowed Mrs Albury at the Hall, who had long designed that fat provision for her nephew, the Reverend Basil Deane. He was working as curate in an East London parish, and when Mr Clench's death took place he had his doubts whether he would be justified in exchanging strenuous duty so early in his career, for the soft cushion of rural ease. But it was now or never for his chance in life; his aunt Emmeline, good gentle soul, was a confirmed invalid, and at her death the Albury property, with the presentation right, would pass under her husband's will to a distant cousin, who would have no concern or care for any Deane.

Mr Clench was only just buried when Mrs Albury wrote: 'I want you to come down for this next Sunday and take the services here, as the churchwardens are in a difficulty, and then we can arrange about your succession to the living. You know it is my earnest wish to have you settled at the Rectory. I cannot be thankful enough that I returned from France to be here at this time. I do not generally leave the Riviera so early in the spring, and it really was as if I had been led. But I caught a severe cold on the homeward journey, and am obliged to keep to my own two rooms, which I know you will excuse.'

Mrs Albury used to spend the greater part of the year abroad, and Basil's visits to her had hitherto been paid either at the Riviera villa or in London: he had not seen Stoke-St Edith since his childhood. So he came with only the faintest recollection of what the place was like, and none of the old man it was proposed he should succeed.

He was unable to get away from his London duties till the Saturday, and his first appearance at the village church was shortly before the eleven o'clock service: there was, he had been told, no celebration, as that took place only once a month, and had been held the Sunday before, after the funeral sermon. Basil reflected that he would change all that, but it was too early yet to announce intentions: at the present moment he was called upon to do no more than carry on the services in the well-worn rut of many previous years.

The clerk, an elderly man wedded to Stoke-St Edith ways, awaited him in the vestry ready with instructions, and looking somewhat askance at the coloured stole Basil took out of his vestment bag. 'We aren't used to that sort of thing here,' the official ventured to hint; but Basil proceeded to assume it, despite the disapproval. It was likely to be a lengthy service. The Litany was expected of him, and also the ante-Communion office, but Basil reflected he might shorten his sermon, and took the opportunity to glance at the notes he had prepared. The choir were not surpliced, so he would have to go in alone; a final instruction from Aldridge dictated where he was to read the service.

'When you come to the chancel, sir, you'll see two reading-desks, one on the right hand side and one on the left. 'Twas the one on the left hand the old Rector always used, and that will be your place. We keep the other for a visiting parson when there is one, like as may be a missionary coming to preach for the Gospel in Foreign Parts collection. I think I mentioned there would be no collection today.'

But when Basil marched into church, feebly accompanied by a voluntary on the wheezy old harmonium, he found the desk on the left of the chancel already occupied, so turned into the other. He felt some slight surprise, concluding he had mistaken Aldridge (who was frowning disapproval from one of the back pews at this insubordination on the part of his pupil). And, when the music ceased and he opened his book, he looked across at his *vis-à-vis*.

It was an elderly clergyman who was seated opposite, wearing a black skull-cap to cover his baldness, and spectacles over which a pair of very keen eyes critically regarded the younger man. He did not stand for the opening of the service, so Basil concluded he was infirm as well as aged; as old, or nearly so, as the nonagenarian priest who had officiated there for so many years. Probably he was a retired parson resident in the village, who came in to give assistance in some part of the service – a part he had not yet reached, but Aldridge ought to have told him.

He made a slight pause on arriving at the Lessons, both the first and the second, but the opposite parson did not budge; and again before the Litany, with the same absence of result. He did not rise for either of the Creeds, but was observed distinctly to frown when Basil turned to the East, which doubtless had not been Mr Clench's practice. When it came to sermon time, however, he got up very alertly, and ascended the pulpit stairs just as Basil was approaching them. Then from that elevation he looked back at the younger priest with a distinctly malicious smile.

What was Basil to do? He could not challenge the usurper of his pulpit then and there, or drag him out in the face of the watching congregation and take his place. He went back to the reading-desk as if for a book; and then, the loudly shouted hymn having come to an end, he became aware that the man in the pulpit was not intending to preach, though he occupied the legitimate place of the preacher. There was an awkward – an extremely awkward – pause. Aldridge was fidgeting at the bottom of the church; the sparsely filled aisles displayed a vista of astonished faces. So in desperation Basil came forward to the chancel step, and from there delivered his address.

He had been in priests' orders close upon four years, and during that time had faced many congregations; the nervousness of the raw hand was no longer his, or so he flattered himself. Why should it be harder to speak to these country bumpkins than to the keener people of the towns? But on this occasion his nerve failed him, he stumbled over his words, lost the place in his notes, and recovered the thread of the argument with agonizing difficulty, while a cold perspiration broke out over him, and he turned from red to white, and then to red again. Yet, had he been cool enough to analyse his feelings, he would have discovered the disturbing element emanated from one only among his hearers, the strange old man who had mounted into the pulpit, and who now bent forward over the tasselled cushion, staring him in the face, and smiling with a sort of evil amusement and triumph.

He had intended to shorten his address, and short it was indeed, as he stumbled through it to a premature and pointless close. The blessing followed, the wheezy harmonium struck up with renewed spirit, and as he turned towards the vestry, the old man descended the pulpit stairs as if to follow him thither. But on reaching the door which Aldridge was holding open, there was no-one to be seen.

Aldridge shook his head more in sorrow than in anger, as he prepared to help Basil off with his vestments.

'People here always make such a talk over any little difference. I'm afraid, sir, they won't half like you preaching to them from the floor, when they have been used to take their sermons out of the pulpit. Begging your pardon, sir, have you always been accustomed to preach so?'

'I have often done so,' Basil answered. 'But today, as you would see, I had no choice. Who was the old clergyman who sat on the left side of the chancel, and then went up into the pulpit, though he did not preach? It was impossible for me to ask him to give place.'

'Old clergyman, sir? I didn't see no old clergyman. Where was he, did you say?'

'In the reading-desk when I went in, and he went up before me into the pulpit. Where do you sit in the church, that you did not see?'

'I could have seen right enough anything that was there,' blurted out Aldridge, forgetful of his manners. 'The pulpit was open to you the whole time, and the reading-desk as well, sure as I am here a living man. Begging your pardon, sir, for being positive.' And then the clerk paled from his usually healthy colour, as a strange thought occurred to him. 'Might I ask, sir, what the gentleman you saw was like?'

'An old clergyman in a surplice and a black stole. An Oxford hood he had too, for I saw the crimson silk as he went up the pulpit stairs. He had on a black skull-cap and spectacles, with sharp eyes looking over them. Bushy white eyebrows, and thin bony hands, with the veins standing out on them.'

'The Lord have mercy upon us!' Aldridge was staring with his jaw dropped. 'It was Parson Clench himself, and you not knowing! And him buried a fortnight come Wednesday! Lord save us: what is to be done?'

'Come, come, my good man, this is rank nonsense.' But Basil was dismayed as well as angry, and a horrid creeping shiver about his scalp might verily have raised his hair had it not been so short-cut. 'Mr Clench is dead and buried. It could not have been Mr Clench in church.'

'It would be him if it was anyone at all,' the clerk said doggedly. He was buried in his vestments just as you saw him. I went to the Rectory for a last look before the coffin was closed, so I know. And I dare say you've heard tell how bent he was on preaching to the last, even after he began to fail. He hated letting anyone else up into his pulpit, and he wasn't one to change. I'd lay odds a feeling he had in life wouldn't be so much different now. Heaven itself would have a tough job to alter Parson Clench, where he had set his mind; begging your pardon, sir, for speaking free. But to think of him in the church, and seen by you!'

This was a last mutter, as Basil assumed his coat. He said no more to Aldridge in the way of assertion or contradiction, but he went out of the vestry utterly dazed. The church as he glanced round it was empty, except for a girl sorting music at the harmonium – no doubt the 'organist' who had officiated at that wheezy instrument: she looked completely undisturbed. Had no-one else shared his vision? Basil was of course aware that there were records of such happenings, and that popular interest in them (or curiosity?) had of late years greatly increased; but hitherto he had been indifferent if not sceptical, and utterly unexpectant of any such experience happening to himself. He would fain, even now, have withheld belief, but it was difficult to remain incredulous when he had seen, and had been able minutely to describe, a man who was a stranger to him, with whose appearance in life he was unacquainted, and of whom he had no thought other than indifference in coming to Stoke-St Edith to fill his place.

He returned to the Hall and the waiting luncheon much perturbed in mind. It was easy to face aunt Emmeline and her affectionate interest: what did he think of the church, and was it easy to fill (a matter of voice) – also had he a full congregation, and did they appear attentive and interested? He hated himself for giving such half-hearted replies to her enquiries, and was sensitively aware of her disappointment in them; and yet how could he help it and what could he say, wishing as he did that he had never seen the Stoke-St Edith church, and might never set foot in it again. And a renewal of his ordeal was before him as close at hand as three o'clock, the custom there dictating that the evening service should be read in the afternoon.

Mrs Albury's catechism did not last long on this occasion, as the butler came to say luncheon awaited him in the dining-room; his aunt had her tiny invalid meal served to her upstairs. 'I shall see you again this evening, my dear, and then we will have *a real talk*,' she said as she dismissed him. Alas! a real talk must mean his acceptance of the Stoke-St Edith living, or a confession of the barrier of the ghost.

As he walked across to the church, which was situated at no great distance from the Hall, he reflected that perception of this species of appearance, may happen to a man on some isolated occasion, once in a lifetime, never to be repeated again. He might take the duty at Stoke-St Edith year in and year out, and never again encounter the wraith of the late incumbent, though the fact that he once had done so would be an unforgotten and unforgettable experience. But, despite all reasoning, the ordeal before him made heavy demands upon his courage, and it was a very dour-looking young man who walked into the vestry, and was assisted by Aldridge to robe.

'I can't make out that anybody else saw what you saw, sir, in the church this morning,' that functionary whispered. 'But I've been told since, there's a talk about in the village that the late rector *walks*. There are some who met him in the lane when he was on his death-bed, stricken so that he could not move; and one at least who saw him going by, out of her cottage window, the day after he was buried. People will tell such-like stories as you know, fancies running away with them, and there are few that heed.'

The wheezy harmonium struck up a voluntary, and Basil went on into the church. Approaching the chancel, he saw that both reading-desks were vacant, and he fully purposed to take possession of the left hand one, which was his own. But he found himself powerless to carry intention into action. It was as if he was firmly seized by the shoulders, and pushed into the right-hand seat by a force he could not resist, or was unable to do so without a struggle, which would have been unseemly in the face of the congregation. What Aldridge was thinking in his place at the west end, Basil could only conjecture, but probably his guess only erred by falling short of the fact.

For the first part of the service the left hand reading-desk remained empty, but on returning to his seat after the second Lesson, he found that it was filled by the same appearance as before – the old man in his vestments and skull-cap, peering at him over spectacles with un-friendly and defiant eyes. It was almost a relief when the presence externalised and became visible, instead of being merely felt in every fibre of his bodily frame.

What was to happen when sermon time arrived? The figure opposite made no movement when Basil was about to leave the desk, and yet in a moment, instantaneous as a flash of light, there it stood at the bottom of the pulpit stairs, barring his way, and facing him with a malignant smile.

Basil did not contest the passage. He delivered this second address from the chancel step, and when he turned at the conclusion, the figure had disappeared.

'Did you see him again, sir?' demanded Aldridge, who was waiting in the vestry, and Basil briefly assented: he was in no humour to discuss the marvel a second time, and Aldridge had no fresh explan-ation to advance.

There was nothing for it now but to be candid with aunt Emmeline, and how she would take the communication he dreaded to think: women were always a mass of nerves, especially invalid women. But his aunt was more reasonable than he had ventured to expect, and was ready to respond to his wish that they should keep the matter to themselves.

'I do not want to be labelled as a man with a supernatural extra sense, or to give Stoke-St Edith a bad name. I am afraid the matter may to some extent have gone abroad through Aldridge, but I'll try to see him tomorrow, and give him an injunction not to talk.'

'Yes, my dear,' the aunt acquiesced. 'It was wonderful, of course, that you should see, and be able to describe a perfect stranger. But it may never happen again, to you or to anybody else. And Basil, I hope, I do trust, that this will not set you against accepting the Living. We know it is likely – I suppose it is likely – that the spirits of the dead are about us always: you know it speaks in the Bible of the great cloud of witnesses. So surely we need not take it as extraordinary if we see one of them now and then. And Mr Clench was a good man. He would do nobody any harm.'

His aunt might have thought differently, Basil reflected, had she seen the malignant eyes of the apparition which barred his way.

'If it went on happening, I could not stay here. Better for someone to come who would not see.'

'I don't want you to decide in a hurry; take a week or two to think it over. I will not have you give me a definite answer tonight. Things may look different on reflection. It is such a chance for you, my dear; and it would be so happy for me to know you were here looking after the people, when I am obliged to be so much away. And there is such an excellent rectory-house, quite a country gentleman's place, the best rectory in the county, so they say, and in very good repair. You need not open the whole of it, if you thought it too large for you alone. It could be made so nice. I was not going to tell you just at once, but I have five hundred pounds put aside to help you with the furnishing!'

What was he to say to all this kindness – how was he to repulse the soft entreating hands held out to him full of gifts? It would make no difference, of that he could be certain; but yes, if she wished he would take a longer time to think the matter over, and he would see the Rectory on the following morning, as he need not take train for London till the afternoon. And then he endeavoured to tell her how deeply he felt her kindness, and what a disappointment it would be to him too, so to put the great chance of his life away.

That ended the Sunday evening, and after Monday's breakfast he went across to the Rectory, in fulfilment of the promise given overnight.

The red-brick Georgian mansion, with its stone pediments and cornice, and formal garden-court, was surely an attractive dwelling, cheerful to look at in the Spring sunshine, a home of which any young divine might well be proud. Probably Parson Clench had some such thoughts of it, when he came into possession at Stoke-St Edith two-and-sixty years before. But he would not have had the same shrinking from the habitation in which his predecessor lived and died, that now disquieted Basil Deane.

Mr Clench's housekeeper opened to him. She was staying on as caretaker, so she told him, until Mr Clench's relatives decided what would be done about the sale. Nothing had been disturbed as yet, she was waiting instructions; and it was what the poor old gentleman had wished, that everything should be kept on just the same. He had spoken of it when he was wandering at the last, thinking he had a journey to go, but that he was coming back.

'Yes, sir, they are handsome rooms, both upstairs and down. A fine old house, just right for a family, but rather large and lonesome for one alone. The dining-room is on this side as you see, with a small breakfast-parlour behind, though it never was used for breakfasting, not in my time. Maybe you are the gentleman who is to succeed Mr Clench, and who preached yesterday up at the church?'

Basil told her that he took the services only as a visitor, and that nothing was decided yet about the living: the last not quite the truth, for in his own mind the decision against taking it was already made.

'Most gentlemen admire the staircase, which is oak as you see, and real old. And here is the drawing-room, but not in order, as we put up the bed you see for Mr Clench when he got feeble at the last, and it was here that he died. It was convenient, being next to the study. A fine room the study is, and looks handsome lined with bookcases. It was a lot of books Mr Clench had, and he was that particular over them. We have put a fire in here to keep away the damp, as I know he would have wished.'

She was opening the door as she spoke, and holding it for Basil to enter. Yes, there was fire on the hearth, and in a chair drawn near it was seated an old man, a man in a black cassock and skull-cap, with sharp eyes peering over spectacles: the old man of the church, though the white surplice was no longer worn. And there was the same hostility in the silent gaze which met and held his own. Basil drew back.

'Who is the old gentleman who is using the room?' he asked in a low voice of the housekeeper.

'No-one is using the room, sir. There is nobody in the house but myself.'

'Why there he is, just before you, sitting by the fire.'

The woman looked round in a seared way, and then shut the door again.

'Are you meaning to put a fright upon me, sir?' she said as they stood together in the hall; she seemed both indignant and alarmed.

Basil disclaimed any such intention.

'I am perfectly serious. I would be the last to wish to frighten you. I saw him so plainly sitting there, that I thought you must see him too. An old man in a skull-cap.'

The housekeeper wrung her hands.

'If I was to see him I could not stay here, no, not for double the wage. People in the village make a talk about the old parson walking, but I never heed such tales. I saw him die, and I saw him buried. It is altogether past belief.'

Basil declined to visit the upper floors: what was the use? It should never be his house; upon that he had now unalterably determined. It remained only to break the decision to aunt Emmeline, and then to return to the mill-horse grind of the East London toil.

Some ten days later he received the following letter:

MY DEAR NEPHEW – I have had you much in mind since we parted, and yesterday our solicitor, Mr Kempson, came down to see me. I wanted to consult him as to what I could best do in your interests about the vacancy at Stoke-St Edith. He thinks it will be quite possible to arrange an exchange of this benefice now vacant for the right to present to another one likely to fall vacant before long, of the same, or nearly equal value.

Of course I did not tell him why you had refused Stoke-St Edith; I left him to suppose you were too much engrossed in your present work to wish to give it up just at once. But, oh my dear Basil, it is indeed a cruel disappointment to me not to have you here.

Your affectionate Aunt,

EMMELINE ALBURY

P.S. – The £500 for Rectory furniture will now be invested in your name, ready for you when the time comes, whether I live or die.

The Wind of Dunowe

It was growing late. The Autumn evening was advanced out of the long northern twilight to be on the edge of dark, when Reginald Noyes left the Dunowe smoking-room where he had been chatting to his host, and dashed upstairs, two steps at a stride, to dress for dinner. The warning bell had rung some time before, so he was not surprised to find his wife already attired in her evening gown. She was seated with her back to him, warming her toes at the wide and glowing fire of peat. Noyes would have been just as well pleased not to find her there – a moderate statement of his sentiments. It was a case of the grey mare being the better horse, and the young man had not always an easy time with his chosen partner. To one sensitive to such indications, the psychic atmosphere of the big state bedroom was charged with displeasure, and this was accentuated by a shrug of an averted shoulder. Surely something more was wrong than the mere fact that Noyes was behind time.

'Why, Flossie, what's the matter?'

The frivolous nickname ill fitted Mrs Noyes, at least in her present mood. And at all times she was rather of the severe type of beauty, even when the sun shone – the metaphorical sun.

'Matter? Matter enough! It's no use: I can't stick it out here for another ten days, to the limit of our invitation. I'm bored to death. Coming to Dunowe has been altogether a mistake. You must make some excuse for a change of plan, and take me back to town.'

'Why – you wanted to cultivate the MacIvors: you even schemed to be invited. You were as pleased as I was when we were both asked – every bit. The shooting is excellent, and MacIvor such a good fellow. And I'm sure his mother received us with every kindness. Have you and she fallen out?'

'Do I ever fall out with anyone? I've no patience with you when you are absurd. Of course there has been no quarrel. But I'm sick to death of this ghostly old barrack. There isn't the least chance here of bringing off any *coup*. And as you know very well, if we don't between now and Christmas – !'

Here there was an effective pause. Noyes winced. Probably he did know what was meant. But he put up a further objection.

'You said, with a view to *coups*, that this visit was the very thing you wanted – to get into a house-party with Mrs Noel MacIvor, and have a chance to draw the feather over her. By George, Noel was a lucky man when he married her, in spite of the snub nose and the American accent. A girl with two millions to her fortune, and likely to have as much again when Poppa dies. And when all the MacIvors are as poor as rats, and he the second son!'

'Two millions – yes. But it seems they were dollars, not pounds sterling, as we heard. And the girl is as sharp and as well able to take care of herself and her money as – as the paternal Yankee himself.'

'Well – she can be fairly generous when she likes. MacIvor tells me she offered to restore Dunowe for him, – put the Castle in complete repair. That was pretty well for a sister-in-law. But of course he wouldn't consent.'

'More fool he to refuse such an offer. But in other ways she is downright stingy: dresses herself like a schoolgirl of seventeen, sweet simplicity unadorned. Not a jewel, even. And she should have had plenty of toilets and jewels in those Saratoga trunks we saw carried in!'

'I dare say you would have liked to have the ransacking of them!'

'I thought of that. But the Noels are far off in the other wing, and she has a dragon of a maid who seems always to be on guard.'

'Good heavens, Flossie! I hope you won't do more than think of it. That sort of thing never pays. And we should be marked for ever!'

'Nonsense. What marks one is not the doing, but being found out. I don't mean to run risks. I said, there is the maid. And I doubt if the jewels are there, though they ought to be. It isn't worth while. But we are bound to get hold of the money – or money's worth – by Christmas.'

Probably Noyes winced for the second time at this renewed reminder, but he was at the moment out of sight. He had plunged into the dressing-room, and was throwing things about there in the course of a hurried toilet. The door between the two rooms was set wide, and now and then he came to the opening to speak.

'I thought you were depending on your bridge. You wanted to play Auction with Mrs Noel – that was the tale in London. You never said a word about her jewels.'

'Right: I meant to play here, and win from her. But the little fool hates cards. And the old lady is puritanical, and hates them too. They are practically barred, or allowed with a limit of sixpenny stakes.'

'Can't you work it some other way? Flatter the heiress, and creep up her sleeve. Get her to restore us, as MacIvor won't let her do up the Castle!' – a laugh here, which was presently extinguished in the folds of a towel.

'I can get round most girls, but she doesn't take to me. She's like a – a glacis with no vantage for the foot. The only human bit about her is that she's curious. She's curious about the ghost here, and wants to find out. I told her I would try to help her – '

'*You* would help her! Why doesn't she question the family? They would know if there is anything in it. But of course there isn't.'

'It is the solitary point on which we touch. A sympathetic interest in ghosts is better than no fellow-interest at all. I've given myself out as psychical – save the mark!' – and here the lady laughed. 'I might personate the ghost, and get at the boxes that way. But the clue of how to make up is still to seek. We do not know what sort of figure is seen.'

'Surely she could ask her husband!'

'Noel told her something, and then he shut up, and would say no more. Lady MacIvor can't bear the subject mentioned, and Sir Ian is just as bad. And she thinks Noel must have been laughing at her. He said the ghost was a gale of wind: a gale which blows inside the castle when the real weather is still. Now a gale of wind won't help me to the boxes. But it is mixed up somehow with an ancestress. I can't find out which, though I asked all the questions I could, quite innocently, about the pictures. Ghosts apart, I tell you there is no chance here, and the sooner we get out of this the better. I wrote today to Juliet in Hampshire: you know she wanted me for her bridge parties, though she says I must not sweep the board as I did last winter. But of course that was only her joke. Gracious, there's the second gong. I must go down at once, and leave you to follow.'

Dinner was served in the hall at Dunowe Castle, a noble but some-what bare room, stone-floored, and so lofty as to be open to the rafters. The diners were, however, well protected from any chill; a great fire blazed, and the table was set within folding screens of Spanish leather, while a thick carpet spread under foot. Dunowe knew nothing of the modern luxury of electric light, and the moderate illumination of the table was effected by candles in tall silver holders. This was all very well within the screens, but the corners of the big room were abandoned to gloom, and only a single lamp burned over-head in the gallery. The piquante little American bride looked round her with a shiver as she descended the staircase. Here was hiding more than ample for dozens of ghosts, and that shrewd draught from the gallery which blew on her uncovered shoulders might be the precursor of the supernatural wind which was supposed to be the MacIvor family omen.

It was not a numerous party which assembled at the table. A married pair with a couple of clever daughters had quitted the Castle that morning, frigid old people, and the girls plain and elderly: impecunious also, and of no account from the point of view of Mrs Noyes. There were Noel MacIvor and Reginald Noyes, and four other men who were 'guns', seven in all with the host; but the American bride and Mrs Noyes were the only ladies remaining, with the exception of the stately old dame who sat at the head of the table, and was Sir Ian MacIvor's mother. Sir Ian had placed the lady guest on his right hand, and his sister-in-law opposite. Mrs Noyes was still in a clouded humour and had little to say, but she must have been well entertained by the pretty American's lively chatter. Ian MacIvor was a handsomer man than his more fortunate brother, but the family honours seemed to have brought with them a weight of care, not to say melancholy, and he looked old beyond his years.

'I went over to Eagles' Cairn today with the mater,' said the bride, whose Christian name was Caryl. 'You know they are all coming to Dunowe for the dance next week, and Mollie Campbell sent you a very particular message. She says they are going to put on fancy dress, as it makes it just twice the fun, and she hopes all the women you expect will do the same. Of course you men will wear the tartan. The mater did not seem to mind. I said I'd be delighted, and I thought Mrs Noyes would dress up too.' Then, with an appeal also to her *vis-à-vis*: 'Say, that was right, was it not?'

'Quite right, if you ladies do not mind the trouble for such a small impromptu affair. It was just like Mollie Campbell to propose it. She is a child still about what you call dressing up!'

'Perhaps we all are. I can answer for one, at least. What do you say, Mrs Noyes?'

'Certainly, if we are still here – I am not sure – '

'Oh, you must stay for it. We cannot let you off. And about costumes: the dear mater and I talked it over in the carriage coming home. She is going to wear a great-grandmother dress that she has stowed away with a lot of others in those chests on the gallery, and I am to try on a particular one that she thinks will suit me. It is like the dress Lady Sibell wears in the picture, where she has on the heirloom pearls and that queer harp-shaped brooch. Oh, Ian,' – with a sudden thought, and striking together the pink palms of her pretty-hands. 'It would be just splendid if you'd lend me the pearls for that one night! Say, will you? I'd take the greatest care of them. That is, if you keep them here, and not lodged at the bank. Are they here at Dunowe?'

'Yes,' he said, 'I have them here.' He did not refuse the request, but he met it gravely, and might have been divined unwilling by one less eager.

'Then you'll let me have them, won't you?' – the piquante little face eloquent with appeal, and the clasped hands held out. 'I'd like – oh, I would like to be Lady Sibell, just for the one night. I'd say I was Lady Sibell come alive out of the picture, if they can't guess who I am. I might even pretend to be the ghost.'

'A good idea,' he admitted, but still there was that air of a reluctance he would not put into words. 'But I wouldn't call myself Lady Sibell, if I were you. She mightn't like it. Couldn't you for the same period find a different name?'

'Why, is Lady Sibell the – ! But I must not ask you that! It's charming of you, Ian. I must tell Noel. I feel as if I could hardly wait for Wednesday. If they are here in the house, could you show them to me tonight?'

'I have them here – yes. In fact, they are in the built-in safe in my den, for they are not allowed to leave Dunowe. They don't often see the light. But you may be disappointed in them. They are not pure white, and some of them are irregular. No doubt they are Scotch river pearls, not oriental.'

The description, though depreciatory, seemed to excite interest in both his hearers. Mrs Noyes was also listening.

'Tinted pearls, are they? I wonder what colour?'

'Pinkish – to the best of my recollection.'

'*Pink* pearls!' Caryl clasped her hands again. 'They must be lovely. And I may wear them, may I not? Just for the one night!'

He smiled now in giving consent; she looked so pretty and childish in her eagerness.

'Yes, you shall have them for the dance. They may only be worn by a MacIvor. An odd provision, is it not; but it is in the deed, which also says they must not be taken out of the castle. But now you are married, you are a MacIvor, Caryl. So that will be all right.'

It is said that lookers on see most of the game. Mrs Noyes, looking and listening, was aware that Noel, who also listened, was rendered uneasy by his wife's request. He was on the edge of a protest, Mrs Noyes thought, but Sir Ian made a slight repressive sign. Caryl the bride was to have her way. Other MacIvor brides had worn the pearls, but they were wedded to the head of the house, and not to a younger son. Noel was aware that Ian thought himself too poor to marry: was it in the elder brother's mind that Caryl in the future would have the right to the pearls as the reigning lady of Dunowe.

'Could you let me see them tonight?' Caryl persisted.

'And may I see them too?' put in Mrs Noyes. 'I admire pearls, and I may not be here when Mrs MacIvor wears them at the dance. Our plans are uncertain. I dare say Reginald told you – ' No, Noyes had said nothing: in fact he had had no opportunity since the conversation in the bedroom. Sir Ian hoped, conventionally, that nothing would hurry them away so soon.

In the husband's case, it would be with him a genuine matter of regret, but he would be able to spare Mrs Flossie with perfect equanimity. He had no great liking for the lady: the surface of her was smooth enough, but he had an instinctive feeling that something unpleasant might be encountered underneath. He would be happy, he said, to show the pearls to both ladies, if they would honour him by paying a visit to his 'den'.

While dinner was in progress the wind was rising, buffeting round the many angles and turrets of the house; and now and then there was a roar in the wide chimney of the hall. It was evident that Lady MacIvor was listening, and listening with apprehension, though was it not the saying that when the ghost wind blew in the castle, the outer and mundane weather was wont to be a dead calm? The old dame was never high-coloured (old she was, to be the mother of those two stalwart sons). Hers was the ivory pallor of age, but a change of tint might have been noted on her cheek and lips, as she sat at the head of the table trying spasmodically to converse. On observing this, Sir Ian remarked, in a voice so far raised as to be sure to catch her ear: 'We are going to have a wild night of it. I could have forecasted as much when we were out today. The equinoctial gales have given us the go-by this year but now it seems as one of them is setting in in earnest.'

Only an equinoctial gale, a natural feature, and Ian cheerful in the forecast. Surely, that should have set her mind at rest, and she contrived to smile back at him down the length of the table. But there was still a quiver about the proud old head, and as she smoothed her lace mittens it was palpable that the thin hands they covered trembled. And when she heard of the display about to be made in the 'den,' it seemed as if her uneasiness increased. She said, however, no word to oppose. Lady Sibell's pearls must be shown and worn, as Ian had given his word. She was a fatalist in her way: what must be, must be: but Heaven grant showing and wearing might bring no evil on the house, which in the past had been stricken enough and to spare.

It was in truth a stormy evening, a gale sweeping over from the western ocean, and buffeting the old castle as it had been smitten many times before during its centuries of existence. But the wind was external, not within the walls, except for such natural draughts as found their way through undefended chinks and crannies. There was a huge fire in the castle drawing-room of logs and peat, but despite of it Lady MacIvor shivered, and drew a voluminous white cloud of Shetland knitting close about her shoulders as she sat alone.

The two younger women had betaken themselves to Sir Ian's den, and there he had the safe set open, and was displaying the contents of an antique casket made of some dark foreign wood, cornered and clamped with steel. Within, on a velvet bed, lay the pearls of Dunowe.

Both ladies admired the string, which was just long enough to encircle a slender throat, and had a ruby clasp. Caryl declared that the faint rosy flush upon the pearls was even more exquisite than the purity of white. She took them out of the case for closer view, and then passed the necklace over for Mrs Noyes also to examine. But when they came into unrelated handling, a queer thing happened.

The room was lighted by four candles in tall holders, two on the table, and two set high on the mantel-shelf. These lights were not extinguished nor did they flicker, but the illuminating power of them died down till each showed only a faint point of bluish flame. The room was almost in darkness, and the three persons grouped at the table could scarcely distinguish each the face of the other in the sudden gloom.

'What is the matter with the candles?' Mrs Noyes exclaimed: *esprit fort* as she considered herself, she was for the moment appalled.

Sir Ian took the pearls from her hand and replaced them in their case, and, as he did so, the lights gradually brightened until they burned as before. He did not answer the question or give any explanation: he appeared not to have noticed the darkness and the return of illumination.

'You shall have them on Wednesday evening,' he said to Caryl as he turned the key. 'I am glad they come up to your expectation.'

'I think they are exquisite,' she said, 'but I am almost frightened of them now. Ian, I know you won't tell me, but is it that Lady Sibell does not want them worn? Was it her doing to put out the candles, and make them burn again when you took back the necklace? No, you needn't answer, for I have found out! You may keep it as secret as you like, but I am certain now she is the ghost!'

Mrs Noyes was awake that night when her husband came up to their rooms; she had also something to say.

'You need not be in too great haste over arranging our departure. The fourteenth will do for me. I have made up my mind to stay over for the dance.'

'You will stay for the dance, and leave the day after: is that it? Rather a mistake if anything should happen to be missing, and there is a hue and cry. Better make it the end of the week, the day set for us, and let me have another good shoot.'

'You think of nothing but your shooting, Reginald. I never knew anyone so selfish.'

'This time, my dear, I am thinking of something quite other than myself. I am thinking of you, and the risk you are running, or are about to run. For of course this change of plan is because you have seen the pearls.'

'Don't speak so loud. Heaven knows who may be outside the door.'

'I am speaking with all discretion, and I want to know. You were there when MacIvor took them out of the safe. What are they like?'

'I had no time to look them over, of course, and there may be flaws. I had them in my own hands less than a minute. But I should say there were twenty at least the size of a large pea, and a dozen that would double that, all faintly tinted pink. The back of the string seemed made up of small ones, an odd and end lot, quite negligible. Whether those at the back were pink I could not see: there was a very bad light. But the middle ones would sell for a fortune in New York, if we can get them there. The latest craze of the Five Hundred is for pearls, and pink pearls head the market.'

'You'll never get them out of this house without detection and exposure, let alone across the Atlantic. Give it up, Flossie: your scheme is a bad egg. I'm off on Monday, and I shall take you with me. That's my last word.'

It might be Reginald Noyes's last word, but it was not Flossie's.

Many words followed on the lady's part: indeed discussions and recriminations raged till the small hours, of which the result only need be noted. The couple would remain over the dance and until the following Saturday, and Mrs Noyes held herself at liberty to pursue the course she had planned, and possess herself (if she could) of the pearls. And the following instructions were issued to the obedient Reginald, a little later on.

'Look here. I want you to engage Mrs Noel for the fourth dance: it is a valse. No, I know you don't valse well, but that does not matter. The big saloon is cleared for dancing on account of the oak floor, but the flirtation nooks and refreshments will be in the hall. Get her to sit out with you, and take her to the nook right in the corner, left of fireplace, the one from which you see the stairs. It is shut in at the back with palms and evergreens, and there is a high-backed seat. Take her there while the dancing is still going on, and the hall is empty: tell her you want to confide in her: keep her engrossed.'

'I can take her there – good: but as to confiding! What the devil am I to confide? She's the last sort of girl to stand love-making, and we haven't an idea in common. As you said once before.'

'Talk to her about the ghost. Tell her you've seen it, with the tallest story you can make up – sulphur and brimstone, horns and hoofs, and all the diabolical horrors. She'll believe you, for on that subject she would swallow anything. If you do that, you'll have her fixed – for as long as will suit my purpose. You understand?'

The morning of Wednesday, Mrs Noyes developed a headache. It was most tiresome of it to come when it did, and she accepted sympathy freely, and swallowed the offered remedies, which was heroic. To lose the dance would disappoint her, more acutely than words could say. No, not the actual dance; she must give up that in any case, for it would be impossible with such a giddy head. But if she could get better ever such a little better – she would still hope to watch the spectacle from some quiet corner, where she would not be in the way. She was sure dear Lady MacIvor would excuse her arraying herself in the elaborate costume which had been arranged, and in which she was to be a *poudre*. But she happened to have with her a dark domino and half-mask, which would do well enough, and this she could throw on at the last moment if she felt able to come down. She would be inconspicuous so attired, and could slip away when fatigued.

So, when the evening came, she assumed a close-fitting sheath-like dress of black satin, in which her spare figure would occupy the least possible space, even when covered by the domino. She would not venture down till the dancing was well begun, but the right moment would find her ready and the headache cured.

Noyes hated the whole business, but had so far fallen under his wife's domination that he was prepared to play his part in the drama. He took the opportunity to acquaint himself with the special flirtation nook she had indicated, to which he was expected to lead his partner. It could not have been better arranged for Flossie's purpose. A large Chesterfield settee was placed across the corner, backed by an apparent grove of tall palms and evergreens, which masked the door into a side passage. This door was not to be used in the service of the night, as the passage did not lead to the kitchens, and indeed communicated only with the gun-room and a side staircase. Flossie would do her part, there was no doubt of that: it only remained for him to act up to the *rôle* for which he was cast, and whisper to a lady psychically interested some thrilling particulars about an imagined ghost.

He foresaw difficulty. The American bride was curious, but she was also an indefatigable dancer, and determined to enjoy herself to the full. Would she be tempted into that retirement, even by a hinted confidence as to ghosts seen at Dunowe?

Caryl was in wild spirits when the hour arrived, enchanted with the effect of her old-world costume, now completed with the heirloom pearls, and a quaint harp-shaped brooch which also figured in the picture. Her hair was dressed after the fashion of Lady Sibell's portrait, and Caryl made the painted lady a mock courtesy as she passed her in the gallery.

'No, you mustn't say you know me,' she said laughing to her intimates. 'I'm not Caryl MacIvor tonight, or Noel's wife. I'm his lady-ancestress instead.' And then, in a following whisper: 'I doubt if the dear old mater really approves of the travesty, though she would not interfere to spoil my fun. You know how she's very superstitious, and in dressing up as Lady Sibell I strongly suspect I'm also impersonating the ghost.'

The Dunowe dance being an impromptu, there were no printed programmes; but those who had pockets – only the men had pockets – carried cards in them, and little stubs of pencils. In this way Noyes had Caryl's name down for Number Four, but when he came to claim it, that young person seemed to be deeply engaged with another partner.

'Do you really want to dance with me?' she queried. 'Because

I'm enjoying myself very much with Freddy.' (Freddy was one of the 'guns'.)

'I do really want this dance, and you know you promised. If you wish, I'll let you off the other; but do try me first.'

She yielded, and they swung off together on the well waxed floor.

'I know I valse badly,' he said presently, 'and I am unpractised in the new steps. What I really want is to get you to sit out with me. I have something to tell you: it's – it's about a ghost. I have just had a horrible experience, and you'll be the first to hear of it: I have told nobody else. We shall get the hall to ourselves – for five minutes – if you don't mind coming this way.'

'About the ghost?'

There was quickened interest in her repetition of his words: his fish was rising to the fly. And perhaps she was not wholly unwilling to cut short her gyrations with an unskilled partner.

'You'll be comfortable sitting here, and that other fellow won't think of looking for you behind this screen. I really want to consult you – ask your advice. For I've had the fright of my life this afternoon.'

She sank down on the soft cushions, leaning well back, which was what Flossie wished.

As he took his seat beside her, he heard a slight rustle in the bower of foliage at the back of the couch, and it did not help to steady his nerves.

'I suppose it would not do to say anything to Sir Ian. My first idea, of course, was that it was a real man. A fellow with bad intentions, and no business where he was. In short, a burglar.'

'A burglar – in broad daylight!'

'Ghosts are not supposed to like daylight, are they, any more than burglars? Though I know next to nothing of the habits of ghosts. But the daylight wasn't – wasn't broad.'

Noyes felt he was floundering, and wondered what Flossie would think of his efforts at narration, in her hiding-place at the back.

'I mean it was getting dark – dusk, you know. If it hadn't been, I could not have seen the flame so distinctly. Yes, there seemed to be a flame about him, or at least a light. It came out of his eyes, I think, but really I don't know. You see, I've had no experience.'

'You thought it was a man first, and then you saw it was a ghost. No, I wouldn't tell Ian: he does not care for these things, and I think they make him uncomfortable. But I would like to hear more about it. Ah-h-h, what's that?'

'Did you see anything?'

'No, but I thought something touched me – at the back of my neck – like a finger!'

Noyes noticed that her hand went up at once to feel for the safety of the pearls.

Flossie's first attempt had been a failure, and he was nearly at the end of ghost-invention. Flames out of the eyes: he had better say next that his apparition breathed them out of its mouth.

'What touched you was a camellia leaf: see, I have broken it off. What were you asking me?'

'Was it the flame made you think the appearance supernatural? Or was there anything else?'

'Well – you see a real man couldn't be on fire, and yet be still and give no sign of pain. But a ghost might look like that, if – if it came from the wrong place. But what made me sure in the end, was that it vanished. It just went right out – while I stood there.'

Noyes was facing sideways as he sat, and, with attention apparently riveted on his companion, he saw with half an eye the two hands again come forward out of the bower of greenery to attack the clasp of the necklace – this time with a lighter and defter touch, which did not alarm the victim. The string of pearls dropped one dangling end, and then was cautiously withdrawn. He made a desperate effort after self-control, continuing to look his partner steadily in the face, as if absorbed in their conversation. The scheme had worked well, Flossie had secured her prize, and now the best thing he could do was to lead Caryl back without delay into the thick of the throng. It would not do for her to recognise too precisely when and where the heirloom disappeared.

'If you'll come a little further out into the room, I can show you whereabouts in the gallery the ghost stood. You never heard of anything like it haunting Dunowe? But you see, they will not speak of the Dunowe ghosts, so whether familiar or not we cannot tell. There is the music ending, and I suppose I must take you back to the dancing-room. Thank you for giving me a hearing. Think it over, and tell me what conclusion you come to. At supper, perhaps; or tomorrow.'

He offered his arm, and at the same moment a slight click of the concealed door informed him Flossie had escaped from her hiding place. Caryl rose, and presently he was pointing out to her an imaginary spot on the gallery above the hall.

'I was just turning out of the corridor on my way down, when there he was straight before me. I give you my word it was horrible. And then to go like that, snuffed out in a moment!'

He had not told his story well; he was conscious of its lack of *vraisemblance*. And it left on the listener's mind an impression of insincerity, eager as she was to believe. Yet there was about Noyes a kind of subdued agitation which was curious: he would hardly have been so moved, she thought, by what was exaggerated or untrue. Yes, they would take an opportunity to speak of it again, and he might tell her husband if he liked, but no word must be said before Ian.

As they crossed the hall, a car drove up with late arriving guests, and now the double doors of the entrance were being set wide. Servants came hurrying forward, and Lady MacIvor at the entrance of the ballroom was ready to receive her guests. Noyes and Caryl passed her going in, and but for the expectation and look beyond, probably she would at once have noticed the disappearance of the pearls. But the moment following a strange thing happened; one likely to be memorable ever after in the annals of Dunowe.

Did the gust of air rush in from those opened doors, or whence did it originate? A whirlwind blast tore through the house, extinguishing lights, swaying the pictures on the walls, tearing down wreaths of evergreens with which the saloon had been decked for the festal night. A wind which blew upstairs, as well as down, shrieking through corridor and gallery, bursting open doors and whirling into closed rooms, so that no portion of the house escaped. There were cries of terror from the women guests, but the blast ceased as suddenly as it began, and Sir Ian's voice was heard above the din, begging everybody to be calm. The room would be quickly re-lighted, and the dancing would go on.

But the lights when they were brought, revealed pale faces which looked questioningly one to another. This was a strange thing which had happened, and beyond nature. The ghostly wind of Dunowe had hitherto been a joke in the neighbourhood: after the experience of that night it would take rank as an article of faith.

The renewed illumination, however, brought with it a diversion. Caryl's loss was noted. Mollie Campbell exclaimed: 'My dear, where are your pearls?' and the bride put both hands to her neck in uttermost dismay.

Had they been torn off and whirled from her by the ghost-wind – the act of an affronted ghost? But common sense suggested they had dropped to the floor, and had been swept away into some corner by a trailing skirt: this was advanced as the most likely explanation, though in these days all dancing gowns are sufficiently abbreviated. The necklace must be close at hand – Caryl was positive she had it in safety not ten minutes before – her dancing-partners could testify they had noticed it about her throat. The idea of theft occurred to nobody: theft was impossible in that secure house, and in the midst of friends.

'Oh, Ian, I am sorry: I am miserable to have lost it,' she said, almost in tears. 'I had no notion that the snap was weak: had I thought of it, I would have tied it on. I ought to have taken more care.'

'You must not let that trouble you,' he said to her kindly. 'It will not be lost – it will come back to us': the last words *sotto voce* to Noel, who was as distressed as his wife. But what he meant by them he did not explain.

Noyes was among the searchers, round the floor and beyond, though well aware it could not be there. The ghostly wind, the darkness, had not helped to steady his shaken nerves, but in a way he welcomed the diversion. Everyone was talking and thinking of the strange event, and if Caryl had been robbed, that darkness would be held thieves' opportunity. No suspicion could rest on Flossie, sick in her room.

But some half-hour later Sir Ian came to him.

'Noyes, I am sorry to tell you your wife is ill. We have a doctor here among our guests, and, if you are willing, I think it might be as well for him to see her. The matter? Oh, only a fainting-fit, but it seems to be obstinate. Some of the women found her lying in the corridor after the rush of wind, and I fear she may have been frightened. She was carried to bed, and the housekeeper and my mother's maid are both with her. If you will go up, I'll send Rawlins. He will know what to do.'

Noyes went upstairs at once, his heart heavy with apprehension. Not so much on account of possible danger, though he was honestly fond of his wife, despite her outbreaks of temper, and the domination of the grey mare. What he dreaded was discovery of what she had done. She must have fainted on her way back to their room, with the pearls upon her. And these women who found her in the corridor, who carried her to bed, would be certain to unfasten her dress in trying to recover her, and there would be the fatal necklace – doubtless well known to both of them, housekeeper and maid. Neither would suppose it a guest's possession, even if unaware of Caryl's loss, and the search going on below. As he hurried upstairs, he felt like a man under sentence, who has just been informed that his hour has come.

He found Flossie laid upon the bed, moaning faintly.

'Madam is coming round nicely now, sir,' said the housekeeper. 'It was the faint going on so long that frightened us. I don't think she will be the worse.'

The woman spoke cordially, not as if she knew them for discovered criminals; but there could be no further interchange, as the doctor was at the door.

While Dr Rawlins examined the patient, Noyes looked round the room. Flossie's dress had been undone as a matter of course, and her few ornaments were unpinned and laid on the dressing-table, but the pearls were not among them. When he drew near the bed on the opposite side to the doctor, Mrs Noyes turned her head on the pillow and looked at him. That she recognised her husband there could be no doubt, but there was a dreadful apprehension in her eyes. No word, however, could then be interchanged.

'Your wife has had a shock of some kind, and collapse has followed. Most likely the wind frightened her. I understand the people here consider it supernatural, and I am ready to confess it was *odd*, though I don't give in to spooks. You had better let the maid settle Mrs Noyes comfortably for the night, and I dare say Mrs Holbrook, the housekeeper, will sit up.'

'No, no,' Noyes objected. 'Nobody need sit up. I can look after her: the women need not stay. You think there is no danger?'

'No danger that I foresee: she is reviving quite satisfactorily. But I will come up again before I leave. I shall find you here?'

Noyes assented, and expressed his thanks. Then, when he had shut the door upon the doctor, he went back to the bed. His wife's eyes met his, filled with the same agony of fear.

'Are – the women – gone?' she panted.

'Yes, for the moment, but they are coming back. Where are the pearls?'

'I don't know – I don't know!'

'You had them. Where did you put them when you left the hall?'

'Inside the bosom of my dress – within everything – next to the skin. When I came to myself, all my clothing had been opened.

'They must have found – ! Unless, indeed, the pearls were taken – when – !'

Speech failed, a violent shudder convulsed her, the apprehension in her face deepened into horror. The hand he had taken in his clutched him hard.

'Why – what – ?'

'The wind came: it was more than wind – it was anger, fury. It seems, when I look back, there was a face with it; or I dreamed the face after. A face that was terrible. I was so near safety when it came: a few more steps: and I was full of triumph. The wind struck me down. I knew no more till I found myself in here, and the women with me. Do you think the pearls – were taken – when I fell?'

After the fateful interruption of the wind, and a general dismay over Caryl's loss, the dance was not kept up late. The first gay frolic of it was only half-heartedly renewed, and the guests did not find much appetite for the excellent supper. It was but little after one o'clock when Sir Ian closed the great doors upon the last departure, and retreated to his den. Caryl had put in his hands the quaint antique brooch worn to fasten her dress as Lady Sibell, and again she made tearful expression of her sorrow over the loss of the pearls.

'I think they will be given back,' he said: this and no more.

His errand to the den was to replace the brooch. He unlocked the safe with his own key, a key that had no duplicate, and never left his possession. He opened the steel-clamped casket to lay the brooch within, and there, safe and unharmed, was the gleaming roseate string, the heirloom pearls of Dunowe.

A few minutes later he knocked at his brother's door.

'Noel! it is I, Ian – I want to speak to you.'

Noel opened at once: he was in pyjamas, and had been on the point of getting into bed.

'What is it, old fellow?'

'Only to tell you that the pearls are found. Let Caryl know. She will sleep all the better.'

'By George, I should think she will, and I, too! Where did they turn up?'

'In their place, in my locked safe. I unlocked it to put the brooch away, and they were there.'

'In your locked safe! Did you leave it undone?'

'No. And I had the key.'

'Then how – who – ?'

'No mortal hand, I think. You know, there is a saying – ! I tell you, but I shall slur it over to the others. Better so. Goodnight.'

Nevill Nugent's Legacy

From Mrs Margaret Campbell to a friend

Yes, you are right; the legacy was a great surprise to us – the surprise of our lives, in fact; and we were ready to bless Cousin Nevill in the beginning – at least I was. Kenneth now says he always had his doubts. But I do not think he had many when he came in to me after the post delivery – just one step from the bedroom to the sitting-room of our flat, with that look upon his face, and the open letter shaking in his hand.

It seemed to have come to us straight from heaven, Cousin Nevill's bequest. For you must know we were at that time very hard up; almost, as the saying is, 'stony-broke'. Kenneth giving up his profession to join the army made a great change in our circumstances. We could not keep on our pretty house, of which I used to be so proud; and, as soon as I was alone, I moved into a tiny flat in town, and got work to do. But when Ken came out of hospital last January so ill and broken, my work had to stop, for I was needed to nurse him. Ever since then the money has been flowing out, with only a little – so little – trickling in: I cried over it only the night before, of course when Ken did not see. For it seemed as if even the wretched flat was more than we could afford, and I did not know where Tom's school-fees were to come from for another term – all important as his education is, the chance of life for such a clever boy.

You will judge what a breaking of sunlight into darkness was the great surprise. Ken's voice had a choke in it as he said: 'I saw Nevill's death in the obituary, but I never dreamed it would benefit us.'

'He was a rich man, was he not?' (I crowded my questions.) 'Has he left us much money? All his money? What does the letter say?'

'All? – No, indeed! But a fair amount of property. It is a Mr Bayliss who writes, an Edinburgh lawyer; and he would like to see me, as soon as I can make it convenient. Here, you can read for yourself.'

He sank into the nearest chair, while I stood, devouring the communication; and now my hands were shaking too. Mr Bayliss wrote that his client, Mr Nevill Nugent, in a will made the week before his death, devised the bulk of his property to Nugent relatives. To Kenneth, as representing his mother's side of the family, he gave the small estate of Mirk Muir, four miles distant from the manufacturing town of R—. It comprised the farms of South Muir, Bull Knowe, and Blackwater, and the residential property of Mirk Muir Grange, generally known as the Chapel House, and let off furnished, but now vacant. There was in addition a street of artisans' dwellings in R—, and most of these were in occupation. If well let, the entire property should bring in about £1200 per annum.

'Twelve hundred a year! Oh, Ken! That will be riches indeed – for us!'

'I wish indeed it was likely. It isn't as good as that. Go on, and you'll see.'

The drawbacks followed, and they were considerable. The rents received the previous year barely amounted to £600. An action at law was pending, which the new owner would do well to compromise even at a loss. There was also an annuity charge for an old servant, passed on to us. And finally Ken was reminded that the death duties would be heavy. My first enthusiasm of greed was somewhat quenched.

'But, even so, there will be enough to make things better for us,' I said more soberly. 'Very – very much better. You can have the change you need so much – Tom's schooling can go on. And – '

'Yes, it will do all that, and more. It will be a change to go to Edinburgh. That is the first thing we must do, Maggie; you and I.'

Two days later we set out on our journey. Tom was left at school, as he was in the middle of a term; and though part of my rejoicing was that his lessons need not be disturbed by our failure to pay, I was irrational enough to regret that he could not be with us. He would have enjoyed the adventure of new scenes and new hopes; and I set out with the thought of my one boy very much in mind – which may have had its share in attuning me to what followed.

We had not exhausted our wonderment during those days of hasty preparation. Ken remarked more than once: 'I'd give a good deal to know what made Nevill think of me at the last. Since he had that row with my dear old dad, we haven't been on speaking terms. And it must be a dozen years since last we met. If I am right in remembering, it was just before Tom was born.'

'I never saw him,' I chimed in. We were now in the great express on our way to Edinburgh – third-class travellers in spite of our accession of fortune. 'Tell me what he was like.'

'Oh – Nevill was a fellow with a crook in him, and looked it all over. He was always queer – about religion, as well as in other matters. Didn't hold with any of the recognised forms, and used to preach as a freelance when he could get anybody to listen. I've no doubt he meant well. I believe he built a chapel for himself.'

'Is that why Mirk Muir Grange is called the Chapel House?'

'I dare say it is. I'm glad he did not saddle his bequest with the provision I should do parson. There are disadvantages enough without that.'

We were to hear more of the disadvantages from Mr Bayliss in Edinburgh. He was a stiff, dry sort of man, but he became slightly more genial on finding Ken willing to take his advice about compounding the action, and selling a portion of the property to meet charges and duty, instead of putting a mortgage on the farms. He thought Ken would be wise to keep on a certain McGregor as his factor, as he had served Nevill Nugent for half a lifetime, and knew the place and the people. We might expect to get something like £300 in the course of the first year, but it was not likely to be more, unless a tenant could be found for the Chapel House: he called it that, I noticed, rather than the Grange. But we had better not be sanguine, as the house was not an easy one to let.

Ken asked why – a question on the tip of my tongue too, though it got no further.

Mr Bayliss did not seem very ready with his answer. It was a good deal out of the way, he said at last. 'Drains bad?' Ken suggested, but was answered 'No'; all the sanitary arrangements had been put in complete order for the last tenant. Of course something might be done by advertising, as the autumn season was coming on; and Mrs Wilding, who was left in charge, was said to be an excellent cook.

Ken turned to me.

'I don't see why we shouldn't go there ourselves, as it is standing vacant. For a few weeks at any rate, until a tenant offers. What would you say to the plan? It would give us the opportunity of looking round.'

I caught at the idea.

'I shall like it of all things,' I exclaimed.

'And you can settle everything else from there.'

It struck me Mr Bayliss looked relieved.

'Yes, you would do well to go, Mr Campbell,' he said. 'You will understand better about the property after seeing over it, and consulting with the factor. I think I told you the Chapel House cannot be alienated so long as Mrs Wilding lives. You are bound to keep it up to afford a home for her, though she works there as a servant. The will provides for that, as well as for the annuity charge of which I spoke.'

A curious provision this, if you come to think of it; and it will be an odd position for us – for me – with a servant in the house over whom I can have no authority, as it is her home by as clear a right as it will be my own. I cannot bid her go, however much she may transgress. But I said nothing of this to Ken, for I did not want to make difficulty; and if it is true we cannot let the Grange, it will be cheaper to live in it ourselves than to pay rent elsewhere. Then the query came up, why could not the Grange be let? – this after we had left Mr Bayliss, and were discussing the matter between ourselves.

'Do you think it can be haunted?' I suggested, but Ken laughed aloud in scorn of the idea.

'What are you fancying about it, Maggie? It isn't an ancestral castle, hundreds of years old, but just an ugly modern house, without a scrap of romance. Ghost, indeed! It's too far from a station, or up and down too many hills on a bad road. Those are the reasons that keep houses vacant, not humbug about ghosts.'

2

Ken was right in part of his description. Mirk Muir *was* a long way out from R—, and on a hilly road; and the Grange certainly was an ugly house. Indeed it could hardly have been plainer, or presented a more dismal exterior, than it did when we turned in through the open gate, one wet cloudy evening on the edge of dusk. The walls were faced with stucco and painted drab, the windows flat, and the slate roof dark with rain. The house itself looked square and compact as it fronted us and the gate; but to the left was a long annexe of one storey only, which appeared to be built of wood. 'By George, that must be Nevill's chapel,' Ken exclaimed. And then our 'machine' drew up at the door.

It was opened to us by Mrs Wilding, a tall gaunt woman, with quite the saddest face I ever saw. She made me think of those people who after a great grief are said never to have smiled again. But she was quite civil, even anxiously so; hoped we should not be inconvenienced because only two rooms had been made ready, but the notice was short, and she could only get in a girl to help. The dining-room was open, and presently there would be the service of a meal; the bedroom we were to occupy looked to the front immediately above. On the morrow, any changes we desired should of course be made.

It would do very well, we told her; and while Ken directed the driver about carrying up our luggage, I turned into the dining-room and sat down. There a lamp was lighted, and the table ready spread with a white cloth; there was even the cheer of a glowing fire which smelt delightfully of peat, and which the chill of the wet evening made welcome, summer as it was. I recognised comfort; but somehow, I knew not why, my spirits had sunk down to zero. There was no visible cause, but I seemed, on entering the house, to have stepped into a cloud of depression which engulfed and swallowed me up. I felt properly ashamed of myself when Ken came in, rubbing his hands.

'Really, this is very snug,' he said. 'And you will be pleased with the room above, for it has three windows, and a view each way. Early Victorian, of course, and a four-post bed with curtains at every corner, but nothing missed out that we can want. The luggage has been taken up, so you can go there when you like.'

To have Ken pleased and cheerful – what more could I desire? I roused myself with an effort, and departed to unpack and make ready. Through the hall window I saw our driver climbing to the box of his vehicle, preparatory to driving away; and a boy was going out and closing the door behind him – a boy of about Tom's age; no doubt he had been got in to assist with the luggage.

I did not give him a second thought, but lighted the two candles which stood ready on the toilet-table, and prepared to change from my travelling-dress. Presently Mrs Wilding brought me a jug of hot water. She seemed anxious to be attentive, and I was ready to like her, only that it gave me a chill at heart to see her face, from which all hope seemed to have gone out. She served our meal, but not quite in the ordinary way, putting it on the table for us to help ourselves. She was alone in the house, she said, except for the girl who came in, and her husband, who was paralysed and a cripple. She thought she could manage for us with the girl's help; that is, if we were satisfied with what she could do. We might find it difficult to get a regular servant to stay. Here again there was reticence and no reason given; and something seemed to tie my tongue from asking why.

I broke Ken's rest that night by an outcry in my sleep, and when he roused me to know what was the matter, I was weeping and trembling, and at first beyond speech. I had heard Tom calling for me, that was my dream; his voice screaming 'Mother – mother!' as if in awful trouble or unbearable pain. I woke with the cry still ringing in my ears, and it needed all Ken's common sense to console me. Even then I could not forget. Something terrible had happened to our child: that was my fear, but what I could not tell. I did not see him in the dream; it was a dream of sound and not of sight; the cries seemed to break out of some strange place which was his prison. Ken talked to me and comforted me till the grey morning light stole into the room, and after that he slept again, but I could not sleep. It was true what he said. Tom had always seemed perfectly happy at school, and the house-master and his wife were our friends, and would let us know at once if any ill befell the boy. And, as he reminded me, they knew of our changed address, as I had written from Edinburgh to say we were going on to Mirk Muir.

The post of that morning brought no ill news; in fact no news of any kind. After breakfast, Mrs Wilding suggested I might like to see the house, and I went alone with her, as Ken had gone to call on McGregor the factor.

There was not a great deal to see: upstairs our bedroom was the only apartment of any size, though there were a number of smaller rooms. One of these I fixed on as a dressing-room for Ken, and another (in my own mind) as just right for Tom, if we stayed on at Mirk Muir and he came for the holidays. On the ground-floor there was a drawing-room, and a small nondescript third sitting-room. The drawing-room, a drab little place, was to the left of the entrance hall; it had only a single window, but on one side of the fireplace was another door, which Mrs Wilding unlocked with a key taken from the pocket of her apron.

'This is the room Mr Nugent built on to serve as a chapel,' she said, drawing back to allow me to look in.

I found myself at the head of about six steps, leading down into an interior chill as a vault. It was a spacious place, bare of furniture, but with a sort of dais at the further end. It was lighted by four windows high in the wall, bordered by ugly strips of blue glass; and a large stove for heating purposes had a black chimney-pipe carried up into the roof. There was also an outer door, which Mrs Wilding said led into the garden.

'McGregor keeps the outer key, but of course he will give it up to Mr Campbell; and I will now leave this one, so that you can enter when you like from the drawing-room. Yes, the chapel-room does strike cold, in spite of the wooden floor having been put in when it was used as a schoolroom. It was all stone flags to begin with, and the stones are still there underneath. Mr Nugent did not use it many times, after going to all the expense of the building. He took a dislike to Mirk Muir and went away; and the tenant next after kept a school for boys, and made it into a classroom – the house has been through many hands in the last eight years.'

'And you have been here with all the changes?'

'Yes, for that was Mr Nugent's wish. I was matron when it was the school; but with the others I have cooked and kept house. Will you like to see the kitchen side?'

I was willing to see all she cared to show, but I understood by a slightly hinted reserve, that the back premises were her own peculiar domain, on which I was not to intrude except by invitation. And I did not wonder when I discovered what was there.

The best kitchen was a spacious apartment, where, I imagine, cooking was rarely done, as there was another and more modern range in the second kitchen behind. There was a fire, however, and set beside it in an elbow chair was the helpless figure of a man.

He was paralysed below the waist, having sustained some injury to the spine, and the malady was creeping upwards; but he must once have been of uncommon strength, with a large and powerful frame. He still had the use of one hand, and he kept a stick beside him. At first he did not appear to notice my entrance, as he kept his eye on a collie-dog, a nice creature, which was sidling round to find a resting-place within the radius of warmth. I shall not soon forget the murderous look on his face, as he struck at the animal with his stick – missing it, happily, for the blow fell harmless on the floor.

'Leave the dog alone,' his wife commanded sharply. And then: 'This is the new mistress, Mrs Campbell,' she said as we passed through.

The man then made some sort of civil salutation, but I could not bring myself to speak to him, except with the merest good-day. If from a man's countenance you may judge the quality of his soul, in this afflicted body must have dwelt a very demon. In the work-a-day kitchen beyond, a stout servant-lass was busy washing dishes at the sink: she had heard what passed, and the blow of the stick on the floor.

'Bassett'll be the death of that dog, missis, just as he was of the other,' she remarked as she bent over her task.

'Who is Bassett?' I asked, though feeling sure what would be the answer.

'The man you have just seen – Thomas Bassett, my husband.'

'But you are Mrs Wilding?' I exclaimed, perhaps unwisely.

'I have taken back my former name, because I will not any longer be called by his. Did not Mr Bayliss tell you?' was her counter-question, to which I answered 'No'.

The tour of inspection ended, I wandered out into the garden, for it was now fine overhead, though everything was still drenched by yesterday's rain. Presently I discovered I had dropped my handkerchief, and as I knew I had it when Mrs Wilding was showing me the drawing-room, I turned in there on re-entering. There it lay on the drab carpet; but I was surprised to come upon the boy who – as I believed – helped overnight with our luggage. Certainly he could have had no business there, in a room I was likely to occupy. Again he was in the act of slipping through a door: it was the front door the night before, and now he was disappearing into the chapel by the entrance Mrs Wilding had left partly open. This time I followed, as I was curious to find out who he was and what was his errand; but the chapel-room was empty.

I shut the door upon the steps and turned the key, though I left it standing in the lock. Then I went back to the dining-parlour and sat down, for I felt suddenly weak. The surprise of that complete disappearance was something of a shock to me, but not such as I would have supposed must be the effect on a living person of seeing what is called a ghost. Indeed I hardly admitted the haunting possibility to myself, even then: my mind was running on the fear of something having happened to Tom. I had heard of *doppelgängers* and apparitions of the living, and this boy was about Tom's size and age, though I could not say the figure was in his likeness: the face I did not see.

I said nothing to Ken when he came in, full of his business with the factor, and wanting me to walk over to South Muir with him in the afternoon, where he had an appointment to view the farm. Nothing then, or through the evening; and I rested quietly that night with no recurrence of my dream. But the next morning I saw the boy again.

I was about to cross the hall, and there he was on the staircase, mounting quickly, but full in view. I called to Mrs Wilding, who was in the room behind me, collecting our breakfast-china on a tray.

'Who is the boy who has just gone upstairs, and what does he want?' I asked.

Mrs Wilding put down the cloth she was folding; she did not seem surprised.

'I do not know, ma'am, but I'll see' – and she ran up, while I waited below. I heard her pass from room to room, and then she came down to me. 'There is nobody there,' she said.

'Then what is it? You must tell me. I have seen this figure twice before. Is it a ghost?'

'Mr Bayliss wrote that we were not to name it to you, but now you have seen for yourself I have no choice. People say it is a ghost, and some see it and some don't. I have never seen it for my part, though I have lived at Mirk Muir for years, and been through the house at all hours, day and night. I doubt if it is a ghost myself. There is no reason for a ghost to be here.'

She looked strangely agitated, as she stood plucking at her apron with nervous hands, while two spots of feverish colour burned on her tragic face. The apparition seemed in some way to concern her nearly, though she professed to disbelieve.

'What do you think it is?'

'I have come to fancy – it is like to be – something made up out of my thoughts, which shows to others, though not to me – never to me. I'm always dwelling on my great trouble, that my son has gone away.'

Here a sort of dry sob choked her voice, but presently she went on.

'He was but a slip of a lad, much like the figure they talk about, when he ran away to sea because his stepfather was cruel. I knew it was in his mind to go. "Mother," he says to me, "I can't bear it any longer, and don't you fret. Whatever hard usage I get on board ship, it can't be as bad as what I've had here; and I shan't write, for I won't be sought for and brought back, but when I've got to an age and a weight so that Bassett can't touch me, then I'll come again to you, and we'll go away together." Bassett had beaten him cruel, not once but hundreds of times. And the next day he was gone.'

'And that is – how long ago?'

'Eight years and two months. It was when the chapel-room was building. And within a year after that, Bassett fell off a ladder and was fixed helpless. Martin need not have feared him then, but I could not tell where my boy was, to let him know. I did put an advertisement in papers I thought he might see, but no notice came. Ma'am, they say that marriage is an honourable estate, and a married woman is respectable. I thought it would be good for me to be married; but I say now that the worst day's work that ever I did, and the wickedest, was when I married Bassett. To give him power over myself, body and soul, was bad enough, he being what he was; but the sin was to give him power over my child. I haven't said it out so plain to anyone else; but I believe it is my thoughts dwelling on Martin that make the ghost, and not anything real.'

Ken looked worried when he came in to lunch, after another confabulation with McGregor.

'I doubt more and more whether Nevill meant well to us when he left us Mirk Muir,' he said when we were alone. 'He has had no end of trouble with the tenants – money going out for repairs and claims, and precious little coming in. And this house won't let at any price; nobody will look at it. There is some confounded story which has got about – '

'The story of a ghost: is that what you mean? The ghost of a boy?'

'Who has been telling you about it?' he asked, frowning.

'I have seen it for myself, three times since we came. I saw it again this morning by broad daylight, and then I asked Mrs Wilding. She says it is seen by some people, and always the same; but she thinks it is a sort of thought-shape, and not a ghost. I am not afraid of it, so you need not mind. What did McGregor tell you?'

'He appears to believe in it, unless he was pulling my leg. He says it has played all manner of what he calls "pliskies", and it began to be active when Grant took the house and brought his school. He was the next here after Nevill. McGregor has a notion Nevill saw it himself, and that was why he gave up living here, after going to the expense of building on that outside room. McGregor says the ghost was never heard of till after the chapel-room was built; the house was quiet up till then, and of good reputation. It was as if the building disturbed something; though that, of course, is absurd. Now tell me what you saw, and what Mrs Wilding said.'

I had the opportunity of questioning McGregor myself that evening, as he came round to see Ken. He was a pawky old Scot, with a twinkle of humour in his eye, but I believe he was sincere in what he told me. Oddly enough, his errand was to ask Ken if he would be willing to sell the chapel-room. He had just received an offer for it from a certain contractor, who would take it down at his own expense, to re-erect for some purpose connected with the war. The contractor would bind himself to take away the brick foundation and stone flagging, as well as the wooden part, and smooth the garden over to be as it was before. The price offered was less than a third of what it cost Nevill to erect, although all materials have gone up in value; but Ken was glad to realise even so much money, and well inclined to consent.

'I didn't tell him he might be buying the ghost along with it,' said the factor with a wag of his head and a smile. 'The ghost came with the chapel-room, and maybe the ghost will go with it. And if it does, so much the better for the Grange.'

'I wish you would tell me what you know about the ghost, Mr McGregor. I'm very interested and not nervous, and my husband will not mind. It seems a very harmless sort of apparition, and I do not see why anybody should be afraid.'

'Just so, ma'am, and I don't know that ever it did harm but once, and that most likely was accident and not intent. We first began to hear about it when Mr Grant was here with his school of twenty boys, and we thought of it at the first as nothing but the young lads' mischief and a tale. To look at, it was much the same as one of them, and they got into scrapes being supposed to go up to the dormitories at wrong hours, and that. Then the dominie, counting heads, would find too many boys in class, and when he counted again they were right: he could not make it out. But the thing that began the trouble was a scribbling on the exercise-books and writing copies and that, scribbling done in pencil, not real writing, but W.W. or M.M., like this' – tracing with his finger on the table – 'the same over and over again. I saw some of it myself. Nobody could make out who did it; and at last Mr Grant locked the books in his own desk, but they were scribbled on even there. He got very angry, and vowed he would flog the whole school, from the senior lad down to the youngest, unless the one that played the trick would come forward and confess. And then there started up a boy who was a stranger and not one of the scholars, and went up to the master's desk with a copy-book in his hand. The dominie was about to take it from him; but no sooner were they face to face than Mr Grant fell down in a fit, and that before ever he touched the book. And in the confusion that followed, the stranger boy disappeared, and no-one could say where he came from or how he went. That was the biggest pliskie that was played. Those who came here after, have just seen him going through the rooms to vanish in some shut up place, and sometimes they have heard cries and knockings, but all the appearances have been much the same.'

3

My last letter ended with McGregor's narrative, did it not, dear Susan? – and now you write to say you are interested, and ask me what more has happened. No more apparitions have happened. I have not seen the boy again, nor has Kenneth seen him: he says he shall not, he is not so made; and, if a healthy scepticism is any safeguard, I imagine he will not. But on the other hand, no eager credulity could in my case have made visible that of which I did not know.

I believe I told you Ken decided to sell the chapel-room, and have it taken away. It is needed for some War object, I am not sure what; so for every reason we are glad to have it go. The contractor's men have been busy all this week taking the timbers to pieces as if it were a child's puzzle, and putting it, not in a box, but on a couple of big lorries. Now they are at work upon the brick foundations and the floor; and the door which led into it from the drawing-room is to have glass panels, and be our way out into the garden.

Only one other event is worth naming since I wrote. That horrible old husband of poor Mrs Wilding's has been taken ill, and I believe the doctor thinks seriously of his state. He hates any sort of change, Mrs Wilding says, and he excited himself over hearing the chapel-room was to be taken away. Imagine this: the first night after the work began, he crawled, nobody knows how, out of the kitchen and through the hall and drawing-room, and himself undid that door. Then I suppose he fell down the six steps, for he was found at the foot of them in the morning, only half alive. It is almost incredible that he could have done it without help. Since then he has had two epileptic fits, and talks the strangest nonsense, so his wife tells us. I wish he could be taken to a hospital – for her sake, poor thing; as well as ours. Ken is going to speak to the doctor, and see what can be arranged.

You ask about Tom. We have had good news of him; two cheery letters, all about cricket, and having got into the first eleven, the height of his ambition. My dream could have meant nothing wrong with him; and now I begin to think it must have been what McGregor calls a 'pliskie' of the ghost's.

I was interrupted yesterday; but now in continuing I can tell you I have seen the boy again. I went out through the drawing-room to look how the work was getting on. The wooden floor has been removed, and now the men are taking up the stone slabs which were underneath, with care not to break them, as they are to be used elsewhere. There were two men at work over this, and the boy was talking to one of them. He seemed to be speaking very earnestly, and pointing to a part of the floor a yard or two away; and the man looked up in his face, and said something (I thought) in answer. I felt a cold shiver pass over me, but in spite of this I walked down the steps into the wrecked place, and, as I approached the group, the boy's figure seemed to slip behind the man with the pickaxe, and so was gone.

'What was that boy doing here, and what did he say to you?' I asked, though my breath almost failed me over the words.

I fancy the workers knew about the ghost, but both of them shook their heads. They had seen no boy, but something was a-whispering in the place – always a-whispering behind them, but they could not make out what it said.

I had but just written that down, when there was a stir outside, of men calling and shouting. Mr Campbell was wanted, and somebody else was bidden to run for the police. I did not know what was the matter, but Ken now tells me 'human remains' have been found under that stone floor. It is very horrible. We have no notion how they came there, but there will, of course, be an investigation. Don't you think we may have happened on a reason for the ghost?

I must post this letter now, if it is to go tonight. I will write again when we know more.

(Five days later)

Oh Susan, this has been a terrible business, and Mrs Wilding is almost out of her mind with grief. The body was that of a boy twelve or fourteen years of age, and from the clothing and certain things found with it, there can be no doubt that it was Martin Wilding, her son. Bassett must have caught him about to run away, and either have killed him on purpose in a homicidal outbreak, or so beaten him that he died; and then buried his body under the floor of the chapel-room, the flags of which were being laid down at the time. Mrs Wilding has charged her husband, and will give evidence against him; and the wretch has been taken away. She says she hopes he will be hanged, but Ken thinks it is not likely the law will go to that extreme, as he is not in his right mind. But he will be shut up as a criminal lunatic for what is left to him of life.

I wonder whether Nevill Nugent foresaw the troubles that would come upon us when he left us the ghost as his legacy! Martin Wilding's remains have been coffined, and will be buried tomorrow.

Ken got me some flowers, and I have made a cross of white lilies for Mrs Wilding to lay on the grave. Is it not strange to think I should have seen him four times, looking as he must have done in life, when all the while his body was lying there? Poor, poor boy, to think what he must have suffered, not able to let his mother know! Now the mystery is cleared up, I don't suppose Mirk Muir Grange will be haunted any more, and Ken may succeed in letting it. As for ourselves, I do not think it likely we shall remain here. Ken says he would rather not, as the associations are too painful: odd that the objection should come from him, the one who saw nothing, and not from me!'

The Crimson Blind

Ronald McEwan, aged sixteen, was invited to spend a vacation fortnight at his uncle's rectory. Possibly some qualms of conscience had
tardily spurred the Revd Sylvanus Applegarth to offer this hospitality,
aware that he had in the past neglected his dead sister's son. Also, with
a view to the future, it might be well for Ronald to make acquaintance
with his own two lads, now holidaying from English public schools.

Mr Applegarth was a gentleman and a scholar, one who loved
above all things leisure and a quiet house: he retained a curate at his
own expense to run matters parochial in Swanmere, and buried
himself among his books. The holidays were seasons of trial to him
on each of the three yearly occasions, and it would not be much
worse, so he reflected, to have three hobbledehoy lads romping
about the place, and clumping up and down stairs with heavy boots,
when it was inevitable he must have two.

The young Applegarths were not ill-natured lads, but they were
somewhat disposed to make a butt of the shy Scottish cousin, who
was midway between them in age, and had had a different upbringing
and schooling from themselves. Ronald found it advisable to listen
much and say little, not airing his own opinions unless they were
directly challenged. But in one direction he had been outspoken,
afterwards wishing devoutly he had held his tongue. Spooks were
under discussion, and it was discovered – a source of fiendish glee to
the allied brothers – that Ronald believed in ghosts, as he preferred
more respectfully to term them, and also in such marvels as death
warnings, wraiths, and second-sight.

'That comes of being a Highlander,' said Jack, the elder. 'Superstition is a taint that gets into the blood, and so is born with you. But
I'll wager anything you have no valid reason for believing. The best
evidence is only second-hand; most of it third- or fourth-hand, if as
near. You have never seen a ghost yourself?'

'No,' acknowledged Ronald somewhat sourly, for he had been more
than sufficiently badgered. 'But I've spoken with those that have.'

'Would you like to see one? Now give a straight answer for once' – and Jack winked at his brother.

'I wouldn't mind.' Then, more stoutly, 'Yes, I would like – if I'd the chance.'

'I think we can give you a chance of seeing something, if not exactly a ghost. We've got no Highland castles to trot out, but there's a house here in Swanmere that is said to be haunted. Just the thing for you to investigate, now you are on the spot. Will you take it on?'

It would have been fatal to say no, and give these cousins the opening to post him as a coward. Ronald gave again the grudging admission that he 'wouldn't mind'. And then, being Sunday morning, the lads said they would take him round that way after church, and he should have a look at the window which had earned a bad repute. Then they might find out who had the keys in charge, if he felt inclined to pass a night within.

'I suppose, as neither of you believe, you would not be afraid to sleep there?' said Ronald, addressing the two.

'Certainly we would not be *afraid*.' Jack was speech-valiant at least. 'As we believe there is nothing in it but a sham, like all the other tales.'

Alfred, the younger boy, did not contradict his brother, but it might have been noticed that he kept silence.

'Then I'll do what you do.' This was Ronald's ultimatum. 'If you two choose to sleep in the haunted house, I'll sleep there too.'

But, as the event fell out, the Applegarths did not push matters to the point of borrowing keys from the house-agent and camping out rolled in blankets on the bare floors – an attractive picture Jack went on to draw of the venture to which Ronald stood committed. After the morning service, the three lads walked some half mile beyond the village in the direction of the sea shore. Here the houses were few and far between, but two or three villas were in course of building, and other plots beyond them were placarded as for sale. Swanmere was 'rising' – in other words, in process of being spoiled. Niched in between two of these plots was an empty house to let, well placed in being set some way back from the high road, within the privacy of thick shrubberies, and screened at the back by a belt of forest trees.

A desirable residence, one would have said at a first glance, but closer acquaintance was apt to induce a change of mind. The iron gates of the drive were fastened with padlock and chain, but the young Applegarths effected an entrance by vaulting over the palings at the side. Everywhere was to be seen the encroachment and over-growth of long neglect: weeds knee high, and branches pushing themselves across the side-paths, though the carriage approach had been kept clear. The main entrance was at the side, and in front bowed windows, on two floors, were closely shuttered within, and grimed with dirt without.

The boys pushed their way round to the back, where the kitchen offices were enclosed by a yard. But midway between the better and the inferior part of the house, a large flat window on the first floor overlooked the flower-garden and shrubbery. This window was not shuttered, but was completely screened by a wide blind of faded red, drawn down to meet the sill. Jack pointed to it.

'That is where the ghost shows – not every night, but sometimes. Maybe you'll have to watch for a whole week before there is anything to see. But, if rumour says true, you will be repaid in the end. Whatever the appearance may be.'

Ronald thought he saw a wink pass between the brothers. He was to be hoaxed in some way; of that he felt assured.

'I'll go, if we three go together, you and Alfred and I. If there is a real ghost to be seen, you shall see it too. What is it said to be like?'

'A light comes behind the red blind, and some people see a figure, or the shadow of a figure, in the room. Perhaps it is according to the open eye, some less and some more. You may see more still, being Highland born and bred. Very well, as you make it a condition, we will go together.'

'Tonight?'

'Better not tonight. There's evening church and supper, and the governor might not like it, being Sunday. We will go tomorrow. That will serve as well for you.'

The fake, whatever it might be, could not be prepared in time for that first evening, Ronald reflected. He was quite unbelieving about the red blind and the light, but firm in his resolve. If he was to be trotted out to see a ghost, the Applegarth cousins should go too. It was a matter of indifference to him which night was chosen for the expedition, so Monday was agreed upon, the trio to set out at midnight, when all respectable inhabitants of Swanmere should be in their beds.

When Monday night came, the sky was clear and starlit, but it was the dark of the moon. One of the lads possessed an electric torch, which Jack put in his pocket. And when it came to the point, it appeared that only Jack was going with him. Alfred, according to his brother, had developed a sore throat, and Mrs Dawson, the housekeeper, was putting him on a poultice which had to be applied in bed.

So it was the younger Applegarth who had been chosen to play the ghost, Ronald instantly concluded: he had no faith at all in the poultice, or in Mrs Dawson's application of it, though he remembered Alfred had complained of the soreness of his throat more than once during the day.

There was little interchange of words between the two lads as they went. Ronald was inwardly resentful, and Jack seemed to have some private thoughts which amused him, for he smiled to himself in the darkness. Arrived at the Portsmouth road, they got over the fence at the same place as before; and now Jack's torch was of use, as they pushed their way through the tangled garden to the spot determined on as likely to afford the best view of the window with the crimson blind. Neither blind nor window could now be distinguished; the house reared itself before them a silhouette of blacker darkness, against that other darkness of the night.

'We can sit on this bench while we wait,' and young Applegarth flashed his torch on a rustic structure, set beneath overshadowing trees. 'I propose to time ourselves and give an hour to the watch. Then, if you have seen nothing, we can come away and return another night. For myself, sceptic as I am, I don't expect to see.'

He could hardly be more sceptical than Ronald felt at the moment. Certain that a trick was about to be played on him, all his senses had been on the alert from the moment they left the road, and he felt sure that as they plunged through the wilderness of shrubbery, he had heard another footstep following. He did not refuse to seat himself on the bench, but he took care to have the bole of the tree immediately at his back, as some protection from assault in the rear.

Some five or six minutes went by, and he was paying little attention to the house, but much to certain rustling noises in the shrubbery behind them, when Jack Applegarth exclaimed in an altered voice: 'By Jove, there is a light there after all!' and he became aware that the broad parallelogram of the window was now faintly illuminated behind the crimson blind, sufficiently to show its shape and size, and also the colour of the screen. Could young Alfred have found some means of entrance, and set up a lighted candle in the room? – but somehow he doubted whether, without his brother to back him, the boy would have ventured into the ghostly house alone. The fake he anticipated was of a different sort to this.

As the boys watched, the light grew stronger, glowing through the blind; the lamp within that room must have been a strong one of many candle-power. Then a shadow became visible, as if cast by some person moving to and fro in front of the light; this was faint at first, but gradually it increased in intensity, and presently came close to the window, pulling the blind aside to look out.

This was so ordinary an action that it did not suggest the supernatural. A moment later, however, the whole framework of the window seemed to give way and fall outwards with a crash of breaking glass. The figure now showed clearly defined, standing outside on the sill with the red illumination behind; but its pause there was one only of seconds before it leaped to the ground and came rushing towards them; a figure so far in ghostly likeness that it appeared to be clad in white. Following the crash of glass came other sounds, a pistol-shot and a scream, but the rush of the flying figure was unaccompanied by noise. It passed close to the bench where they were seated, and young Applegarth grasped Ronald's arm in a terror well-acted if unreal.

'Come away,' he said thickly. 'I've had enough of this. Come away.'

The light behind the blind was dying out, and presently the window was again in darkness, but these spectators did not stay to see.

Jack Applegarth dragged Ronald back towards the road, and the younger lad broke from the bushes and followed them, sobbing in what seemed to be real affright, and with a white bundle hugged in his arms. They climbed the palings and went pelting home, and not till the distance was half accomplished did any one of them speak. Then Ronald had the first word. 'Why Alfred, I thought you were in bed. I hope your throat will not suffer through coming out to trick me with a sham ghost. I made sure all along that was what you and Jack would do.'

Alfred hugged tighter the bundle he was carrying: did he fear it would be snatched off him and displayed? – it looked exceedingly like a white sheet.

'I had nothing to do with *that thing*,' he blurted out between chattering teeth. 'I don't know what it was, or where it came from. But I swear I'll never go near the blamed place again, either by night or by day!'

2

Whether there was any natural explanation of what they had seen, Ronald never knew. His visit to his Applegarth relatives was drawing to a close, and, shortly after, the old Rector died suddenly during the service in church. The home was broken up, the two schoolboy cousins had their way to make in the World, and, whether ill or well made, this history knows them no more. And between the just concluded chapter, and this which is now begun, must be set an interval of twenty years.

Ronald had done well for himself in the meantime. He had become an alert hard-headed business man, a good deal detached from the softer side of life, for which, he told himself, there would be time and to spare by-and-bye. But now, at thirty-six, there began to be a different telling. He could afford to keep a wife in comfort, and it seemed to him that the time for choice had come.

This does not pretend to be a love-story, so it will only briefly chronicle that it was the business of wife-selection which took Ronald again to Swanmere. He happened to act as best man at his friend Parkinson's wedding, and one of the bridesmaids seemed to him an unusually attractive girl, happy herself, and likely to make others happy, which is better than mere beauty. Probably he let fall a wish that he might see Lilian again; anyway, some time later, he was invited to run down and pay a weekend visit to the newly-married pair, when Lilian was at the same time expected to stay. And, as it happened, the Peregrine Parkinsons had settled at Swanmere.

'Do you know this place at all?' queried Mrs Parkinson, who was meeting him at the station with the small pony-carriage, of which, and of her skill as a whip, she was inordinately proud.

'I was here once before, many years ago,' was Ronald's answer. 'I was only a schoolboy in those days, visiting an old uncle, who then was rector of the parish. Swanmere seems to have grown a good deal bigger than I remember it, or else my recollection is at fault.'

'Oh yes, it has grown; places do grow, don't they? There was a great deal of new building before the war; villas you know, and that style; but 1914 stopped everything. Peregrine and I were fortunate in meeting with an older house, in a quite delightful well-grown garden. Oh no, not old enough to be inconvenient, and it has been brought up-to-date for us. We were lucky to get it, I can assure you: it is so difficult in these days to find anything moderate-sized. They are snapped up directly they are vacant, the demand is so much in excess of the supply.'

Ronald did not recognise the direction taken, even when the pony willingly turned in at an open pair of iron gates, which he had last seen chained and padlocked – or if not these gates, their predecessors, as gates have a way of perishing in untended years. All was trim within, pruned and swept and gravelled, and the garden a riot of colour with its summer flowers. But the front of the house, with double bows carried up to the first floor, did strike a chord of association. 'I wonder!' he said to himself, and then the wonder was negatived. 'No, it isn't possible; it would be too odd a coincidence.' And upon this he dismissed the thought from mind.

It did not return during the evening, not even when he went up – in a hurry, and at the last moment – to dress for dinner in the bedroom allotted to him; a spacious and well-appointed one, where his port-manteau had been unpacked and habiliments laid out. After dinner there was the diversion of some good music; Mrs Parkinson played and Lilian sang. The Swanmere experience of twenty years ago was quite out of mind when he retired for the night; pleasanter thoughts had pushed it into the background and held the stage. But the recollection was vaguely renewed last thing, when he drew aside the curtains and opened the window, noting its unusual square shape, divided into three uprights, two of which opened casement fashion.

It was the only window in the room, but so wide that it nearly filled the outer wall. Certainly its shape recalled the window of twenty years ago which was screened by a crimson blind, and his watch in the garden with Jack Applegarth. He was never likely to forget that night, though he was far from sure whether the ghost was ghost indeed, or a sham faked by the Applegarth boys for his discomfiture. Probably these suburban villas were built all upon one plan, and an older foundation had set the note of fashion for those that followed. He never knew the name or number of the haunted house, or locality, except that it was entered from the Portsmouth road, so in that way he could not identify it. And again he dismissed the idea, and addressed himself to sleep.

Neither this recollection nor the dawning love-interest was potent to keep him awake. He slept well the early part of the night, and did not wake till morning was brightening in the east. Then, as he opened his eyes and turned to face the light, he saw, and was aston-ished seeing, that the window was covered with a crimson blind, drawn down from top to sill.

He could have declared that nothing of the sort was in place there over night. The drawn-back curtains had revealed a quite ordinary green venetian, which he had raised till it clicked into stoppage at its height. To all outward seeming this was a material blind, swaying in the air of the open casement, and with no light behind it but that of the summer dawn. And yet, for all that, he lay staring at it with nerves on edge, and hammering pulses which beat thickly in his ears and throat: something within him recognised the nature of the appearance and responded with agitation, despite the scepticism of the outward man. That was a bird's song vocal outside, wheels went by in the road, the ordinary world was astir. He would rise and assure himself that the blind was a mundane affair, palpable to touch; it had of course slipped down in the night owing to a loosened cord, and was hung within the other.

And then he discovered that his limbs were powerless: it was as if invisible bands restrained him. He writhed against them in vain, and in the end, despite those rapid pulses of the affrighted heart, he fell suddenly into trance or sleep.

He had had a seizure of nightmare, he concluded when he awoke later, with the servant knocking at the door to bring in tea and shaving-water, and the open window cheerful and unscreened, letting in the summer air.

His first act was to examine the window-frame, but – of course, as he told himself – there was no crimson blind, nothing but the green venetian, and the curtains drawing on their rod. He had dreamt the whole thing, on the suggestion of that memory of a schoolboy visit long ago.

He was well assured of the folly of it all, and yet he had again and again to reason the thing out, and repeat that it was folly – himself in colloquy with himself. This was still more necessary when in the course of the morning he strolled out into the garden and round the shrubbery paths. Though the wild growth of long ago had been pruned back and certain changes made, he had no difficulty in finding the spot – what he thought the spot – where he and Jack Applegarth had watched. There was still a rustic seat under the trees, full in view of the square window of his room where the red blind no longer was displayed. He sat down to light a cigarette, and presently his host appeared, pipe in mouth, and joined him on the bench in the shade.

'You have a nice place here,' Ronald said, by way of opening conversation. 'Yes,' Parkinson agreed. I like it, and Cecilia likes it, and in every way it suits us well. Convenient for business you know, and not too pretentious for young beginners. We both fell in love with it at first sight. But I heard something the other day' (poking with his knife at a pipe which declined to draw) 'something that rather disturbed me. Not that I believe it, you know; I'm not that sort. I only hope and trust that no busybody will consider it his, or her, duty to inform Cecilia.'

'What did you hear?'

'Why, some fools were saying the house used to be haunted, and that was the reason why it stood long unlet, and fell into bad repair. Stories of that sort are always put about when a place happens to be nobody's fancy, whether the real drawback is rats or drains, or somebody wanting to keep it vacant for interests of their own – as you know. In this case I should say it was the latter – because the man told me lights were seen when the place was shut up and empty. A thieves' dumping ground, no doubt. Or possibly coiners.'

This in pauses, between whiffs of the pipe. Parkinson ended: 'I don't want Cecilia to know. She is fond of the place, and I wouldn't like her to be nervous or upset.'

'Couldn't you warn the man?'

'I did that. But there are other men who know. And, what is worse, women. You know what women's tongues are. Especially when they think they have got hold of something spicy. Or what will annoy somebody else!'

'Why not tell your wife yourself, and trust to her good sense not to mind. Better for her to learn it so, than by chance whispers from a stranger. She won't like it if she thinks you were aware, and kept it up your sleeve.'

But Parkinson shook his head. Fond as he was of his Cecilia, perhaps his opinion of her good sense had not been heightened by the experience of four or five months of marriage. And Ronald checked his own impulse to communicate the history of that former episode, together with the odd dream – if it was a dream – which visited him the night before. But he had found out one thing: now it was beyond doubt. This smartly done-up villa with its modern improvements, was identical with the closed and neglected house of long ago.

That day was Saturday. He had been invited to stay over the weekend, so there were two more nights that he was bound to spend at the villa. He did not enjoy the anticipation of those nights, though some slight uneasiness would cheaply purchase the intermediate day to be spent with Lilian. And what harm could any ghost do him, and what did it matter whether the window was covered with a crimson blind, or a white or a green!

It mattered little when regarded in the day, but during the watches of the night such affairs take on a different complexion, though Ronald McEwan was no coward. He woke earlier on this second night: woke to be aware of a faint illumination in the room, and of – he thought after, though it was hardly realised at the time – the instantaneous glimpse of a figure crossing from wall to wall. One thing he did distinctly see: over the window there hung again – the crimson blind! Then in the space of half a dozen heart-beats, the faint light faded out, and the room was left in darkness.

This time the paralysis of the night before did not recur. He had been careful to place within reach at the bedside the means of striking a light, and presently his candle showed the window unscreened and open, and the door locked as he left it overnight. He did not extinguish that candle, but let it burn down in the socket; and he was not again disturbed.

During Sunday he debated with himself the question to speak or not to speak. That spare room might next be occupied by someone to whom the terror of such a visitation would be harmful; and yet, he supposed, all turned on whether or not the occupier was gifted (or shall we say cursed?) with the open eye. He felt thankful he had been quartered there and not Lilian. Finally, he resolved that Parkinson must be warned, but not till he himself was on the point of leaving – not till he had passed a third night in the haunted room, disturbed or not disturbed. And, after all, what had he to allege against it in this later time? Could a room be haunted by the apparition of a crimson blind?

Saturday had been brilliantly fine throughout, but Sunday dawned upon unsettled weather, and a wet gale rushing over from the not distant sea. He went to rest that night resolved to keep a light burning through the dark hours, but found it necessary to shut the window on account of the driven storm. He strove to reason himself into indifference and so prepare for sleep, which visited him sooner than he expected, and for a while was profound. It was somewhere between two and three o'clock when he started up, broad awake on the instant, with the consciousness of something wrong.

It was not the moderate light of his candle which now illuminated the room, but the fierce glow of mounting flames, though he could not see whence they proceeded. The red blind hung again over the window, but that was a negligible matter: some carelessness of his had set the Parkinsons' house on fire, and he must give the alarm. He struggled up in bed, only to find he was not alone. There at the bed-foot stood gazing at him a man, a stranger, plainly seen in the glare of light. A man haggard of countenance, with the look of a soul that despaired; clad in white or light-coloured garments, possibly a sleeping-suit.

Ronald believed he made an attempt to speak to this creature, to ask who he was and what doing there, but whether he really achieved articulate words he does not know. For the space of perhaps a minute the two stared at each other, the man in the flesh and he who was flesh no more; then the latter sprang to the window, standing on the low sill, and tore aside the crimson blind. There was a great crash of glass like that other crash remembered, a cry from below in the garden, and a report like a pistol-shot; the figure had disappeared, leaping through the broken gap. Then all was still and the room in darkness; those fierce flames were suddenly extinguished, and his own candle had gone out.

He groped for the matches and struck a light. The red blind had disappeared from the window, there was no broken glass and no fire, and everything remained as he had left it over night.

No-one else appeared to have heard that shot and cry in the dead middle of the night. After breakfast he took Parkinson into confidence, who heard the story gloomily enough, plainly discomforted though unwilling to believe.

'You have been right to tell me, my dear fellow, and I am sure you think you experienced all these impossible things. But look at probability. Those Applegarth boys hoaxed you years ago, the impression dwelt on your mind, and was revived by discovering this house to be the same. Such was the simple cause of your visions; any doctor would tell you so. As for my own action, I don't see clear. It is a horribly awkward affair, and we have been to no end of expense settling in. Cecilia likes the place, and it suits her. So long as she does not know – !'

'Look here, Parkinson. There is one thing I think I may ask – suggest, at least. You have another spare bedroom. Don't put any other guest where I have been sleeping. Couldn't you make it a storeroom – box-room – anything that is not used at night?'

Parkinson still was doubtful: he shook his head. 'Not without an explanation to Cecilia. She happens to be particularly *gone* on that room on account of the big window. It was just a toss-up that she didn't put Lilian there, and you in the other. And – if in time to come a nursery should be needed, that is the room on which she has her eye. She would never consent to give it up for a glory-hole or a store-room without a strong reason. A very strong reason indeed.'

Ronald could do no more: his friend was warned, the responsibility was no longer his.

It was some comfort to know that Lilian was leaving two days later, going on to another visit, and the fatal house did not seem to have affected her up to now.

After this, a couple of months went by, during which the Parkinsons made no sign, and he for his part kept his lips entirely sealed about his experiences at Swanmere. It might be, as Jack Applegarth said long before, his Highland blood which rendered him vulnerable to uncanny influences, and the Parkinsons and their Southron friends might remain entirely immune. But at the end of two months he received the following letter:

DEAR OLD CHUM – It is all up with us here, and I think you will wish to know how it came about. I am trying to sub-let Ashcroft, and hope to find somebody fool enough to take it. I haven't a fault to find with the place, neither of us have seen or heard a thing, and really it seems absurd. The servants picked up some gossip about the haunting, and then one of them was scared – by her own shadow, I expect, and promptly had hysterics. After that, all three of them went to Cecilia in a body, and said they were willing to forfeit their wages, and sorry to cause us inconvenience, but nothing would induce them to stop on in a haunted house – not if we paid them hundreds – and they must leave at once. Then I had to have it out with Cecilia, and she was not pleased to have been kept in the dark. She says I hoodwinked her – but if I did, it was for her own good; and when we took the place, I had not the least idea. Of course she could not stay when the servants cleared out – and nor could I; so she has gone to her mother's, and I am at the hotel – with everyone asking questions, which I can assure you is not pleasant. I shall take jolly good care not to be trapped a second time into a place where ghosts are on the loose.

There is one thing that may interest you, as it seems to throw light on your experience. The house was built by a doctor who took in lunatic patients – harmless ones they were supposed to be, and he was properly certificated and all that: there was no humbug about it that I know. One man who was thought quite a mild case suddenly became violent. He locked himself into his room and set it on fire, and then smashed a window – I believe it was that window – and jumped out. It was only from the first floor, but he was so badly injured that he died: a good riddance of bad rubbish, I should say. I don't know anything about a red blind or a pistol-shot: those matters seem to have been embroidered on. But the coincidence is an odd one, I allow.

We were pleased to hear of your engagement to Lilian, and I send you both congratulations and good wishes, in which Cecilia would join if here. I suppose you will soon be Benedick the married man.

Yours ever,
PEREGRINE PARKINSON

Fingers of a Hand

'In the same hour came forth the fingers of a man's hand and wrote . . .
and the king saw the part of the hand that wrote.'

The children were supposed to need a seaside change, and I dare say they did, poor wee things, as they had had whooping-cough in the spring, and measles to follow. As you know, we are taking care of them for Bernard, who is in India with his wife, and so we are even more anxious about them than if they were our own. That is one great use of unmarried aunts – to shoulder other people's responsibilities; and I, for one, think the world would be a poorer place if the 'millions of unwanted women' were, by some convulsion of nature, to be swept away. I only mention the children's measles as the reason why we took those lodgings at Cove at the beginning of July, for, now one has to economise, we should not have gone in for a seaside change as a luxury for ourselves.

The lodgings were clean and fairly comfortable, and we took them for two months certain, letting our own pretty cottage in the midlands for a similar term. And that was why we had no home of our own to retreat to when – but I am telling my story upside down, as Sara says I always do. You would not be likely to understand, if I did not begin in the right place, with what went before.

The house was Number Seven, Cliff Terrace, a row of detached villas above the road, on the other side of which was the esplanade and the sea. There were no other lodgers, as we took both Mrs Mills's 'sets'; nobody in the house but ourselves and the bairns, and that important person, Nurse, except Mrs Mills herself, and her daughter who waited on us. So you see there was no-one who could have played tricks – but again I am getting on too fast.

We had never been to Cove before, or to St Eanswyth either, the larger watering place which lies to the east of Cove; but we thought our choice of place for a summer holiday was amply justified by the pretty inland neighbourhood and the sweet air, and a safe beach close at hand, where the children could be out playing early and late under the guardian wing of Nurse. For the first fortnight we were all satisfied and happy, and, both in metaphor and actually, there was not a cloud in the sky.

Then the rain began, not brief summer showers and sunshine in between, but the worst weather of a wet July – a continuous downpour with hardly ten minutes intermission, and going on for days: such rain as Noah must have witnessed before the beginning of the Flood.

Of course the poor children had to keep the house, and, though they and Nurse had the dining-room set to themselves, there was but little space for them to play about. Sara and I occupied the drawing-room, and she had been sketching from the window – not that there was much visible to make into a picture: a leaden sea and slanting lines of rain, and boats drawn up on the beach. At last she pushed away colour-box and pencils.

'I can't stand this any longer,' she said. 'Rain or no rain, I am going out. It will be a good opportunity to test the resisting powers of my new cloak. You must stay in today, as I believe you have caught cold.'

I did not dispute her fiat. Sara always decides what is, or what is not to be done, and I, who am a biddable person, submit to be ruled. And, to say the truth, I was not particularly anxious to get wet. I went on with my sewing till it was nearly time for Miss Mills to appear with the luncheon-tray, and then I began to clear the table of Sara's scattered possessions.

Some blank sheets of paper were lying about, besides the one pinned to her board with the half-finished sketch; and on one of these I noticed some large scrawled writing. Not Sara's writing, which is particularly small and neat; not the writing of anyone I knew. The words were quite legible, but they were very odd. GO – by itself at the top of the sheet; and the same word repeated twice below, followed by GET OUT AT ONCE.

Of course I showed Sara this when she came in to luncheon, and she could not account for it any more than I. The sheets were unmarked when she took them out of her portfolio; of that she seemed to be certain.

'Someone has been playing a trick on us,' she said. 'If it is Mrs Mills, it is an odd sort of notice'; and at this very mild witticism both of us laughed.

But the idea of a trick being played was absurd: I had been in the room the whole time, as I said.

'Unless you think I dozed off while you were out, and did it in my sleep!'

Sara laughed again, and began to sort the loose papers back into place.

'Why, here is more of it,' she exclaimed; and I saw on the sheet she held out, in the same large scrawl, a repetition of the words – GET OUT – GET OUT AT ONCE.

Now I could have sworn – had swearing been of any use – that I had looked those papers over on both sides after finding the first writing, and with that sole exception they bore no mark whatever. So these last words must have been written after my discovery and before Sara's return, and while I was beside them in the room. Surely they had been traced by no mortal hand!

You will not wonder that such a curious happening was the subject of discussion between us during the rest of that wet day. 'I'd give anything to know who did it,' Sara was saying, while I added: 'I should like better still to know what it means.' I am more credulous than Sara, and it seemed to me there must be some meaning in anything so unaccountable. I had this feeling from the very first, and, as you will see, both the conviction and the reason for it grew.

I pass on to the following Sunday. The weather was still wet, and the children were kept mainly to the house. For the sake of variety for them, Sara had little Dick and Nancy upstairs in our sitting-room for their Sunday lessons, which as a rule devolve on her to give, as she is a cleverer teacher than I. Lessons of the simplest, as they generally consist of showing pictures and giving explanations; and to be allowed to look at Sara's illustrated Bible is a frequent Sabbath treat. The children had gone down again to Nurse, and Sara was about to tidy the book away, when she gave a sharp exclamation.

'Grace, look here. Who can have done this?'

The volume was lying open at the nineteenth chapter of Genesis, and these words in the twenty-second verse were scored under blackly in pencil – *Haste thee: escape*.

Now Sara, who is particular in everything, is especially so about her books. She hates any soil or mark upon them, and nothing irritates her more than to have a lent volume returned with 'purple passages' scored beside in the margin, whether in approval or other-wise. 'Tut-tut,' she was saying, at the usual pitch of exasperation. 'It is really unpardonable. *Where* is my india-rubber? I must see if I can take it out. It could not have been the children. And the Millses would never – ! But there is nobody else.'

'You would have seen, had it been the children. They are good little things, and would not: besides, they had not a pencil' (thus I weakened an argument based on their righteousness). 'And what odd words to have chosen to mark, when you think of the other scrawls. I wonder if this is all. It is possible there may be more.'

'I shall look the book right through and see, and then I shall lock it in my box.'

Sara sat down to her task armed with the piece of rubber, and by no means in a Sabbath spirit of peace and good-will. She did find two other texts scored under, and these were the marked words:

> 2 Kings, ninth chapter and third verse.
> *Open the door and flee and tarry not.*
>
> St Matthew, seventh chapter and twenty-seventh verse.
> *The . . . house . . . fell, and great was the fall thereof.*

I was superstitious, because disturbed by these happenings – so I was told, yet who would not have been affected in my place? I believe Sara too was disquieted in her secret mind, though she would not allow it. But then she was used to pride herself on being an *esprit fort*.

I kept saying to myself, 'What next?' – and the next came quickly. I did not tell Sara what I purposed doing, but I left a couple of sheets of paper and a freshly-cut pencil displayed on the table when we were going out. More writing might be done with the opportunity given, and 'it' might vouchsafe to make clear 'its' meaning. I could not then have analysed what I meant by the convenient impersonal pronoun, nor am I clear of the exact meaning now.

We were about to do some shopping in the town, and I had stupidly left my purse on the mantel-shelf in the sitting-room, so I was obliged to turn back to get it. As I opened the door, my eyes fell at once upon the papers, and I saw some dark object moving across the white surface, and then quickly disappearing over the table edge. It was too big for a mouse; could it have been a rat? The thought of a rat gave me a nervous shiver; I think I would have a greater terror of rats than of ghosts. I looked at the papers though I did not touch them; yes, a vague scrawl was begun upon the upper one, not developed into legible words. I had disturbed the writer too soon. But what could the writer be, coming in the form of a rat, or the shadow of a rat, and yet able to write words which appeared to convey a message? I left the papers as they were, but the scrawl was not continued; no doubt that unexpected first return had scared away the writer.

I said nothing to Sara of my failed experiment; but next day about the same time I laid my trap again, this time staying in the room, but retired into a distant corner, where I set myself to watch.

For a long while there was nothing. Then an object ill-defined and shadowy crept across the paper, stealing towards the pencil as it lay. I hardly dared breathe, the excitement was so tense. Over the pencil this shadow paused, and now became denser, taking solid form. It was not the whole of a hand, but a thumb and two fingers, forming something like a claw. But, if you consider, a thumb and two fingers are all a hand needs to manipulate a pencil, and 'it' may not have cared to materialise anything superfluous. The pencil now slanted upwards between these fingers and the thumb, and – yes, no doubt remained – the claw was writing. Now we would know all, such was my sanguine thought, not forecasting how deep the mystery would remain.

It was Sara this time who interrupted, coming in. The pencil dropped, the claw from a solid form became a shadow, and slipped away over the edge of the table, as I had seen it vanish before. Sara noticed nothing; she was too full of her news, and the letter open in her hand.

'Look at this. We ought to have had it two days ago, but there was a mistake in the address. It is from Mrs Bernard's mother.' (Mrs Bernard is our brother's wife.) 'She is at Diplake for ten days before they go to Scotland, and she wants one of us to bring the children there just for the time they stay. She says she is sorry she cannot have us both, but it is a case of a single room, as the house is full. She is expecting us tomorrow, so I shall have to wire, and tell Nurse to get ready. Will you go, Grace, or shall I?'

'Of course you must be the one. I should never get on at Diplake, and with a large, gay party. You must go, Sara, and put your best foot foremost, for Bernard's sake. And – I'm glad you have to take the children. For look what is written here!'

I showed her the paper on which the claw had scrawled. Over and over again the word DANGER, as if it could not be too often insisted on. Then, also repeated: GO. GET OUT. Then an attempt at *children*, afterwards clearly written: DANGER. CHILDREN MUST GO.

I think Sara was impressed at last, though she hardly believed in the claw I had seen writing. As to that, I must – she said – have been hallucinating, or else slept and dreamed. But little time remained for argument, as all was in a hurry of preparation – boxes to be packed, and the children to be consoled, for their enjoyment of the seaside pleasures was very keen, and the attraction small of going to stay with an almost unknown grandmother. 'But we are coming back?' said little Nancy. 'We are coming back again here?' I believe I told her 'Yes', but as to what will happen in the future, who can say?

They set out early next morning, Sara and the three children and Nurse, and I saw them off at the station. Sara said almost at the last: 'I don't half like leaving you alone here, Grace. If you find the lodgings too solitary, why not take a room at the hotel for the days I am away?'

I said I would think of it, but in truth I felt no special nervousness or concern, only an intense curiosity to see what would happen now we had (by pure accident) obeyed the dictation of the writing, and sent the children away.

The lonely evening passed for me without disturbance; Miss Mills came at the usual time to carry down my supper tray, and wished me goodnight, and shortly after this I went to bed.

I slept, and do not remember any warning dreams. But in the very early daylight I was suddenly startled broad awake – not I think by any noise, but by an alteration in the level of my bed. My head was low, almost on the floor, and my feet were high in air. Everything in the room was sliding and altering; basin and ewer slipped from the washstand, crashed and broke, and pictures flapped from the wall. Then came a greater crash like the jolting of a thunder-clap, and it was close at hand; chimney-pots falling, walls and roofs collapsing: was it an earthquake that had happened? I heard screams and shouts, but the sliding movement had stopped.

I struggled up and to my feet, for I had been half buried by the bedclothes falling back upon me; and there opposite was a great crack or rent in the outer wall, wide enough to admit my arm, with the new morning looking through, and a waft of air blowing in keenly from the sea. It was as if the house had broken in two. What but an earthquake could have caused such a disaster? – and again I heard people screaming. The often repeated warning, the scored words in the Bible ran in my head. I could be thankful indeed that Sara and the children were safe at Diplake out of the way: what an agony had they been still here, and those screams possibly theirs!

I do not know how long it took me to scramble up the slanting floor, to find my clothes, my shoes, where all was confusion, so that if it were possible to get out of the house I might go forth clad. Then I tried the door.

It was in some way jammed, and it seemed as if ages passed before

I could wrench it open. When at last it gave way, the wreck revealed without was worse than the wreck within. The staircase was a heap of broken wood, and the back wall had fallen inwards; there was no getting down that way. What had become, I wondered, of Mrs Mills and her daughter, and was it their screams that I heard? I called to them by name, but there was no answer.

Baffled so, I looked from the window, which had hardly a whole pane left. It was as if the terrace had disappeared: the road was broken up, and the house had been carried down with the sliding earth, many yards nearer the sea. A crowd had assembled, staring at this phenomenon, but at a safe distance. I shouted to them, and a man called up to me instructions to stay where I was, as a ladder would presently be brought.

I knew later that they feared at first to touch the house, lest it should collapse in total ruin like the one next on the terrace, where, alas! two people had been killed, overwhelmed and buried in their sleep.

This was a danger indeed, about which that warning came. The part of our house which fell was where the children would have been sleeping. I was told that tons and tons of masonry had crushed in their little beds; even now it makes me sick to think of what we so narrowly escaped. The Millses, mother and daughter, were dug out of the basement quite unharmed, but I am afraid, poor people, they are heavy losers. I myself had not a scratch.

The great landslip at Cove, with all its damage and disaster, will surely pass into history: the slide of the undercliff down into the sea, the gaping fissure torn above, hundreds of feet in length – the alteration of the ground below, heaped into mounds and billows like the waves of the sea, while the buildings in the course of the slide are broken up and displaced like a set of children's toys, playthings in the hands of a giant. People who are wise about the geological formation talk of a bed of slippery clay underlying the upper strata, and say water had percolated down to it owing to the wet spring, and, following upon that, the heavy rains of that dismal week in July. But they are wise after the event and did not forecast it: indeed it was anticipated by no-one other than the writer of those mysterious words.

The Next Heir

Fryer and Fryer, solicitors, of Lincoln's Inn, the original firm and their successors, have for the past hundred years acted as guardians of the interests of the landed gentry, buying and selling portions of estates, proving wills, drawing up marriage settlements and the like. And a glance at the japanned deed-boxes in their somewhat shabby office would discover among the inscriptions sundry names of note.

The original Fryers have long been dead and gone, but there is still a Fryer at the head of the firm. And on a certain day of spring, this ruling Fryer was alone in his private office-room, when his clerk brought in a message. 'Mr Richard Quinton to see you, sir. He has no card to send up, but he says you will know his name and his business, as he has called to answer an advertisement.'

Without doubt Mr Fryer did know the name of Quinton, as it was legibly painted on a deed-box full in view, but something in his countenance expressed surprise. He signified his willingness to see Mr Richard Quinton, and presently the visitor entered, a pleasant-faced youngish man, brown of attire, and indeed altogether a brown man, except for the whitish patch where his forehead had been screened from the sun: bronzed of skin, brown of short cut hair, and opening on the world a frank pair of hazel eyes, which looked as if they had been used to regard the wide spaces of waste lands, and were not fully used to the pressure and hurry and strenuousness of our over-civilised older world.

'I have called, sir, about an advertisement inserted by Fryer and Fryer in a Montreal paper. I have it here to show you. It was posted to me at the London hospital, where I have been since my wound. I see that the representative of Richard Morley Quinton, who emigrated to Canada in 1827, will hear on applying to you of something to his advantage.'

'*May* hear of something,' corrected the man of law. 'Are you the representative in this generation?'

'I am, sir. Richard Morley Quinton was my grandfather.'

'Great-grandfather, surely? You are under thirty, and he was twenty-six years old when he left England.'

'No, grandfather. He had a hard struggle in his first years on the other side. His English brother was not the sort to help him, and he never asked for help: he would not. He did not marry until late in life, and my old dad was the only son who survived infancy. There was a daughter who married and had children. But I don't suppose you want to know about her.'

'We want the male heir. Or at least to know where he might be found.'

'My dad married earlier, but he had no children by his first wife. He was well over fifty when he married my mother, and I am their only child. I can put you in the way of certificates you want, and vouchers from responsible people who have known the family. And now, tell me. Why am I advertised for? Is it an inheritance?'

'Not at the present moment, but it may be.'

'Of Quinton and Quinton Verney – is that so? My dad would have been pleased. He thought much about Quinton, hearing about it from his father, who was born at the Court.'

'If the present Mr Quinton, your second cousin, makes no will, the Quinton property goes to the heir-male of your mutual great-grandfather. But he has the power of willing the whole where he pleases – to a hospital, or to a beggar in the street. You can count on no certain inheritance. You understand?'

'Then why – ?'

'We advertised because Mr Quinton wished to ascertain who represented the Canadian branch of the family, and also to make your personal acquaintance. We can give you no certainty, but I gather from what he has written, that, if your cousin likes you, and if you agree to certain stipulations respecting the property, he intends to make you his heir. When the particulars you give me are verified, you will have to go down to Quinton, but he will reimburse any expense you may be put to, through loss of time and detention in England. You can hold yourself at our disposal?'

'If military orders do not interfere – yes, gladly, for the sake of a look at old Quinton Court, even with nothing to come after. But perhaps Mr Quinton may prefer to meet me in London.'

'You will have to go down there. Mr Quinton is a complete invalid, and keeps a resident doctor: he is still under sixty, but most unlikely, I should say, to marry. His father was killed in the hunting-field; he had not been long married, but his wife, who was one of the Pengwyns, gave birth to twin sons, posthumous children. This Clement was the younger of the two, but his elder brother died at nineteen, also from an accident. There you have the family history in a nutshell. Give me an address, where a letter will certainly find you when I have looked into this.'

Richard had not long to wait for the expected letter. Mr Clement Quinton seemed disposed to take his young kinsman on trust, without holding aloof till his story was verified. Mr Fryer was still in correspondence with Canada when the summons came for Richard to present himself at Quinton Verney. The young Canadian was prompt in obeying, and on the day following he took train for the nearest railway point. No day or time had been named for arrival, so, after changing at the junction and alighting at a small wayside station, no conveyance was there to meet him. Nor, on enquiry, was any trap to be hired. His portmanteau could be sent by a returning cart in the course of a couple of hours, but for himself there was no alternative. He would have to walk the four miles, or rather more, which separated the station from Mount Verney.

Mount Verney, these people styled Mr Quinton's dwelling, and not Quinton Court as he expected; the Quinton Court his old father used to talk of, told by the grandfather reminiscent of his youth. Why had the original name been changed? – that should be a first question when the time for putting questions came. Meanwhile he was not ill-pleased to be approaching Quinton on foot and alone, and a walk of four miles and over was but a light matter.

Four miles of lovely country verdant with the early green of spring, hill and dale unfolding wooded glimpses here and there, and the ancient Roman road stretching its white line before him, enduring still after all these centuries. He could hardly mistake the way, but after a while he thought it better to ask direction. There were iron gates and an avenue leading to Mount Verney, so he was told, and when he came to the iron gates he must turn in.

Gates and an avenue! His father had spoken of no such appendage to Quinton Court, but no doubt they were additions of a later time. He had his father much in mind during that walk, and the interest he would have felt in this possible – nay, probable – inheritance for his son. His grandfather too; the grandfather who died before his birth: it was as if the two old men went beside him along the green-fenced way, made fair by the sunshine of late April. And he had another person in mind, one who up to now has not been named. Nan, his girl, who waited for him far off across the Atlantic, full of love and faith. If this succession truly came to pass, if it were even an assured future to him and to his heirs, marriage would be no longer an imprudence, it might be entered into at once on his return, released from war-service.

That hope was enough to gild the sunshine, and spread the pastures with a brighter green. And then he came to the gates, and they stood open.

Mount Verney did not boast a lodge, though the drive was a long one. The avenue had been closely planted with ilex and pine, too closely for the good of the trees, and it was consequently dark in shadow: as he turned in he was conscious of a certain chill.

The open gates were hung on stone pillars, and the ornamentation of these uprights caught his eye. On either side, inwards and outwards, a face was carved in relief, but a face that was not human: the mask of a satyr, with pricked animal ears and sprouting horns, and an evil leering grin. Richard had seen nothing of this sort in his backwoods experience, though possibly other things that were starker and grimmer. The leering faces filled him with repugnance; they should not remain there, he thought, to watch over the comings and goings of the house, did ever that house become his own.

The dark avenue had a bend in it; he could not see to the end, but he thought he knew well what he would find there, the old Quinton homestead had been so often described to him. The grey stone house, with its gables and mullioned windows, diamond-paned; the steep roof, up and down which the pigeons strutted and plumed themselves; the paved courtyard with its breast-high wall and mounted urns. He had a clear picture of it in his mind, and this was what at the turn of the avenue he expected to see. But when the turn was reached, his joyful anticipations fell dead. This was quite another place. Had he been misdirected after all?

What lay before him was a white stuccoed villa, spreading over much ground, but so pierced with big window-spaces that it presented to the beholder scant solidity of wall. This was the entrance side; towards the valley the walls rounded themselves into two semi-circles with a flat central division, and here again were the big sash windows of plate-glass, overlooking the view. But there was no mistake. This was Mount Verney.

A grave-looking elderly manservant answered the bell, and it became evident the Canadian visitor had arrived too soon. Mr Richard Quinton was expected, yes certainly, but the day had not been named, and Mr Quinton was at present out in the car, and Dr Lindsay with him. If Mr Richard would step into the library, tea should be brought to him – unless he preferred sherry. His room had been so far prepared that it could be quickly made ready; he, Peters, would tell the housekeeper. And would Mr Richard come this way?

So tea was served to Richard in the library, and his first meal under the Mount Verney roof was taken in solitude, as the master of the house did not return. The library possessed one of the wide bows overlooking the valley, but in spite of the tall sash windows the room was a dark one. They were, it is true, heavily draped with crimson curtains, and the furniture was also heavy, and of an inartistic period. He tried to picture Nan in these surroundings, sitting in the opposite big chair (it would have swallowed her up entirely unless she perched on the arm) and pouring out for him from the huge old teapot, but the effort was in vain. The fancy portrait of his little love would not fit into this frame, but doubtless the frame could be altered: like the grinning masks on the gates, there was much it would be possible to change. Meanwhile hurrying footsteps were heard on the floor overhead, housemaids were busy there; and presently Peters came again to ask if he should conduct the guest to his room.

Richard left the dull library with a sensation of relief. The chamber immediately above had been prepared for him, of equal size, and with windows commanding the view. Richard made some appreciative comment, which seemed to please the old servant.

'Yes, sir,' he said, 'this is the best bedroom, it has the finest lookout. Mr Quinton himself gave orders for it to be yours. It used to be Lady Anna Quinton's.'

'Lady Anna Quinton!' Richard repeated the name in his surprise. 'I did not know Mr Quinton had ever been married.'

'No, sir, and he never was. Her ladyship was his mother. She went away to France and died there; it is getting on for thirty years ago, but Mr Quinton couldn't bear to take the room to be his, though it is the best in the house. I'll send up your portmanteau, sir, directly it arrives.' And with that, Peters withdrew.

Here Richard was certainly well lodged. He stood at the middle window which had been set open, and looked out over a wide prospect. The sun was now beginning to decline, and the first flush of rosy cloud was reflected in the chain of pools which filled the valley to the right, widened out almost to the dimensions of a lake – no doubt artificially formed by damming up the natural stream, which rushed over a weir out of sight. In the middle distance, between the house and the water, was a grove of young oaks, not thickly set like the planting of the avenue, but high-trimmed and rising tall and bare-stemmed out of evergreen undergrowth. The shimmer of water was visible through them in the background, not wholly concealed, though it might be when leafage was full.

The name of Quinton Verney was familiar, cherished among those legends of the importance of the family which the Canadian branch had preserved and handed down; but the lake was to Richard another innovation and surprise. Was it good fishing water, he wondered, and would rainbow trout flourish and breed there? As he stood looking, a boat shot out from the headland to the right, and, crossing the field of view, was lost behind the grove: it was only after it had disappeared that Richard began to wonder what had been the motive power. He could not recall any flash of oars or figures of rowers, or indeed any occupier of the boat.

This might have puzzled him still more, but his attention was diverted by the sound of an arrival below. A car had drawn up at the entrance, voices were now heard in the hall, footsteps on the stairs. After a brief interval, a sharp, rather authoritative knock came at his door and a man entered, a man still on the younger side of middle-age, reddish-haired and short of stature, with a close-trimmed bristly moustache.

'Mr Quinton?' Richard exclaimed, coming forward. If this was his host, he was quite unlike the fancy picture he had formed. But then at Mount Verney everything was unlike and unexpected.

'No – my name's Lindsay – I'm the doctor. Mr Quinton is sorry you were not met, but he had not understood you were arriving today.'

'I hope my coming has not been inconvenient?'

'Not at all – not at all, unless to yourself. But I do not suppose you minded the walk from the station; it is pretty country, and you came here especially to acquaint yourself with the place and its surroundings. One thing more. I have to ask you to excuse Mr Quinton for this evening, and put up with my company only. Mr Quinton is, as you know, an invalid, and I have been with him today to his dentist for some extractions under an anaesthetic. He is a wreck in consequence' – here the little reddish man shrugged his shoulders – 'and will not leave his own rooms again tonight. You are comfortable here, I hope?' – this after Richard had expressed concern at his host's condition. Now it was necessary he should praise his quarters, which he did without stint.

'Mr Quinton would have it that Lady Anna's room should be made ready for the heir, and we were all surprised, as it has been long out of use. Well, adieu for the present: come down as soon as you are ready. Dinner is at seven: we keep early hours here in the country. What! your portmanteau not come? Then never mind about dressing; we will not stand on ceremony for tonight.'

With that, Lindsay the doctor took himself off. But, after he had closed the door, some of his last words kept repeating in Richard's mind. *Made ready for the heir*! That was taking intention for granted in a way for which he was not prepared; and, suddenly, he felt strangely doubtful of his own wish in the matter. Did he really desire to be the owner of the Quinton property, and, if not, from what hidden root did disinclination spring?

Presently a gong sounded from below, and he went down to find the dining-room lighted up, though it was scarcely more than dusk without, and the window-screens were still undrawn. The table was set out with some fine old silver and an abundance of flowers, the service of the meal was faultless, and Lindsay made an excellent deputy host. Good food has a cheering influence, and the causeless depression which had threatened to engulf Richard's spirit was lifted, at least for the time.

'I hope you will like Quinton Verney,' Lindsay was saying with apparent heartiness. 'Mr Quinton is particularly anxious that you should like the place, and take an interest in his hobbies. He will explain better than I can what they are. But be prepared to hear a great deal about Roman remains in Britain, and to be cross-questioned about your knowledge.'

'Then I can only avow ignorance. It is a study that has not come in my way, but I am at least ready to be interested.'

'Ah, well, interest won't be difficult in what has been discovered on your own land, for that is his especial pride. A fine tessellated pavement down there by the pools, and an altar in what is now the grove. I am a duffer myself in these matters, but Mr Quinton is a downright enthusiast about the old pagans and their times. It was he who replanted the grove where it is supposed that a sacred one existed, and set up in the midst of it a statue of Pan copied from the antique. I chaff him sometimes about it, and tell him I believe there is nothing he would like better than to revive the *Lupercalia*, and convert the entire neighbourhood. That's an exaggeration, of course, but the element of mystery appeals to him. As you will discover.'

Following this touch of personal revelation, Richard remarked: 'You know Mr Quinton very well. I suppose you have been with him a long time?'

'Eighteen months – no less, no more. But you can get to know a man pretty well in that time, especially when you happen to be his doctor as well as his house-mate. He has been an invalid for many years – since boyhood in fact: a sad case; you'll know more about it after a while. I was at the war before that: got knocked out, and when free of hospital could only take on a soft job, and fate or luck sent me here. Quinton and I have got on well together. Indeed I may tell you in confidence that he offered to leave me all he possessed, provided I would bind myself by his conditions.'

So the Quinton inheritance had been offered and refused else-where. Here was a matter that might well give Richard food for thought.

'And why did you not – ?' he began impulsively.

'Why didn't I grasp at such a chance? Well, I allow it was tempting enough, to a man who is a damaged article – a damage that will be lifelong. But I couldn't consent to bind myself as he would have me bound; and there was another reason. I would have been suspected of using my position here to exercise undue influence, and that I couldn't stomach. It was I who suggested to Mr Quinton that he should seek out his next of kin – eh, what; what is the matter?'

The query was to Peters, who was whispering at his elbow.

'Pray excuse me. I am sorry, but my patient is not so well.' And the little doctor hurried away.

Peters brought in the next course.

'Dr Lindsay hopes you will go on with the dinner, sir, and not wait for him. He may be detained some time.'

For the rest of the meal Richard was solitary. He declined after dinner wine and dessert, so Peters, who felt himself responsible towards the guest, suggested that he might like to smoke in the library, and coffee would be brought to him there. Richard rose from the table, and, as he did so, turned towards the unscreened window behind his chair, and experienced the shock of a surprise. There stood a strange-looking figure, gazing in at him and at the room, with face pressed against the glass. His exclamation recalled Peters, who was in the act of carrying out a tray; but by the time the old butler returned, the figure had disappeared.

Who, or what was it? But Peters could not tell.

'I'll have it enquired into, sir. No-one had any call to be there.

These windows look into the enclosed garden, that is always kept private. A man, did you say, sir? Like a tramp?'

'A man,' Richard assented, but he did not add in what likeness. Surely it must have been some freak of fancy that suggested those lineaments, the white leering face which resembled the bestial masks at the gate of the avenue, with their pricked ears and budding horns; and suggested also the naked torso, of which a glimpse was afforded by the light.

Peters brought word with the coffee that no-one was found in the garden, but he meant to be extra careful in locking up, 'lest it should be somebody after the plate'. And indeed, were ill characters about, the unscreened window was likely to bring danger, as the display of silver on sideboard and table might well excite the cupidity of a looker-in.

Dr Lindsay came down an hour later, but it was only to ask whether Richard had all he wanted for comfort and for the night.

'I shall be sitting up with Mr Quinton,' he explained. 'Unluckily, haemorrhage has followed these extractions, and he is morbidly affected by the sight and taste of blood. No, not a sufficient loss to be alarming: it will be subdued by tomorrow I don't doubt: it is serious only as it affects his special case. You'll give Peters your orders, will you not, and tell him when you wish to be called, and all that. I understand your portmanteau has arrived.'

So Richard found himself back again in the best bedroom at an early hour, with the night before him, and his luggage unpacked, and despatch-case set on the writing-table. Now was the time for the letter he had promised Nan, with his first impressions of Quinton Verney, about which she was naturally curious; the old homestead he had described to her, which might some day be his home and hers. But when he spread paper before him, he felt an overmastering reluctance to write that letter. What could he say if he told her the truth – and surely nothing less than the truth and the whole truth was due to Nan, however much it might disappoint and puzzle her. Could he tell her, with no reason to allege, of the distaste he felt for this place, for the house and all that it contained? – a distaste which began with the first sight of those leering masks at the avenue gate: how tell her of that other living face which resembled them, seen peering into the lighted dining-room, pressed against the glass of the shut window a couple of hours ago? Better delay, than that he should fill a letter with maunderings such as these, when another day's experience, or a personal interview with the invisible cousin, might bring about an altered mind.

He was tired and out of spirits, and though he rejected with scorn the suggestion that a walk of less than five miles could have fatigued him, he was only lately out of hospital, and it was long since so much pedestrian exercise had come his way. And there had been throughout a certain excitement of highly strung expectation, from which, no doubt, reaction played its part. No, he would not attempt to write to Nan; the letter should be postponed until the morrow. And he would betake himself at once to bed.

2

It has been said that the chamber allotted to him was spacious and well-appointed, a private bathroom opened from it, and with one notable exception, it fulfilled every modern requirement. The rest of the house had been wired, and electric light installed, but here there were no means of illumination but candles, and, though these had been abundantly supplied on toilet and mantelpiece, and also at the bedside, the result was curiously dull. It was as if the walls and hangings of the apartment absorbed and did not reflect the light; a room of ordinary size would have been as well illuminated by a farthing dip. One of the windows was opened down a hand's breadth behind the curtains, and they stirred faintly in the air. Richard drew them apart to push up the lower sash, and then was struck by the beauty of the scene below. The valley had put on a veil of silvery mist, so delicate as hardly to obscure, and away to the left the moon was rising, a full yellow moon, magnified by its nearness to the horizon.

How still it all was. He had been used of late to the roar of a great city, audible even through hospital walls; before that to the thudding of great guns, and the scream of shell. How silent, and how peaceful: but presently not completely silent, for music broke into the stillness.

Somebody down below was playing on the flute, long-drawn notes and a simple air, but of enthralling sweetness. The music was difficult to locate; sometimes it seemed to come from near the house, sometimes from the grove of trees, and now to be a mere echo from a greater distance still. Could some rustic lover be serenading a housemaid? But no, that seemed impossible. Richard was himself no musician, but he knew enough to appreciate the rare quality of the performer. And then the final notes died away, and silence reigned under the rising moon.

He dropped the curtain over the window, leaving it open, and now applied himself quickly to prepare for bed. Tired as he was, he expected to sleep as soon as his head touched the pillow: such was his custom in high health, and the habit had served him in good stead when recruiting strength. But on this first night at Mount Verney sleep and he were to be strangers. No doubt there was some excitement of nerve or brain, the cause of which might be looked for entirely in himself. This at first; but by-and-by there was something external, something more, though it was nameless and undefined.

A change had set in: this was no restlessness of his own that he was suffering, it was the misery and torture of another; a misery all the greater that it could not be expressed. It seemed to him that he was divided; he recognised that he was lying on the bed, but he was also walking the room from wall to wall, with tossed arms, with hands clenched and threatening, and then spread open; gestures foreign to his nature under any extreme of passion. He, or the entity which absorbed him, did not weep: no tears came to the relief of this distress, and his own voice was dumb in his throat; there could be no cry of appeal. Whether the passion which tore him was fury solely, or grief solely, he could not tell; or whether in its extreme anguish it combined the two.

For a while he was completely paralysed by this strange experience; he was walking the room with the sufferer; he *was* the sufferer: and then again he knew the personality and the agony were not his own; that his real self was stretched upon the bed, though he could neither lift a finger nor move a limb. How long did this endure in its alternations? Keen as was his after memory, he could not tell: moments count as hours when under torture, and in an experience so abnormal time does not exist, even as we are told it will be effaced for us hereafter. One fragment of knowledge informed his brain; how he knew cannot be told, for no voice spoke. The entity was a woman. It was no man's agony into the vortex of which he had been drawn; this was a woman who knew both love and hate, a mother who had possessed and also lost.

Then, in a moment, the strain upon him snapped: he could move again, he had the government of his limbs, he was in his own body and not that other, if the other was a body indeed. Candles – the means of striking a light – were at his hand; in less time than it takes to write, both flames were kindled: the whole room was plain to see, and there was nothing, nothing but empty air. And yet he knew, he knew that the woman was still there – that she was pacing up and down from wall to wall – that she was still torn with fury, from the vortex of which his own spirit was scarcely yet set free, as consciousness of it remained.

This would have been a staggering experience, even to one versed in psychic marvels, but of such matters Richard Quinton was completely ignorant. To him the ordeal he had passed through was as unique as it was unaccountable – a horror to have so penetrated another's being, and also in a way a thing of shame, to be covered up shuddering from the light of day. He leapt out of bed; he must seek the window, the free air, if he would not choke and die. In his rush forward it seemed as if he encountered and passed through the frantic figure that yet was invisible and disembodied; but the collision, if it was collision, affected neither: roused as he was, the grip of individuality was too strong. He tore the curtains apart, and there at last was the cool night, the serene moon, the wafting of free air, in which, behind him in the room, the lighted candles flared.

The moon was now high in heaven, the scene was bathed in white light, the shadows, where shadows fell, were black and sharply defined. The silvery mist of the earlier evening had disappeared, the light veil of it withdrawn, rolled up and swept away before that stirring of air. There was a path of reflected light across the quiet water of the pool, the headland stood out dark. And, strange to relate, from behind it again shot out the mysterious boat, the boat he had seen before, but now there were two men on board. He saw, or thought he saw, one man attack the other; for a dozen seconds they were locked together struggling. Then the rocking boat capsized and sank, and the men also disappeared.

Richard saw this, and yet in some dim way he realised that he had witnessed no actual disaster for which he need give the alarm: it was a scene projected into his mind from the mind of another. It did not even occur to him that there, within a bowshot of the house, were men drowning who might be saved. The moon-path on the water was smooth again now, undisturbed by even a ripple, the night utterly still. But a moment later the silence was broken by the same flute music which had discoursed so sweetly earlier in the night. It was, however, tuned to a livelier measure this second time, one that might accompany dancing feet. It sounded from the grove, and underneath the clear light Richard could distinguish moving figures, leaping among the trees.

There were five or six of them apparently, men or boys, and the figures looked as if naked above the waist. And the dance was not solely a dance, for they seemed to be chasing, or driving before them, some large animal which fled with leaps through the undergrowth, a goat possibly, or a sheep. The animal and the pursuing figures disappeared among the trees, and then appeared again as if they had made a circuit of the grove; the goat (if it was a goat) leaping in front, and the others pursuing. This was the end; a cloud drifted over the moon, and when it passed there was no more sign of movement in the grove, and the jocund fluting had ceased.

Richard turned back into the room, and now his perception of that fury and distress, if not wholly effaced, was dulled as if here, too, was the shadowing of a merciful cloud. But stretch himself on that bed he could not, nor address himself to sleep, lest it should be renewed with all the former horror. He would keep the lights burning, if only he had a book he would occupy himself with reading, but literature had formed no part of his light luggage.

He might seek one in the library below, treading softly in stocking-soles so as not to disturb the sleeping house.

But as he issued forth, candle in hand, he found a burner switched on on the landing, and the dressing-gowned small doctor crossing over from an opposite door. Lindsay at once accosted him.

'Can I do anything: what is the matter? – oh, can't sleep, and want a book: is that it? I can find you one close at hand, and mine are livelier than the fossils in the library. Come this way.'

Lindsay's room opened over the entrance, next to Mr Quinton's bedchamber. A set of bookshelves filled a recess.

'Help yourself. The yellowbacks on the top shelf are French – I dare say you read French. But you'll find English ones below, and perhaps they are more likely to put you asleep.'

He snapped on an extra light, and then turned for a fuller scrutiny of his companion. 'You look pretty bad,' was his remark. 'Does a sleepless night always knock you up like this? I'm doctor to the establishment you know, and I prescribe a peg. Whisky or brandy will you have? Both of them are here, and so is a siphon. Sit down while I get it ready. Three fingers – two – one? Good: you do well to be moderate. Get outside that, and you'll feel better. And then you can pick your book.'

Lindsay did not question further as to the cause of disturbance, though he looked inquisitive, as if suspicions were aroused. Richard for his part remained tongue-tied; time was needed to digest and try to understand his experience: he might speak of it later on, but not now, while still his nerves were vibrating from the strain. The human companionship was, however, reassuring, and by the time the prescribed dose was swallowed, he felt altogether more normal. He enquired for Mr Quinton, sat for a while conversing on indifferent subjects, and then departed with a book.

He did not venture again to lie down, but installed himself in a deep chair, the candles burning at his elbow. The effect of the novel may have been soporific, though he was an inattentive reader. After a long interval he fell asleep, and waked to find morning already brightening in the east.

The night was over, its perplexities and distresses had sunk into the past, and a new day had begun. It was refreshing to spirit as well as body to wash and re-clothe, to undo the bolts and chains which guarded the front door, and find himself in the free air. Though it was still the air which breathed over Mount Verney, he was delivered from the evil shadow of that roof. He retraced his steps of the day before, down the dark curving drive, out through the satyr-headed gates, to the high road which was free to all, the road traversed by Roman legions in centuries that were past. He turned to the right, with the eastern sky behind him, and walked on, without object, but steeping himself in the freshness of the newly awakened world.

At first he appeared to be the only person astir and observant, but presently an old man of the labouring class pushed open a gate some way ahead and came towards him, a shepherd accompanied by his dog. Richard would have liked to exchange ideas with an English working man, but felt suddenly too shy to venture on more than a good-morning as they drew abreast. The man, however, stopped and accosted him.

'Beg pardon, master, but as you came along, did you mebbe happen on a straying sheep? A ewe she is, and has taken her lamb with her, one getting on in size, as it was dropped early. Me and the dog have been after her since first it was light.'

Richard had no information to give; he had not seen the ewe and her lamb. And then he bethought him.

'I stayed last night at Mount Verney, and, looking out in the moonlight, I saw a sheep leaping about in the grove, the coppice of oaks by the water. Would that be the one you have lost?'

The man shook his head.

'No, sir, that would be Mr Quinton's sheep. I drove it down myself, a prime wether, only a day ago; and my heart was sore for the poor thing. It seemed as if the dog here was sorry too, for he didna like the job. Mr Quinton he buys one at the spring full moon, and again at harvest, of my master or one of the other breeders, always to be driven into the coppice and left there, and I doubt if ever the creatures live as much as two days. What he wants them for 'tis beyond me to say. Seems a waste of good meat and good wool, for it is just a hole in the field and dig them under, so I am told, and not a soul the better. Some folks will eat braxy mutton, meat being dear as it is; but not one of them would touch a sheep that had died up there in the wood, poisoned as like as not. 'Tis just a mystery to all of us. But I've no call to be passing remarks, seeing you know Mr Quinton, and are staying at Mount Verney.'

Richard might have replied with truth that he did not know Mr Quinton, their acquaintance was still to make. But he asked instead for direction, and was told to cross a stile to the right into a certain field-path, which would bring him out opposite the house, by the bridge over the water.

The bridge was a rustic affair of planks, and a hand-rail, and beyond it the way diverged to right and left, the path on the left entering the grove, barred only by a light iron turnstile. Was it curiosity, or another sort of attraction which drew Richard thither, to see by daylight the spot on which he had looked down under the moon the night before? Now it seemed ordinary enough; the paths cut through it were grassed over and green, but here and there, where the turf was soft, he noticed they were trampled by divided hoofs, larger than those of sheep.

The trees, young and slender, shorn of their lower branches, were now faintly green with unexpanded leafage; the undergrowth, which was chiefly rhododendron, was here and there breaking into purple and pinkish flower. While still some way from it, he could distinguish among the trees the statue of which Lindsay had spoken. It was mounted on a pedestal, and was, as he said, a modern copy of the antique. Pan with his pipes in bronze, an abhorrent half-animal figure; the brooding face less repulsive perhaps than those of the satyrs at the gate, but the regard it appeared to bend on the observer who approached had a keener expression of intelligence and evil power. Richard as he drew near, his attention riveted on that face and crouching figure, almost stumbled over an object lying at the foot of the column.

It was the dead sheep. Had it been dragged thither with a purpose, or hunted till it fell exhausted where it lay? There was no mark upon it that he could see, of the knife of the executioner, but the swollen tongue protruded from the half open jaws, and thick blood had flowed from both nostrils, staining the ground.

Truly Mount Verney was a spot where there were strange happenings. The shudder of the night again passed over Richard, and he had now not the least desire to linger in the grove, or to make further discoveries. Passing through another gate he gained a steep slope of lawn, leading up to the gravelled terrace on which the windows of the library opened. His approach had been observed, and here was Lindsay waving him a cheerful greeting, with the intelligence of waiting breakfast.

3

'Been for an early ramble? – that was well done. Mr Quinton wants you to see as much as possible of the place before he speaks to you of the future. A lovely morning. And this house stands well, does it not, above the valley? Gives you a first rate view.'

Richard assented. And then put the question he had been meditating.

'Was this house built on the site of another, do you know? The house my father used to speak about was called Quinton Court. It was built long before his father's time, and was of stone; it had a walled courtyard and mullioned windows. I don't suppose it was ever a grand mansion. But that was what I expected to find in coming down here.'

'Quinton Court is still in existence; the man lives there who has the farm. It is a fine-looking old place, but I expect it has gone a long way downhill since it was given up as the family residence. You will find it about a mile from here, on the other side of the hill.'

'I should like to see it. I should greatly like to see it – !'

'Make it the object of your next walk. Go the length of the lake to the head water, and through the field beyond, and you will come upon a cart-road. I would show you the way, but I may have difficulty in leaving. And perhaps you would rather go alone.'

That he would prefer to make the visit alone was so true that Richard left the suggestion uncontested. Lindsay passed lightly to another subject; one on which he was not improbably curious.

'I hope the novel and the "peg" helped you to sleep? – I hate to lie awake myself, but sometimes a strange bed – ! There is fish, I think, under that cover. Or do you prefer bacon?'

'I am a good sleeper usually, in any sort of bed, strange or familiar. Dr Lindsay, I am sorry to be a troublesome guest, but can I change my room? And, if you will allow me, I will do so before tonight.'

'You can, without doubt. There are other guest-rooms, though with fewer advantages than the bow-room, as we call it. I will see about the exchange. But – may I be so indiscreet as to ask why? Because Mr Quinton will put the question to me, and I had better be prepared to answer him.'

'Then perhaps I may put a question on my side. I understand that bedroom has been long out of use. I know nothing about ghosts, and have never believed in them, but – it is not like other rooms. Is it supposed to be haunted? And, if so, why was it chosen for me?'

'I can't tell you much about it; remember I only came here eighteen months ago. As for why it was chosen, you must ask Mr Quinton: it was his doing, not mine. I never heard of any ghost being seen there. The only queer thing said about the room sounds like illusion, and could not disturb a sleeper. Nor would it, I suppose, be visible at night. But perhaps you, as a Quinton, would be more sensitive than a stranger.'

'What is the queer thing?'

'Why it seems absurd, but they say whoever looks through that window sees a boat on the lake. I saw something like it myself on one occasion, but I expect it is a flaw in the glass. Was there a ghost last night?'

'No ghost in the sense you mean, but such an impression of misery – and not misery only, anger – that I found sleep imposs-ible. That is all I have to tell. If Mr Quinton is affronted by my wish to change, I must find quarters elsewhere till he is ready to speak to me.'

'Nonsense: he won't be affronted, it would be absurd. I doubt if you will see him today, but he is decidedly better, and I shall not need to sit up another night. You'll like him, I think. He has his eccentricities, that must be allowed. But you would be sorry for him from your heart if you knew all.'

'He is eccentric? I heard a strange story about him this morning, from an old shepherd I met in the road. Is it true that he purchases a sheep twice a year, and that it is driven into the grove to die? There is one lying dead there now, at the foot of the statue of Pan.'

Lindsay shrugged his shoulders.

'I told you he was half a pagan, and I don't defend the sheep business. That sacrifice is one of the things he wants continued, and makes a condition; but I told him straight out that no successor would pledge himself to a thing so out of reason, and you had better be firm about it when he speaks. Of course it is natural he should wish Mount Verney kept up as the residence of the owner; there one can be in sympathy. His grandfather built it, and his father planned the grounds, and the ornamental water and all that. Odd about the lake, seeing what happened after. Why, don't you know? The elder son was drowned there. Mr Quinton's twin brother. Archibald, his name was. He was the Quinton heir.'

Richard saw again, in a flash of memory, the two figures struggling in the boat and disappearing under water; but where was the good of taking Lindsay into confidence? He had said enough, and made it plain he would occupy the room no more, nor look from it over the lake: he did not care to what sort of apartment he was transferred; it would serve him for the time, however mean.

The doctor hurried away as soon as they had breakfasted, apologising for his enforced absence, but Richard was well content to be alone. He wanted to think out the warning again given about conditions. That which concerned the sheep was unthinkable, and could hardly be pressed; but evidently there were others, by reason of which Lindsay had refused the offered heirship. If he was required to live at Mount Verney in the future, and make it his home and his wife's home – what then? In one way the prospect of the inheritance was tempting enough to him, and would be to any man – an inheritance that would at once convert him into a person of importance, with a stake in the country as the saying is; a good position to offer his wife, ample means, provision for the children that might be born to them.

But if what he began dimly to suspect was fact; if the place had somehow fallen under a curse, in pagan times or now – such a curse as affected inanimate building, and tainted the very ground – it would be no fit home for her. And Nan was not covetous of riches – she would not mind struggling on with him and being poor; she would approve, so he justly thought, of a refusal made for the sake of right.

There was nothing to detain him indoors, so with these cogitations in mind, he set out in the direction Lindsay had indicated, following the north shore of the artificial lake, and crossing the headland which, viewed from above, had been the departure point of the mysterious boat. On the western side of the headland, furthest from the house and half hidden by the bank, were the remains of what certainly had been a boathouse; but in these days no boat sheltered there, and the timbers of the roof had rotted and fallen in decay. He passed through the gate by the head-water, a clear and fast running stream; found and followed the cart-road, which after a while was merged in a superior approach, now well nigh as worn and deeply rutted as the other.

He came upon the old Court suddenly, round a fold of the hill, and there he stood for a while, his heart moved by a mysterious feeling of kinship – if not utterly fantastic to suppose flesh and blood can feel itself akin to walls of stone. The old homestead had fallen from its first estate, but there was a dignity about it still, the dignity of fine proportion and high quality, differing widely from the jerry building of today. The grey gables were there as of old, the roof of slabbed stone, the panes of diamond lattice; there the flagged courtyard with its breast-high boundary wall, and five of the six urns mounted in place; the sixth had fallen, and lay broken at the foot.

The front door was fast shut, an oak door studded with iron, but Richard drew near and knocked, treading the very stones the footsteps of the dead had worn. Why, why had the later degenerates forsaken this dear place, and fixed their abode at Mount Verney?

A neatly-dressed young woman opened to him, and looked enquiringly at the stranger.

'I'm sorry, sir, my father is not in, if so be as you come seeking him.'

No, Richard said, that was not his errand; but might he be allowed to see inside the house, if only a couple of the rooms?

'Why certainly, if you are thinking of taking the place. I didn't know as it had got about that we are leaving, but news do fly apace. But we shall not be out until September.'

'My name is Quinton, and I am from Canada. My great-grandfather lived here, and it was here that my grandfather was born. I am anxious to see the Court now I am in England. If you would be so good as to allow – '

'Come in, sir, and look where you like; you are kindly welcome. My father would make you so I know, for he is the oldest tenant on the estate. We have no fault to find with the place, but the farm is too big for father now he has no son with him, and the house too large for us too. I am the only one at home, and mother is laid by with the rheumatics. These long stone passages take a lot of cleaning, to say nothing of the many rooms, though more than half of them we shut away.'

So upon this invitation Richard had his wish, and saw over the house upstairs and down. In some of the rooms put out of use there were still pieces of old furniture, Quinton property, his guide told him: an oak chest or two, corner cupboards with carven doors, a worm-eaten dresser, chairs in the last stage of decrepitude. They were let with the house, having been thought unworthy of removal to Mount Verney. In the best parlour sacks of grain were stored, and on the threshold of two of the empty bedrooms he was warned to step warily, as the floors were thought to be unsafe.

Quinton Court had fallen from its first estate, but it was still lovely in the eyes of this late descended son. It had been cleanly kept, however roughly, and there was an air of purity about its homeliness, of open casements and scents of lavender and apples. He could picture his Nan here, a happy house-mistress under the ancient roof of his forefathers; but not as the chatelaine of Mount Verney with all its wealth: never at Mount Verney. Ah, if only Mr Quinton would make this place his bequest to the next heir, the old Court and the surrounding farm which he might work for a living; and leave Quinton Verney and his accumulated thousands, where else and to whom else he pleased!

4

Such were Richard's thoughts as he walked back along the green shores of the lake, and under the midday sun. He and the doctor were again *tête-à-tête* at luncheon; but he was told Mr Quinton desired to see him that afternoon in his private room above stairs; also that he intended to dine with them, being greatly better than the day before. So the first interview with his host came about earlier than he had been led to expect.

The appearance of his elderly cousin took him by surprise. Mr Clement Quinton was strikingly handsome, though older-looking than his two and fifty years. He might have been taken for a man advanced in the seventies, though his tall thin figure was still upright. He owned a thick thatch of grey hair, a close-cut white beard, and bushy grey eyebrows above eyes of steely blue, rather unnaturally wide open. He welcomed Richard cordially, shaking him by the hand: a cold hand, his was, and yet the younger man felt uncomfortably, the instant they were palm to palm, that he touched something sticky and moist. Mr Quinton's left hand was gloved, and Richard remembered after that he held a dark silk handkerchief in the other while they talked together.

There was nothing embarrassing or noteworthy about the earlier conversation. Mr Quinton appeared kindly interested in Richard's past history, asking about his father and home, how he had been educated and where, and also the details of his military service. They had been talking together for half an hour, before any reference was made to the future.

'I want you to be interested in this place,' he said with emphasis. 'I want you to be particularly interested. For there are various things I am bound to leave to the doing of others, and much will depend on their punctual carrying on. It will smooth my pillow – as the saying is – if I may be assured of the co-operation of my successor.'

This was not very easy to answer, as Richard could not assume successorship on a hint so vague. So he struck out into an account of his visit to Quinton Court, and pleasure over the discovery that the old house of which his grandfather had spoken with affection was still solidly existent.

'I was afraid it had been pulled down, and Mount Verney built on its site.'

'No, we destroyed nothing. My respect for antiquity is too great. As I will show you later, it has been my great desire to – call back into life, I may say – associations from the dead past of an earlier period still. Traces of what had been were thick on the ground hereabouts: you shall have the complete history of how, and why, and what. You will find it remarkable indeed. I will tell you frankly, my young cousin, it is here and on Mount Verney I want your interest focussed. This place dates back to the Roman occupation of Britain, and in comparison with the relics here, Quinton Court is but a thing of yesterday.'

'Dr Lindsay told me Roman remains had been unearthed. I think he said some portions of a pavement.'

'There was a villa here, on this very spot; baths in the valley, with the water running through them; and an altar where you see the grove, which was once a dense thicket of wood. I have other means of knowing, besides conclusions drawn from the fragments that remain, and these communications the excavations have strikingly confirmed. I was directed where to dig. There was a special cult connected with this place. The worship of Pan.'

'I observed the statue in the grove.'

'It marks the site of the old altar. Pan is a deity about whom little

has been known and much mistaken. From the sources of information at my command, I have compiled a treatise. And that is one
thing I require of my successor. If unpublished at the time of my
decease, I wish it given to the world.'

The posthumous publication of a treatise! It would be well if other
conditions were no more formidable than this.

'Some writers have made the mistake of confounding Pan with
Faunus; surely an extraordinary error. My theory is entirely different. Cain was his prototype. Cain.'

Here the recluse seemed to be stirred by some inward excitement,
and he got up to pace the room.

'Cain!' he repeated. 'Of course you know the scriptural narrative,
and probably little else about that founder of an early race. There are
mistakes in that account – it is libellous, the fabrication of an enemy.
Eve put about unworthy slanders. If Cain did truly kill his brother, it
was in self-defence, or in a fury of panic anger: I say if, for I do not
allow it to be the truth. Abel, the favourite, was a sneak and a coward,
and he knew whatever lie he set up, so long as it was against the
other, would stand as unassailable truth. He was better blotted out,
than left to be the father of a degenerate race. Cain was at least a
man – and it is said the Lord put a mark on him. What did that
mean, think you?'

'I have not the least idea. Does anybody know?'

'I know this much, that it was the curse of the partly animal form.
Cain was crippled into that likeness, and some of his sons took after
him. Not the daughters, for they were in the likeness of Eve. And
it is on record that they were beautiful. The sons of God saw the
daughters of men that they were fair. But that does not come into the
argument, nor concern us now. It was because of the mark set on him
that Pan loved solitary places, the cool depths of caves and the
shadow of woods. It was he in the beginning, and not Abel, who was
the keeper of flocks. Abel did nothing but laze in the sun and watch
the fruits ripen, and then gather them for an offering. I told you that
the record lied. Do you wonder how I know all this?'.

Richard could do nothing but assent.

'I will tell you – show you. I wish to instruct you in my methods,
that they may be yours hereafter. It is not all who have the gift of
sight. Lindsay is psychically blind. But something tells me you have
it, or will have it. Come here with me.'

He opened a door and showed an inner, smaller room, probably
intended as a dressing-closet in the original design of the house.

There was a writing-table and chair in the sole window, but the only other furniture was a high stand, on which was some object covered over with black velvet drapery. Mr Quinton turned back part of the covering, and directed Richard to seat himself before it. The lifted flap revealed the smooth and shining surface of a large crystal, or ball of glass, set into a frame.

'You know what this is, and what its use? I want to test whether I can make a scryer of you. The black cloth is used only to prevent confusing lights. Now look steadily into the crystal, and tell me what you see.'

Richard looked, in some amusement and complete incredulity.

'I see the reflection of my own face,' he said presently. 'Nothing more. Except – yes – something which looks like smoke.'

'Go on looking, and be patient. There will be more.'

As Richard gazed, his own reflection disappeared, the smoke cleared away, and there were the gates of the avenue with the leering faces, exactly as he saw them the day before. Then the cloud of smoke returned, blotting them out; cleared again, and showed the spy of the evening, peering in at the window of the dining-room. Succeeding this, came the scene of the grove by moonlight, with the figures leaping among the trees, and driving the doomed sheep.

'I am seeing a procession of scenes,' he replied to a further question. 'But only what are in my mind and memory. Nothing new.'

'Go on looking,' was again the command. 'What is new will come.'

The next scene was, as Richard half expected, the grove as he entered it that morning, with the statue of Pan on its pedestal, and the sheep before it lying dead. This persisted, not small as dwarfed within the limits of the ball, but now as if a window opened before him on the actual scene. But a change was taking place in the figure of the god. The bronze seemed to soften and warm into flesh, the terrible, wise face was no longer serene and meditative, the eyes looked into his, and now there was mockery in them, revelling in his surprise. The thing was alive, moving, surely about to descend.

But no. The figure, without leaving its pedestal, stretched out one hairy ape-like arm, and clutched the body of the sheep, drawing it up to rest on his crossed hocks, while the mocking face bent closer, as if to snuff or lick the blood. Was the monstrous creature about to tear the victim open, ready to devour? The action of the hands looked like it.

Richard could look no longer. A sweat of horror broke out over him, and stood in beads on his forehead; he started up gasping for air. 'Let me go,' he cried out wildly: 'let me go!'

Mr Quinton replaced the velvet covering.

'That is enough for today,' he said. 'I am sufficiently answered. You can see.'

Richard hardly knew how he got out of the room, whether it was by Mr Quinton's dismissal or his own will. Or how long a time elapsed before, finding himself alone, he happened to look at the palm of his right hand, which had felt curiously sticky after contact with Mr Quinton's. The smear on it was dry and easily effaced by washing, but without doubt what he had touched was blood.

Mr Quinton seemed to have been in no way affronted by Richard's abrupt withdrawal. He was in a genial mood when he joined the two younger men at dinner, now with his loose wrapping gown put off, and faultlessly attired in evening dress. A handsome man; and Richard noticed that his hands were beautifully shaped and white. But, to the guest's vision, there was one striking peculiarity about his appearance, a peculiarity which seemed to increase as the meal went forward. Perhaps the opening of Richard's clairvoyance, artificially induced some hours before, had not wholly closed. For doubtless what he now perceived would not have been visible to ordinary sight.

Most of us in these later days have heard of the existence of auras, a species of halo which is supposed to emanate from every mortal, indicative of spiritual values and degrees of power; but it is doubtful whether our backwoodsman was aware. What he saw, however, was an aura, though formed of shadow and not light. It encompassed the seated figure of his host with a surrounding of grey haze, spreading to a yard or more from either shoulder, and equally above the head; not obstructing the view of the room behind him, but dimming it, as might a stretched veil of grey crêpe. It was curious to see Peters waiting on him and passing through this, evidently unaware; his hand and the bottle advancing into the full light as he filled Mr Quinton's glass, and then withdrawing to leave the veil as perfect as before.

Mr Quinton made an excellent dinner, and chaffed Richard on his want of appetite; he also drank freely of the wines Peters was handing round, and pressed them on his guests. The glasses were particularly elegant, of Venetian pattern, slender stemmed and fragile. Peters had just replenished his master's glass, when Mr Quinton in the course of argument lifted and brought it down sharply on the table with the result of breakage. The accident attracted little notice;

Peters cleared away the fragments and mopped up the spilt wine, and another glass was set in its place and filled. But as Mr Quinton raised the fresh glass to his lips, Richard noticed that blood was dripping from his right hand in heavy spots, staining his shirt-cuff and the cloth.

'I am afraid, sir, you have cut yourself,' he exclaimed impulsively; and almost at the same instant Peters appeared at his master's elbow offering a dark silk handkerchief.

Mr Quinton did not answer, but uttered an exclamation of annoyance, and abruptly rose from table and left the room. Lindsay followed him, but presently returned, looking unusually grave. Richard enquired if the cut was serious.

'Mr Quinton did not cut his hand,' Lindsay answered. 'I am charged to tell you what is the matter. Though it is as far as possible kept secret, he thinks it better you should know.'

The gravity of Lindsay's countenance did not relax. He poured out half a glass of wine and drank it, as if to nerve himself for the telling of the tale.

'When I came here as resident doctor eighteen months ago, I heard the story: it was, of course, necessary I should be informed as I had to treat his case. I shall have to go a long way back to make you understand. Lady Anna, Quinton's mother, had twin sons, born shortly after her husband's death. She must have been a strange woman. They were her only children, but almost from infancy she made a difference between them, setting all her affection on Archibald, the elder, and treating the other, Clement, with coldness and every evidence of dislike. Quinton says he can never remember his mother caressing him, or even speaking kindly. He was always the one held to blame for any childish fault or mischief, and pushed into the background, while everything was for Archibald the heir. We cannot wonder that this folly of hers led to bad feeling between the lads. It was active in their schooldays, though they were educated at different schools, and met only in the holidays. Whenever they met they fought. What the last quarrel was about I cannot say, but Archibald was entering an expensive regiment, and the army could not be afforded for Clement, though it was his great desire: he owns to having been very sore. They were in a boat on the lake, and they fought there, and the boat capsized.

'It was said that Archibald hadn't a chance; he had been stunned by a blow on the head, or else had struck his head in falling. They both could swim a little, but he went down like a stone, and Clement reached the shore: the distance could not have been great, nor could one have expected such an accident to result in anything worse than a ducking. The horrible part of it was that Lady Anna saw what happened from her window in the bow-room.'

'Ah – !'

'Yes, the room you had, and where you were disturbed last night. She saw the fight and the struggle, and was convinced of Clement's guilt: that he had plotted the occasion and killed Archibald, so that he might take his place. She wanted to have the boy tried for murder; ay, and would have had her way, had it not been for her brother, Lord Pengwyn, who was guardian to both the lads. He got the thing passed over as an accident, as no doubt it was. But the point I am coming to, though I've been long about it, is this. When Clement was drawn from the water, and brought in, sick and dazed, Lady Anna met him in a fury of passion. He was Cain over again, the first murderer who slew his brother: I wonder, did Eve do the like! "Your brother's blood," she said, "will be upon your hands for ever." Quinton says he would not have cared, after that, if they had hung him then and there. He had an illness, and the palms of his hands began to bleed – from the pores as it were, without a wound – and they have continued to bleed at intervals from that day to this. You saw what happened tonight.'

'It sounds like a miracle. Is there no cure?'

'Everything has been tried – styptics, hypnotism even. Sometimes the symptom remits for two or three weeks, and the bleeding is generally early in the day; he thought himself safe this evening. Miracle? no, unless the power of the mind over the body is held to be miraculous. You have read of the stigmatists – women, ay and men too – on whom the wounds of Christ have broken out, to bleed always on Friday?'

'I have heard of them – certainly. But I set it down as a fraud – a monkish trick.'

'It is as well vouched for as any other physical phenomenon. And this case of Quinton's is nearly allied, though horror created it in his case, and not saintly adoration. It has spoiled his life; for over thirty years he has been an invalid, and will so continue to the end. His aberration of mind has all arisen from this root: his queer fancies about Cain and Pan, blood-sacrifices to pagan gods – satyrs and fauns and hobgoblins, and I know not what!'

'You speak of aberration and yet assert that he is sane?'

'He is sane enough for all practical purposes – a good man of business even, with a sharp eye to the main chance. Take him apart from these cranks of his, I like him – I can't help liking him. You'll like him too, when you know him better. You have seen the least attractive side of him, coming down like this, with the misgiving he is driving you into a corner. I'd have you stand up to him and speak your mind about what you will and will not do. And I believe he will hear reason in the end.'

Next morning's post brought Richard a letter, forwarded on from London: a notice requiring his appearance before a certain Medical Board, and obliging his return to town. He sent a message to Mr Quinton by Lindsay, explaining his abrupt departure, but saying he was willing to return if desired. The reply message requested an interview, in the same upstairs room as before. It proved to be a long one. Lindsay, waiting in the hall for the car to come round, wondered what was the delay, and what was passing between the two. At last a door in the upper regions opened and shut, and Richard came down the stairs. He was white as chalk, staggering like a man dizzy or blind, and a cold sweat stood in beads on his forehead, as happened after the scrying of the day before. Lindsay sprang forward to meet him, and propped him with a hand under his arm. He leaned against the wall, and gasped out: 'It's all over – I've refused – you were right to refuse too. The thing he asks is impossible. This house is full of devils – of devils, I tell you – and they come out of Quinton's crystal. He made me look again – against my will, and I saw – what I can't speak of – what I never can forget – !'

'Come into the dining-room with me, and I'll give you a dram. You have been upset; you may think differently when you are calm.'

'No – no. Never this place for me. He is beyond reason: he is given over to the fiend. I told him I would thank him for ever for just Quinton Court and a farm, but he would not part the property. It had to be all or nothing. And not even to gain Quinton Court would I be owner here. No, I'll have no dram. I want to get away.'

The car was now heard coming round, and drawing up at the door.

'Goodbye, Lindsay, and thank you for your kindness. We may never meet again, but I shall not forget.'

These were his last words, and the next moment he was shut in and speeding away, the open gates with their watchful faces left behind.

5

Richard reached London only to fall ill. The doctor diagnosed influenza, but seemed to think his system had received a shock: as to this he was not communicative. He had a week in bed, and another of tardy convalescence, a prey to depression and all the ills resulting from exhaustion. A fortnight had gone by since he left Mount Verney, when he received a communication from Fryer and Fryer asking for an interview. Mr Fryer wished to see Mr Richard Quinton on a matter of business, and would be obliged if he could make it convenient to call.

'I ought to have written to the old bird, to tell him I am out of the running,' was Richard's comment, spoken to himself. 'But, as I have been remiss, I had better go and hear what he has to say. I shall have to take a taxi.'

He had no strength left for the walking distance, and even the office stairs were something of a trial. He was shown in at once to Mr Fryer, and began with an apology.

'I have only just ascertained your address,' said the man of law. 'Are you aware, Mr Quinton, that your cousin and late host is dead?'

'Indeed no, sir, I was not aware.' And that Richard was shocked by the intelligence was plain to see.

'He died suddenly of heart-failure the night after you left. And, so far as Dr Lindsay and I can ascertain after a careful search through all his papers, he has left no will.'

This communication did not seem to inform Richard; he was still too dazed by what he had just heard.

Mr Fryer tapped the blotting-pad before him, which was a way he had when irritated.

'You don't realise what that means? The whole property goes to you, both real estate and personal. Mount Verney, and all that it contains.'

Richard gave a cry, which sounded more like horror than elation.

'You are telling me – that I am the owner of Mount Verney?'

'If no will is discovered later, certainly you are the owner.'

'And does this bind me to live there? Because I cannot – I will not. I told Mr Quinton so before leaving, and, as he made it a condition, I refused the inheritance.'

'So I understand from Dr Lindsay. No, you are bound to nothing. You can live where you please. And, as soon as the legal processes of succession are gone through, you can sell the property, should you prefer investment abroad.'

Richard still sat half-stunned, slowly taking it in. He could rid himself of Mount Verney and all that it contained, and Quinton Court, the home of his desire, would be his own.

'You would have wished, of course, to attend your cousin's funeral, but you had quitted the address left with me, and we were unable to let you know in time. He was cremated, according to his own often expressed desire. There is one thing, Mr Quinton, I would like to say to you – to suggest, though you may think I am exceeding my province. Your cousin's intestacy benefits you, but there are others who suffer by it. Old Peters, a servant who had been with him from boyhood: he would have been provided for without doubt. Probably there would have been gratuities to the other domestics, according to their length of service; and his resident doctor, Lindsay, would have come in for a legacy. Of course it is quite at your option what to do.'

'I will thank you, sir, to put down what you would have advised Mr Quinton in all these cases, had you prepared his will, and I will make it good.'

It was not always easy to divine Mr Fryer's sentiments, but he seemed to receive the instruction with pleasure. Lawyer and client shook hands, and then Richard was in the street again, hurrying away. O, what a letter – what a letter he would have to write to Nan!

*   *   *

Legal processes take time, and summer was waning into autumn before Richard was fully established as owner of the Quinton property. Up to now he had sedulously avoided Mount Verney, though he had been in the near neighbourhood, and had several times visited Quinton Court. He knew only by the agent's report that his orders were carried out, the heads removed from the gate-pillars and the statue from the grove, which was a grove no longer, as the young oaks had been felled and carted away. The Roman relics had been presented to a local museum, and the house was now shut up, and emptied of most of its furniture. Lindsay, at Richard's desire, had chosen such of the plenishings as he cared for and could make useful, receiving these in addition to the money gift advised by Fryer.

All this was accomplished, the last load removed, and now the big white villa was shut up and vacant, and Clement Quinton's heir was about to enter for the first time as its possessor. But, strange to say, he had elected to make the visit late at night and in secret, so planning his approach across country that his coming and going might be unnoticed and unknown. A thief's visit, one would have said, rather than that of the lawful owner, who could have commanded all.

The latter part of the journey was made on foot, and throughout he carried with him, under his own eye and hand, a large and heavy gladstone-bag. He had studied incendiary methods when serving in France, and materials for swift destruction were contained within.

It was a wild evening; a gale, forestalling the equinox, hurtled overhead, tearing the clouds into shreds as they flew before it, and making clear spaces for some shining of stars. Rain was not yet, though doubtless it would fall presently. The wind would help Richard's purpose, rain would not, though he thought it could hardly defeat it. That intermittent shining of the stars gave little light. The night was very nearly 'as dark as hell's mouth', and Richard had much the feeling that he was venturing into the mouth of hell.

It had needed the mustering of a desperate courage, this expedition on which he was bent, but he could entrust his purpose to no other hand. Purification by fire: there could be, it seemed to him, no other cleansing. He intended no oblation to the infernal gods, that was far from his thought: what he dimly designed was a final breaking of their power.

With this purpose in mind he turned into the dark avenue, the shut gates yielding to his hand, between the pillars from which the satyrs' heads were gone. Did faces pry on him from between the close-ranked trees? He would not think of it: and for this night at least he would shut the eyes of his soul, the eyes with which he had perceived before, or he might happen upon something which would make him altogether a coward. In the darkness he left the road more than once, and blundered into the plantation, needing to have recourse to the electric torch in his pocket before he could find the way. But at last he came upon the open sweep of drive, and there was the villa before him, stark and white, eyeless and shuttered, the corpse of a house from which the soul had gone out.

This new owner had been careful to carry with him the keys which admitted. He unlocked a side door and entered, and now the torch was a necessity in the pitch darkness which prevailed within. His first act was to go through the lower rooms, unshuttering and opening everywhere, so as to let in a free draught of air. Here a certain amount of the heavier furniture still remained: Lindsay had been moderate in his selection, though he might, with Richard's approval, have grasped at all. Then he mounted to the attics, opening as he went, and here the incendiary work started. The flames were beginning to creep over the floors and about the back staircase, when he turned his attention to the better apartments on the first floor, entering and igniting one after another. He left Mr Quinton's private rooms until the last; the rooms where those momentous interviews had taken place, and where the devils had issued from the glass.

The private den had been wholly stripped, both of furniture and books; no doubt Lindsay, who was free to take what he pleased, had valued these mementoes of a patient who was also a friend. Richard was glad to find the apartment empty; there was less to recall the past. But as he moved the illuminating torch from left to right in his survey, it seemed to him for an instant that a tall figure stood before him – long enough to realise its presence, though gone in the space of a couple of agitated heartbeats. He never doubted that it was Quinton, present to reproach him, to arrest the course of destruction if that were possible. But in spite of what he had seen – if indeed he did see – he gritted his teeth and went on.

The inner cabinet was next to enter. Here nothing had been removed or changed; the writing-table in the window still had its equipment of inkpot and blotting-pad, and on the latter, Richard noticed, a sheet of blank paper was spread out. The velvet cover thrown over the high stand, no doubt concealed the uncanny crystal into which he had been forced to look. No-one would look into it again after the destruction of this night! And then somehow, he knew not how, his attention was drawn to the white paper on the table.

Most of us have seen the development of a photographic plate, and how magically the image starts into view on a surface which before was blank. That was what appeared to happen under his eyes upon the paper, and the image was the imprint of a large hand, a man's hand, red as if dipped in blood.

The same awful sensation of sick faintness, experienced before with the crystal, overcame him once again. It was a marvel to him afterwards that he did not fall unconscious, to perish in the burning house. He saved himself by a desperate effort of will, flinging what was left of his incendiary material behind him on the floor. As he gained the staircase, a rush of air met him from below, and this was perhaps his salvation. But the house was now filling with smoke, and from the upper regions came already the crackle of spreading flame.

The crackle of flame, and something more. Something which sounded like the clatter of hoofs over bare floors, and a cackle of hellish laughter; unless his senses were by this time wholly dazed and confused, hearing bewitched as well as sight. He found the door by which he entered, locked it behind him and fled into the night, now no longer bewilderingly dark, but faintly illuminated by the rising moon.

He did not take the direction of the avenue and the road, but climbed fences and made his way up the hill behind; and when on the wind-swept summit he turned to look back. He had done his work effectually; the white villa was alight in all its windows, fiercely ablaze within, and, as he still lingered and watched, a portion of the roof fell in, and flame and smoke shot up into the sky.

From the local paper of the following Saturday:

We regret to state that the mansion of Mount Verney, recently the residence of the late Clement Quinton, Esquire, and now the property of Mr Richard Quinton, was destroyed by fire on Tuesday night. The origin of the fire is wrapped in mystery, as the house was unoccupied and shut up, and the electric light disconnected, so there could have been no fusion of wires. Much valuable property is destroyed, and part of the building is completely gutted. The blaze was first noticed between twelve and one o'clock, by a man driving home late from market. He gave notice to the police, but by the time the fire-engines arrived, the conflagration had taken such hold that it could not be checked, though abundant water was at hand in the Mount Verney lake. The loss to Mr Richard Quinton will be very considerable, as we understand no part of it is covered by insurance.

From the same paper in the following December:

We understand that a gift has been made to our hospital fund of the shell of the Mount Verney house with the grounds that surround it, to be converted into a sanatorium for the treatment of tuberculosis, and Mr Richard Quinton also adds to the subscription list the sum of £1,000. This munificent donation of money and a site will enable the work to be put in hand at once; and it is believed that what is left of the original mansion can be incorporated in the scheme.

The Mount Verney house, which, as will be remembered, was destroyed by a disastrous fire about three months ago, was not insured, and Mr Richard Quinton had no wish to rebuild for his own occupation. He will, we understand, make his future residence at Quinton Court, the ancestral home of his family, so soon as he returns from Canada with his bride.

Anne's Little Ghost

We had planned to take a holiday as soon as I was demobilised, and I claim that we had abundantly earned it, Anne and I. She had been a war worker all the time I was serving abroad – (for there were, alas! no children to tie her to the duties of home) – and she needed relief and change as much as I. It was to be a real holiday and in full measure – no wretched scrap measured by days, but lasting several weeks, and at our own option to extend into months if we so pleased. This gave a peculiar feeling of wealth and spaciousness; for once we were to be millionaires in the holiday line. But from the pound.s.d. point of view, a quite separate matter, the holiday was bound to be cheap. So Anne decreed, and I left it to her to arrange what it should be, and where.

She was in high spirits the last time she came to see me in hospital, about a week before my discharge. She had heard of the very place for us, if I agreed – and of course I was ready to agree. Her friend Adelaide Sherwood recommended Deepdene, but there was no time to be lost; we must write or wire at once if we wanted to secure the rooms. Farmhouse lodgings in Devonshire; would not that be delightful? – with trout-fishing for me thrown in, and the sea not many miles away. It was really half a house, and the farm-mistress would board and cook for us: we could either bring a servant (we did not possess one) or a day-woman would come in from the village to order the rooms. Some friends of Miss Sherwood's had stayed there the previous autumn, and were abundantly satisfied with everything, cleanliness included; the charge was, besides, astonishingly low.

'Just think, Godfrey, of getting the farm produce fresh on the spot – eggs and vegetables, to say nothing of dairy luxuries beyond. And in such pretty country as they say it is. I cannot fancy getting tired of the quiet, but perhaps you may feel differently. A large sitting-room with glass doors on to a verandah, and such a view from it; the farm-buildings quite away on the other side. The bedroom is on the same floor: that will be right for your lame leg, will it not? And then upstairs two more bedrooms, roomy attics. We shall not need to use these, but they are part of the half house, and are let with it. What do you say?'

A prompt telegram secured us the tenancy of the half-house, and a week later Anne and I were *en route* for our new abode. We took the journey leisurely – a fit prelude to a holiday which was to be all leisure – and stayed a couple of nights at Exeter on our way. So the journey of the last morning was a short one. We arrived at our destination soon after noon, to find all gilded with the cheer of midday sunshine, and a white-aproned landlady hospitably welcoming us at the door.

The house was neither picturesque nor old, but it promised comfort, and seemed likely to justify the encomiums of Anne's friend and correspondent. Mrs Stokes the landlady was openly proud of it, and showed us round expecting appreciation. The kitchen and offices occupied the lower floor, but we had a separate entrance through the garden wicket up steps to the verandah, our private portion of it, which was cut off from the other set of lodgings by a light railing thrown across. This second set was at present vacant, but would be occupied in another fortnight by two ladies, sisters, who came always at this time of year, bringing with them their own maid.

The attic rooms were also shown, though we were not intending to occupy them. My lame leg excused me from a further mounting of stairs, but Anne accompanied Mrs Stokes aloft. The occupiers of both sets had an equal right to these stairs, and the attic accommodation was impartially divided, two falling to our lot, and two to that of the sisters and their servant.

They were airy rooms, Anne told me, and would make pleasant bedrooms, looking out through smaller windows on the same lovely view that we commanded on the lower floor. This was all that was said at the time, but later, when tea was spread and we were partaking of it, she told me more.

'People must have been here with children,' she said presently in an interval of filling my cup. 'The attic over our bedroom has evidently been used as a nursery, for there are coloured pictures pasted on the wall, and a child's bed is pushed into one corner. Mrs Stokes said she would take it out if it was in our way.'

There was just the slightest sigh with this communication, and the least possible droop at the corners of Anne's sensitive mouth, but enough to give me a clue to what was in her mind. I can often read Anne's mind as plainly as the page of a book – though I do not tell her so; perhaps because of long association, to say nothing of affection. We two are singularly alone in the world, and so are drawn all the closer, each to each. We have been married rather more than eight years, and in our second year together we possessed, for a brief space of only weeks, a baby daughter. So brief a space that one might suppose both joy and grief would be easily forgotten; but those who so think, know little of a mother's heart – at least, little of Anne's. From the dear memory of that joy and that grief (the sword piercing her soul, as was foretold of another mother) comes the wistful interest she takes in all children. And I could divine her thought: 'If only little Clarice had lived and had been with us here, the pictured attic would have been her nursery, and the little bed in the corner would have been ready made for her.' But of this I said nothing.

'Perhaps Mrs Stokes's own children sleep there when they are without lodgers,' I suggested, but Anne shook her head.

'No, for I asked the question. They have only three big boys, all in their teens. The eldest works on the farm, and the other two are away at school. None of the Stokes family sleep under this roof; a stable is converted into quarters for them, so that the house may be set apart as lodgings' – and again there came the slight and smothered sigh. I should be giving a false impression if it were thought from this that there is anything dreary about Anne. No-one is more resolutely cheerful, or more keenly and alertly practical, than this wife of mine. These inner feelings of hers, tender regrets and constant thoughts, have their own secret chamber in her mind, the door of which is shut and barred; a sacred threshold, which even I dare not openly approach. No more was said about the empty cot and the pictures, and that first evening of our stay at Deepdene passed delightfully amid country sights and sounds, and the sweet Devonshire air. Miss Sherwood's recommendation was, we thought, justifying itself to the full.

And at night, when the veil of dimness, not quite darkness, was drawn over the garden and the hills, what a healing silence prevailed: bird notes stilled, and at last even the plaintive cry of a lamb which had wandered from its mother, satisfied and at rest. I slept profoundly, but presently what was this? Anne's voice: Anne shaking me awake.

'Godfrey! Godfrey, listen! Do you hear?'

I was for the moment deaf and dazed with sleep.

'No,' I said. 'What is it? What is the matter?'

'It is a child sobbing. A little child in trouble. A child that has been shut out. I cannot hear it and do nothing. Can you?' Anne was thrusting her feet into slippers, and was already arrayed in her dressing-gown – blue and white, the colours of the Virgin Mother. 'I can't make out where the sound comes from – whether it is overhead or out of doors. Listen, and you will hear it too. There are no words, only cries and sobs. I heard it again the instant before you awoke.'

I was out of bed by this time and broad awake. I heard no crying, but I did hear footsteps: a child's pattering run across the floor overhead, once from end to end of the room, and then again in return.

'Now I know,' said Anne, quite composedly, proceeding to light a candle. 'It is upstairs in the attic I told you of; the room like a nursery, which is over ours. I wonder what child it can be. Mrs Stokes should have let us know. I am going up to see.'

That was so entirely Anne-like I was not surprised. She went out carrying the light, and I followed on to the landing in case I should be wanted. As I went, I heard again the pattering feet overhead, and I think Anne heard them too. I waited at the foot of the stairs, not wishing to affright the child by the sight of a grim soldier-man in pyjamas. No child, not even the most nervous, could be frightened at the sight of Anne.

Waiting there, I could be certain that no living soul came down the stairs. I heard Anne pass from room to room, and then she called to me.

'Godfrey, I wish you would come up here.'

I went up in the soft twilight that was not wholly dark, even in that enclosed place, entering where I saw her candle shine. She was in the attic with the pictured walls, sitting on the little bed, and her face was white and awe-stricken.

'I can't find anything,' she said. 'The rooms are all empty, and there is no place in which a child could be shut. I wish you would look too.'

Of course I looked with her, and, equally of course, our search was fruitless. Then I persuaded her to go back to our room and listen there, while I hurried on some clothes and made search round the house outside. I talked some nonsense about the way in which sounds reflect and echo, and the difficulty there is about locating their direction, especially at night; but I do not think she believed me: unconvinced myself, I could hardly expect to convince another.

And I was privately certain I had heard the footsteps of a child, not echoed over floors from a distance, but distinctly overhead. There must be some way of getting up to those attics, and down from them, that we did not know.

But in the morning Mrs Stokes could tell us nothing, and had no explanation to offer. No child could have got in without her knowledge. It must have been one out of the village wandering round outside, scared by the darkness, and afraid to go home because it had been threatened with the stick. That was how the good dame dismissed the matter, and we might have been satisfied about the crying, but not as to those footsteps overhead.

It will be well believed that I was eager to sample the fishing, and the next day saw us on the banks of the stream, Anne sitting near me with a book. But somehow in the week following she managed to catch cold, and after that I had for a while to pursue my sport alone, and she spent solitary hours at the Deepdene farm.

I think it was on the second day of her seclusion that she said to me when I came back in the evening: 'I have seen the child.'

I had better mention here that in the interval we had heard no more of the sobbing voice at night, nor of the footsteps overhead. Anne looked as if something had moved her profoundly, even to the shedding of tears.

'Did you find out whose child it is, and why it is here?'

'No. She did not speak, and it seems so odd that Mrs Stokes does not know. I was on the landing when I saw her first, and she was running upstairs. There is no carpet on those stairs, and I heard quite plainly the patter of her feet. A little girl. I went up after her, and she ran straight into that room which was a nursery, the room with the pictures.'

'And you followed?'

'Yes, I followed, but she was not there. I was puzzled – almost frightened, and I went back again to the sitting-room. I think it must have been half an hour later when I saw her again. If you remember, it began to rain. It was so chilly, I was obliged to shut the glass doors.'

'Yes?' I said. Anne had paused again, with that odd breathlessness which was new.

'*She* was out there on the verandah, and the rain was slanting in upon her. Such a pretty little girl, and about the age – '

I knew what Anne so nearly said, and why she checked herself and altered the phrase to 'about six years old'. (Clarice would have been six years old had she lived.) 'Not a poor woman's child. She had a pretty white frock on, worked cambric and lace, and a silk sash of a sort of geranium red. No cottagers' child would be dressed so. And she had such an appealing little face, as if she was longing to be sheltered and comforted. It was raining, you know, all the time.'

'And what did you do?'

'Why of course I opened the window and said, "Come in, my dear, you will get wet." I held out my hand and she put hers into it; oh, such a cold little hand, as cold and soft as snow. I can feel the touch of it still. I drew her into the room. "We should be warm in here," I said. No, I'm not crying, Godfrey; not really crying; but there was something in her face that touched me: a sort of surprise, as if no-one had ever welcomed or been kind to her before. I asked her where she lived, but she only made a sign and put a finger to her lips. She heard me – I am sure she heard me, but I cannot help fancying the poor child is dumb.

'She heard me, for when I said, "My darling, will you give me a kiss?" she put up both her little arms, and her face was close to mine. I would have had that kiss, only just then that tiresome Mrs Stokes knocked at the door; the butcher, it seemed, had called, and she wanted to know if we would take a joint. The instant there came the knock, the child slipped away out of my arms. I had left the window open behind us, and she was gone.'

'Mrs Stokes did not see her?'

'No. She saw nothing, and could tell nothing; only I thought she looked a little *odd* when I was putting questions. I couldn't help wondering if there was any secret about it which she was bound to keep.'

As the days went on, I began also to wonder this, and after a while that wonder shaped itself into action. But I anticipate.

That night we heard again the footsteps overhead: both of us heard them. It was still completely dark, and the rain, driven against our windows, was mixed with hail. The pattering steps crossed the floor above once, twice, and after an interval a third time. I was still awake, holding my breath to listen should they come again, when I heard another sound beside me. Anne was crying, very quietly, her face buried in the pillow so that all sound should be hushed. I put out my hand to touch her.

'What is the matter?'

'Oh Godfrey – oh Godfrey, that poor child,' she sobbed. 'It is so sad for her to be up there all alone in the cold and darkness, and only six years old. Six years old! Clarice would have been just that age.

Can it be Clarice trying to come back to us? It felt as if she were Clarice when I held her in my arms.'

I was not surprised. It was as if I had seen the thought taking shape, somehow, as crystals form. But what could I do but dub it foolishness, born out of the sweet fond folly of a mother's love?

We heard no more that night. Next morning, without telling Anne of my intention, I went up to examine the attics for the first time by daylight. The rooms over ours were vacant, and in the one with pictured walls the little bed was gaunt and undraped, with its stripped mattress and uncovered pillow. There was no closet or recess in which it was possible for even the smallest child to hide, and as the walls were of thin modern building, secret entrances and passages were out of the question here.

I was to hear again later of that little bed. Nothing more passed between us touching that strange fancy of Anne's, the confession I had surprised from her in the night, until she said in a sort of shamefaced fashion (but again there were tears in her eyes): 'I made a pretence to Mrs Stokes today; I hope it was not untrue enough to be wrong. I said we might be expecting a child visitor: we might expect any visitors you know, and some of our friends have children. And I asked her to have the pictured attic put ready, and the bed made up – in case. She did it this morning, and I did not want you to go up there and be surprised. It does not look nearly so miserable now the furniture is in order, and sheets and blankets are on the little bed. Anyone who was up there in the night, and who was cold and tired, could lie down.'

What was I to say to this, but again that it was folly? – but I could not charge Anne with folly when she looked as she did then. And hardly a night passed without the pattering footsteps overhead.

The parish to which Deepdene belonged was a scattered one; the church was a long half-mile away, and a mere cluster of cottages called itself the village. That cluster, however, contained the post-office, and the inevitable general shop, which included among its wares a few toys of the simpler sort. One day Anne returned from a post-office errand the purchaser of a doll, pretty of head and face, but with its nudity barely covered by a scant chemise of waxed muslin. She said nothing of her intention, but for a day or two that doll lay about in our sitting-room, while her skilful fingers were busied shaping for it more befitting garments – pink and frilly, and with a pinafore of lace. Then it disappeared, but I did not remark, nor for a while did she explain, not until I asked her a week later if she had seen the child again.

'She often comes when I am alone, peeping in at me from the verandah,' was the answer. 'And she was pleased when I gave her the doll. She took it from me and kissed me, but still she does not speak.'

She took the doll! With this the mystery grew. How could an immaterial creature, one we dimly guessed to be spirit and not flesh, accept a material gift, removing it when she withdrew? Yet Anne had given her the toy in exchange for a kiss, and the doll was certainly gone.

Next day when I came in from the stream, Anne was out, and some impulse urged me to go up again to the attic, the attic prepared for our supposed guests, which no-one had arrived to occupy. It was vacant as before, but a couple of small vases held fresh flowers, of Anne's filling doubtless, and on the white pillow of the little bed there lay the pink-frocked doll.

I was beginning to be anxious about Anne. There was a change in her I did not like to see; a feverish spot on her cheek, and, slight as she was before, she had fallen away in the few weeks of our sojourn to be very thin. She laughed over it herself, and said her gowns must be taken in; but to me it seemed no laughing matter. Was vitality being drawn from her for the shaping of the child apparition in material form; and, if so, what would be the effect upon her health? I am not instructed in such matters, but I vaguely recalled some of the explanations put forward – material forms built up from the medium, and life-substance drawn away. Ought I to make some excuse, and cut short our stay at Deepdene? That was one question, but another followed it. Now that she fancied the appearance might be that of her dead baby, our little Clarice, would Anne be content to go?

Our little Clarice! Mine as well as hers; the father's tie as valid surely as the mother's, if not so close and fond. If to one of us, why not to both? But in the end I could no longer say this. Though only once, she was to me too.

Was it a projection from Anne's mind influencing mine? I have wondered since; but these are questions I can only indicate: they are beyond my power to answer.

We were sitting in the early twilight, the lamp unlit, as Anne had a headache: her head often ached in these days. The glass doors were open, and I dimly saw, first a glimpse of white on the verandah, misty and indefinite, which presently resolved itself into the figure Anne had described to me – the dainty figure of a girl-child in white frock and red silk sash, a cloud of dusky hair hanging about her little head. She was peeping in at me and drawing back; then with more confidence peeping again. Anne took no notice; she was, I think, asleep. I remained motionless, scarcely daring to breathe, lest I should startle this exquisite small creature, as one might fear to affright a bird. Presently she ventured as far into the room as where Anne was sitting, and stood resting her little elbows on her friend's knee, and looking me straight in the face.

I was able now to understand Anne's meaning about the child's pathetic eyes with their wistfulness of appeal, and also to appreciate something more: something that Anne herself had not noticed, was not likely to notice, as people seldom see likenesses to themselves. It was very marked – the eyes, the brow, the hair: here was Anne as she must have been a quarter of a century ago. Could I doubt that it was our child; and did a longing for the earthly parents' love draw her down to us, away from her safe and happy cradling in the satisfaction of Heaven?

I was still gazing when my wife moved and sighed, waking from her sleep; and the childish figure was gone in a flash, too abrupt for any real withdrawal. In spite of the evidence of those material-sounding footsteps – in spite of the handling of the doll – I never again thought of her as compacted of ordinary mundane flesh and blood.

I had seen her with my own eyes, and I could no longer doubt. But there was a point which I still desired to probe, despite that evidence of the resemblance. I wanted to find out whether the half-house we were renting could be haunted, and whether the child-ghost had been seen or heard by other people than ourselves.

It would be a difficult matter to ascertain, for in defence of their property against depreciation, very good people have before now thought it hardly a sin to pervert the truth. But I reflected that the clergyman of the parish had no interest in letting Deepdene. I would go in the first place to him, and then see what I could make of sounding Mrs Stokes.

My errand to Mr Fielding bore only negative fruit. He was a man of advanced years, a gentleman and a scholar, and he received me with suave politeness; if he could serve me in any way he would be glad. But when I put my question, I could see that a faint flicker of amusement underlay his grave attention; he, the minister of the Unseen, was wholly sceptical as to its demonstration.

I said very little, merely asking did the house where we were lodging bear the reputation of being haunted? We – I, that is, for I left Anne out of it – had heard sounds that could not be explained, and seen a small figure that appeared to vanish. I should like to know whether it was a matter of common report.

The answer to this was 'No'. There might be some vulgar story of the sort, it was just possible, but it had never reached his ears. Had it done so, he would have discredited it. I would readily see on reflection how easy it was to mistake sounds and their origin; and not only did our ears trick us in such matters, but also our vision. A supposed phantom generally meant that the percipient would do well to resort to an oculist.

I did not argue the point. As I told him, I only wished to ascertain whether there was, or was not, any local tradition. I wished him good-morning, and my next resort was to Mrs Stokes.

Here I was met by indignation, and the good woman was not easy to appease. I was interested, I told her, I was not objecting; rather than otherwise, it increased my interest in Deepdene. I only wished to know if any of the other lodgers – and doubtless in the course of the year she would have many – had mentioned to her any similar sights or sounds.

Her first answer was a flat negative; but there was, I thought, an uneasy consciousness in the eye that did not meet mine as before, and presently modification came. For her own part she knew nothing, as she never slept in the house herself, nor did Stokes *père*, nor the boys – (was this, it occurred to me to wonder, a suspicious circumstance?). She had never seen or heard anything 'worse than herself', and I might take that as on her Bible oath; but, now she came to think, some of the lodgers had mentioned a running about on those upper floors, happening when they had the rats in at threshing time. They got some virus when they heard of it, and there were no more complaints after that was put down. If I had been disturbed, no doubt the rats were getting in again. But, certain sure, there were no ghosts.

I wondered, and I wonder still, whether some houses have a psychical atmosphere which can be variously moulded and used; the child employing it to approach us, and the spiritual environment of others putting it to a quite separate use. I think this is not impossible, but as to the truth of the matter, who can say?

As I have shown, I gained nothing by my enquiries, and this is nearly all I have to tell. The end of our sojourn followed quickly. I remember once discussing psychical matters with a friend. He was a believer, and he said to me: 'I always know how to distinguish a true ghost-story from a faked one. The true ghost-story never has any point, and the faked one dare not leave it out.' This ghost-story of mine, though not faked, has a point, but it is one the ordinary reader would overlook, and I do not insist on it. I am abundantly content to be disbelieved, and Anne is content too.

It was Anne's health which brought our stay at Deepdene to an abrupt close. I think I have said that for some time I had noticed she was looking ill, and wondered vaguely whether her vitality could be drained away to supply material for those manifestations we had witnessed and heard. It was, however, no case of gradually lessened strength, but a threatened crisis which demanded prompt attention – surgeon's investigation and a nursing-home. So, in figurative language, we struck our tents, seeking another encampment, and Deepdene knew us no more.

Over the Wires

Ernest Carrington, captain in the 'Old Contemptibles', was in England on his first leave from the front. There he had a special errand, hoping to trace a family of the name of Regnier, which had been swept away in the exodus from Belgium, then of recent date. Two old people, brother and sister, harmless folk who had shown him the kindest hospitality before their home was wrecked and burned; and with them their niece, Isabeau, who was his chosen love and his betrothed wife. He had endured agonies in these last weeks, receiving no news of them, though he fully believed they had escaped to England: it was more than strange that Isabeau did not write, as she knew his address, though he was ignorant of hers.

A friend in London had made enquiry for him where the thronging refugees were registered and their needs dealt with, but nothing seemed to be known of the Regniers. Now he would be on the spot, and could himself besiege the authorities. Hay might have been lukewarm over the quest, but it seemed impossible that he, Carrington, could fail. His friend, Hay, with whom he was to have stayed, had just been transferred from Middlesex to the coast defence of Scotland, but had placed at Carrington's disposal his small flat, and the old family servant who was caretaker.

The flat was a plain little place, but it seemed luxurious indeed to Carrington that first evening, in sharp contrast to his recent experiences roughing it in the campaign. His brain was still in a whirl after the hurried journey, and it was too late to embark upon his quest that night; but the next morning, the very next morning, he would begin the search for Isabeau.

Only one item in Hay's room demands description. There was a telephone installation in one corner; and twice while Carrington's dinner was being served, there came upon it a sharp summons, answered first by the servant, and secondly by himself. Major Hay was wanted, and it had to be detailed how Major Hay had departed upon sudden orders for Scotland only that morning.

Now the meal was over and cleared away, and the outer door closed, shutting Carrington in for the night. Left alone, his thoughts returned to the channel in which they had flowed for many days and nights. Isabeau – his Isabeau: did the living world still hold his lost treasure, and under what conditions and where? And – maddening reflection – what might she not have suffered of privation, outrage, while he was held apart by his soldier's duty, ignorant, impotent to succour! He could picture her as at their last meeting when they exchanged tokens, the light in her eyes, the sweetness of her lips: the image was perfect before him, down to every fold of her white dress, and every ripple of her hair. His own then, pledged . . . to him, and now vanished into blank invisibility and silence. What could have happened: what dread calamity had torn her from him? Terrible as knowledge might be when gained, it was his earnest prayer that he might know.

A groan burst from his lips, and he cried out her name in a passion of appeal. 'Isabeau, where are you? Speak to me, dead or alive!'

Was it in answer that the telephone bell began to ring? – Not sharply and loudly, like those demands for Major Hay, but thin and faint like their echo. But without doubt it rang, and Carrington turned to the instrument and took down the receiver.

'Yes,' he called back. 'What is it?'

Great heaven! it was Isabeau's voice that answered, a voice he could but just hear, as it seemed to be speaking from far away.

'Ernest – Ernest,' she cried, 'have you forgotten me? I have forgotten many things since I was tortured, but not you – never you.'

'I am here, my darling. I have come to England seeking you, with no other thought in mind. Tell me, for God's sake, where I can find you. Can I come tonight?'

There was a pause, and then the remote voice began again, now a little stronger and clearer. 'Ernest – is it really you? I can die happy, now you tell me that you love me still. That is all I wanted, just the assurance. All I may have in this world – now.'

'Darling, of course I love you: you are all in all to me. Where are you speaking from? Tell me, and I will come?'

'No, no: it is all I wanted, what you have just said. It will be easy now to die. I could never have looked you in the face again – after – I am not fit. But soon I shall be washed clean. What does it say – washed? And they gave them white robes – !'

The voice failed, dying away, and when Carrington spoke there was no answer. He called to her by name, begging her to say if she was in London or where, but either the connection had been cut off, or she did not hear. Then after an interval he rang up the exchange. Who was it who had just used the line? But the clerk was stupid or sleepy, thought there had been no call, but was only just on after the shift, and could not say.

It was extraordinary, that she could know where he was to be found that night, and call to him. And how was it that the voice had ceased without giving him a clue? But surely, surely, it would come again.

To seek his bed, tired as he was, seemed now to be impossible. He waited in the living-room, sometimes pacing up and down, sometimes sitting moodily, his head bent on his hands: could he rest or sleep when a further call might come, and, if unheard, a chance be lost. And a call did come a couple of hours later; the same thin reedy vibration of the wire. In a moment he was at the instrument, the receiver at his ear, and again it was Isabeau's voice that spoke.

'Ernest, can you hear me? Will you say it over again: say that you love me still, in spite of all?'

'Dearest, I love you with all my heart and soul. And I entreat you to tell me where you are, so that I can find you.'

'You will be told – quite soon. They are so kind – the people here, but they want to know my name. I cannot tell them any more than Isabeau; I have forgotten what name came after. What was my name when you knew me?'

'My darling, you were Isabeau Regnier. And you were living at Martel with our old uncle Antoine Regnier, and his sister, Mademoiselle Elise. Surely you remember?'

'Yes; yes. I remember now. I remember all. I was Isabeau Regnier then, and now I am lost – lost – lost! Poor old uncle Antoine! They set him up against the wall and shot him, because they said he resisted; and they dragged the Tante and me away. But the Tante could not go fast enough to please them. They stabbed her in the back with their bayonets, and left her bleeding and moaning, lying in the road to die. Oh, if only they had killed me too. Don't ask me – never ask me – what they did to me!'

'Do not think of it, Isabeau dearest. Think only that I have come to seek you, and that you are safe in England and will be my wife. But I must know where you are, and when I can come to see you.'

'I will tell you some time, but not now. The nurse says I must not go on talking; that I am making myself more ill. She's wrong, for it cannot make me ill to speak to you; but I must do as I am bidden. Tell me that you love me; just once again. That you love what I was: you cannot love what I have become.'

'Darling, I loved you then, I love you now, and shall love you always. But tell me – you must tell me where.'

She did not answer. This seemed to be the end, for, though he still watched and listened, the wire did not vibrate again that night, nor for many following hours.

He did not spend those hours in inaction. He was early at the London office, and then took the express to Folkestone, but at neither place was there knowledge of the name of Regnier. Nor had he better fortune at the other seaports, which he visited the day following. But where there had been such thronging numbers, despite the organisation vigilance, was it wonderful that a single name had dropped unnoted? And if what had been told him was correct, about the murder of her uncle and aunt, she must have reached England alone.

His next resort was to a private inquiry office, and there an appointment was arranged for him at three o'clock on Friday afternoon.

He had arrived in London on the Monday, and it was on Monday evening and night that those communications from Isabeau came over the wire. Each of the following nights, Tuesday, Wednesday and Thursday, he had spent in Hay's rooms, but from the installed telephone there was no sound or sign.

No sign came until midday on Friday, when he was just debating whether to go out to lunch, or have it brought to him from the service down below. The thin, echo-like call sounded again, and he was at once at the receiver.

'Isabeau! Is it you? Speak!'

'Yes, it is I.' It was Isabeau's voice that answered, and yet her voice with a difference: it was firmer and clearer than on Monday night, although remote – so remote!

'Where are you? Tell me, that I may come to you. I am seeking you everywhere.'

'I do not know where I am. It is all strange and new. But I rejoice in this: I have left behind what was soiled. I would tell you more, but something stops the words. I want you to do something for me: I have a fancy. You have done much, dear Ernest, but this is one thing more.'

'What is it, dearest? You have only to ask.'

'Go to the end of this street at two o'clock. That is in an hour from now; and wait there till I pass by. I shall not look as I used to do, but I will give you a flower – '

Here the voice failed; he could scarcely distinguish the last words. Strange, that one thing could be said and not another, never what he craved to know. But in an hour he would see her – speak to her, and their separation would be at an end. Not as she used to look! Did she mean changed by what she had suffered? But not so changed, surely, that he would not know, that she would need to identify herself by the gift of a flower. And was the change she spoke of, of the body or the mind? A chill doubt as to the latter, which had assailed him before, crept over him again. But even if it were so, there would be means of healing. She was ill now, shaken by what she had suffered: with love and care, and returning health, all would be well.

He was punctual at the place of appointment. A draughty corner this street-end; but what did he, campaign-hardened, care for chill winds, or for the flying gusts of rain? The passers-by were few for a London street; but each one was carefully scrutinised and each umbrella looked under – that is, if a woman carried it. There was not one, however, that remotely resembled Isabeau. Taxis went by, now and then horse-drawn vehicles; presently a funeral came up the crossing street. A glass hearse with a coffin in it, probably a woman's coffin by its size. A cross of violets lay upon it within, but a couple of white wreaths had been placed outside, next to the driver's seat. A hired brougham was the only following.

They had done better to put the wreaths under shelter, but perhaps no-one was in charge who greatly cared. As the cortège came level with the corner, a sharper gust than before tore a white spray from the exposed wreath, and whirled it over towards him; it struck him on the chest, and fell on the wet pavement at his feet. He stooped to pick it up: he loved flowers too well to see it trodden in the mud: and as he did so, a great fear for the first time pierced him through. What might it not signify, this funeral flower? But no, death was not possible: scarcely an hour ago he had heard her living voice.

He waited long at the rendezvous, the flower held in his hand, but no-one resembling her came by. Then, chilled and dispirited, but still holding the flower, he turned back to his lodging. It was time and over for his appointment at the inquiry office, but the rain had soaked him through, and he must change to a dry coat. The servant met him as he came in.

'A letter for you, sir. I am sorry for the delay. You should have had it before, but it must have been brushed off the table and not been seen. I found it just now on the floor.'

Could it be from Isabeau? – But no, the address was not in her writing. Carrington tore it open: it was from the Belgian central office, and bore a date two days back.

We have at last received information respecting Mademoiselle Regnier. A young woman who appeared to have lost her memory was charitably taken in by Mrs Duckworth, in whose house she has remained through a recent serious illness, the hospitals being over full. She recovered memory last night, and now declares her name to be Isabeau Regnier, formerly of Martel. Mrs Duckworth's address is 18, Silkmore Gardens, S. Kensington, and you will doubtless communicate with her.

Here at last was the information so long vainly sought, and it must have been from the Kensington house that Isabeau telephoned, though her voice sounded like a long-distance call. He would go thither at once; his application to the inquiry office was no longer needed: but still there was a chill at his heart as he looked at the white flower. Was some deep-down consciousness aware, in spite of his surface ignorance; and had it begun to whisper of the greater barrier which lay between?

As he approached the house in Silkmore Gardens, he might have noticed that a servant was going from room to room, drawing up blinds that had been lowered. At the door he asked for Mrs Duckworth.

'I am not sure if my mistress can see you, sir,' was the maid's answer. 'She has been very much upset.'

'Will you take in my card, and say my business is urgent. I shall be grateful if she will spare me even five minutes. I am a friend of Mademoiselle Regnier's.'

Carrington was shown into a sitting-room at the back of the house, with windows to the ground and a vision of greenery beyond. It was not long before Mrs Duckworth came to him; she wore a black gown, and looked as if she had been weeping.

'You knew Isabeau Regnier,' she began with a certain abruptness. 'Are you the Ernest of whom she used to speak?'

'I am. She is my affianced wife, so you see I enquire for her by right. I have been searching for her in the utmost distress, and until now in vain. I have but just heard that you out of your charity took her in, also that she has been ill. May I see her now, today?'

The lady's eyes filled again with tears, and she shrank back. 'Ah, you do not know what has happened. O, how sad, how dreadful to have to tell you! Isabeau is dead.'

'What, just now, within this hour? She was speaking to me on the telephone only at midday.'

'No – there is some mistake. That is impossible. She died last Tuesday, and was buried this afternoon. Her coffin left the house at a quarter before two, and my husband went with it to the cemetery. I would have gone too, only that I have been ill.'

At first he could only repeat her words: 'Dead – Tuesday – Isabeau dead!' She was frightened by the look of his face – the look of a man who is in close touch with despair.

'Oh, I'm so sorry. Oh do sit down, Mr Carrington. This has been too much for you.'

He sank into a chair, and she went hurriedly out, and returned with a glass in her hand.

'Drink this: nay, you must. I am sorry; oh, I am sorry. I wish my husband were here; he would tell you all about it better than I. It has been a grief to us all, to everyone in the house; we all grew fond of her. And we began quite to hope she would get well. When she came to us her memory was a blank, except for the wrong that had been done her. That seemed to have blotted out all that was behind, except her love for Ernest – you. But she said she could never look Ernest in the face again, and she wanted to be lost. She took an interest in things here after a while, and she was kind and helpful, like a daughter in the house – we have no children. And then her illness came on again; it was something the matter with the brain, caused by the shock she had sustained. She was very ill, but we could not get her into any hospital, all were too full. But she had every care with us, you may be sure of that, and I think she was happier to be here to the last. So it went on, up and down, sometimes a little better, sometimes worse. Last Monday evening delirium set in. She fancied Ernest was here – you – and she was talking to you all the time. It was as if she heard you answering.'

'Have you a telephone installed? Could she get up and go to the telephone?'

'We have a telephone – yes, certainly. But she had not strength enough to leave her bed, and the installation is downstairs in the study.'

'I declare to you on my most solemn word that she spoke to me over the telephone – twice on Monday night, and once today. It is beyond comprehension. Can you tell me what she said, speaking as she thought to Ernest?'

'She asked you to remind her of her forgotten name. We did not get Regnier till then, nor Martel where she lived; it was as if she heard the words spoken by you. I wrote at once to the organising people to say we had found out: I had no idea then that her death was so near. With the recollection of her name came back – horrors, and she was telling them to you. It seems she lived with an old uncle and aunt: would that be right for the girl you knew? They shot her uncle, the Germans did, when they burnt the house, and stabbed her poor old aunt and left her to die. I can show you a photograph of Isabeau, if that will help to identify. It is only an amateur snapshot, taken in our garden, at the time she was so much better, and, we hoped, recovering. It is very like her as she was then.'

Mrs Duckworth opened the drawer of a cabinet, and took out a small square photograph of a girl in a white dress sitting under a tree, and looking out of the picture with sad appealing eyes. Carrington looked at it, and at first he could not speak. Presently he said, answering a question of Mrs Duckworth's: 'Yes, there can be no doubt.'

He had heard enough. Mrs Duckworth would fain have asked further about the marvel of the voice, but he got up to take leave.

'I will come again if you will permit,' he said. 'Another day I shall be able to thank you better for all you did for her – for all your kindness. You will then tell me where she is laid, and let me take on myself – all expense. Now I must be alone.'

There was ready sympathy in the little woman's face; tears were running down, though her words of response were few.

Carrington still held the photograph.

'May I take this?' he said, and she gave an immediate assent. Then he pressed the hand she held out in farewell, and in another moment was gone.

The sequel to this episode is unknown. Carrington sat long that night with the picture before him, the pathetic little picture of his lost love; and cried aloud to her in his solitude: 'Isabeau, speak to me, come to me. Death did not make it impossible before: why should it now? Do not think I would shrink from you or fear you. Nothing is in my heart but a great longing – a great love – a great pity. Speak again – speak!'

But no answer came. The telephone in the corner remained silent, and that curious far-off tremor of the wire sounded for him no more.

A Water Witch

We were disappointed when Robert married. We had for long wanted him to marry, as he is our only brother and head of the family since my father died, as well as of the business firm; but we should have liked his wife to be a different sort of person. We, his sisters, could have chosen much better for him than he did for himself. Indeed we had our eye on just the right girl – bright-tempered and sensibly brought up, who would not have said 'No': of that I am assured, had Robert on his side shown signs of liking. But he took a holiday abroad the spring of 1912, and the next thing we heard was that he had made up his mind to marry Frederica. Frederica, indeed! We Larcombs have been plain Susans and Annes and Marys and Elizabeths for generations (I am Mary), and the fantastic name was an annoyance. The wedding took place at Mentone in a great hurry, because the stepmother was marrying again, and Freda was unhappy. Was not that weak of Robert? – he did not give himself time to think. We may perhaps take that as some excuse for a departure from Larcomb traditions: on consideration, the match would very likely have been broken off. Freda had some money of her own, though not much: all the Larcomb brides have had money up to now. And her dead father was a General and a K.C.B., which did not look amiss in the announcement; but there our satisfaction ended. He brought her to make our acquaintance three weeks after the marriage, a delicate little shrinking thing well matched to her fanciful name, and desperately afraid of mother and of us girls, so the introductory visit was hardly a success. Then Robert took her off to London, and when the baby was born – a son, but too weakly to live beyond a day or two – she had a severe illness, and was slow in recovering strength. And there is little doubt that by this time he was conscious of having made a mistake.

I used to be his favourite sister, being next to him in age, and when he found himself in a difficulty at Roscawen he appealed to me. Roscawen was a moor Robert had lately rented on the Scotch side of the Border, and we were given to understand that a bracing air, and the complete change of scene, were expected to benefit Freda, who was pleased by the arrangement. So his letter took me by surprise.

DEAR MARY (he wrote, and, characteristically, he did not beat about the bush.) – Pack up your things as soon as you get this, and come off here the day after tomorrow. You will have to travel via York, and I will meet you at Draycott Halt, where the afternoon train stops by signal. Freda is a bit nervous, and doesn't like staying alone here, so I am in a fix. I want you to keep her company the weeks I am at Shepstow. I know you'll do as much as this for –

Your affectionate brother,

ROBERT LARCOMB

This abrupt call upon me, making sure of response and help, recalled bygone times when we were much to each other, and Freda still in the unknown. A bit nervous, was she, and Robert in a fix because of it: here again was evidence of the mistake. It was not very easy then to break off from work, and for an indefinite time; but I resolved to satisfy the family curiosity, to say nothing of my own, by doing as I was bid. When I got out of the train at Draycott Halt, Robert was waiting for me with his car. My luggage was put in at the back, and I mounted to the seat beside him; and again it reminded me of old times, for he seemed genuinely pleased to see me.

'Good girl,' he said, 'to make no fuss, and come at once.'

'We Larcombs are not apt to fuss, are we?' – and as I said this, it occurred to me that probably he was in these days well acquainted with fuss – Freda's fuss. Then I asked: 'What is the matter?'

I only had a sideways glimpse of him as he answered, for he was busy with the driving-gear.

'Why, I told you, didn't I, that it was arranged for me to be here and at Shepstow week and week about, Falkner and I together, for it is better than taking either moor with a single gun. And I can't take Freda there, for the Shepstow cottage has no accommodation for a lady – only the one room that Falkner and I share. Freda is nervous, poor girl, since her illness, and somehow she has taken a dislike to Roscawen. It is nothing but a fancy, of course, but something had to be done.'

'Why, you wrote to mother that you had both fallen in love with the place, and thought it quite ideal.'

'Oh, the place is right enough, it is just my poor girl's fancy. She'll tell you I dare say, but don't let her dwell on it more than you can help. You will have Falkner's room, and the week he is over here I've arranged for Vickers to put him up, though I dare say he will come in to meals. Vickers? Oh, he's a neighbour on the opposite side of the water, Roscawen Water, the stream that over-flows from the lake in the hills. He's a doctor of science as well as medicine, and has written some awfully clever books. I understand he's at work on another, and comes here for the sake of quiet. But he's a very good sort though not a sportsman, does not mind taking in Falkner, and he is by way of being a friend of Freda's – they read Italian together. No, he isn't married, neither is the parson, worse luck; and there isn't another woman of her own sort within miles. It's desperately lonely for her, I allow, when I'm not here. So there was no help for it. I was bound to send for you or for the mater, and I thought you would be best!'

We were passing through wild scenery of barren broken hills, following the course of the river upstream. It came racing down a rocky course, full and turbulent from recent rains. Presently the road divided, crossing a narrow bridge; and there we came in sight of the leap the water makes over a shelf of rock, plunging into a deep pool below with a swirl of foam and spray. I would have liked to linger and look, but the car carried us forward quickly, allowing only a glimpse in passing. And, directly after, Robert called my attention to a stone-built small house high up on the hillside – a bare place it looked, flanked by a clump of firs, but with no surrounding garden-ground; the wild moor and the heather came close under the windows.

'That's Roscawen,' he said. 'Just a shooting-box, you see. A new-built place, raw, with no history behind it later than yesterday. I was in treaty for Corby, seventeenth century that was, with a ghost in the gallery, but the arrangement fell through. And I'm jolly glad it did' – and here he laughed; an uncomfortable laugh, not of the Larcomb sort, or like himself. And in another minute we were at the door.

Freda welcomed me, and I thought her improved; she was indeed pretty – as pretty as such a frail little thing could be, who looked as if a puff of wind would blow her away. She was very well dressed – of course Robert would take care of that – and her thought appeared to be of him. She was constantly turning to him with appeal of one sort or another, and seemed nervous and ill of ease when he was out of her sight. 'Must you really go tomorrow?' I caught her whisper later, and heard his answer: 'Needs must, but you will not mind now you have Mary.' I could plainly see that she did mind, and that my companionship was no fair exchange for the loss of his. But was not all this exaction the very way to tire out love?

The ground-floor of the house was divided into a sitting-hall, upon which the front door opened without division, and to the right you entered a fair-sized dining-room. Each of these apartments had the offshoot of a smaller room, one being Freda's snuggery, and the other the gun-room where the gentlemen smoked. Above there were two good bedrooms, a dressing-room and a bathroom, but no higher floor: the gable-space was not utilised, and the servants slept over the kitchen at the back. The room allotted to me, from which Captain Falkner had been ejected, had a wide window and a pleasant aspect. As I was hurriedly dressing for dinner, I could hear the murmur of the river close at hand, but the actual water was not visible, as it flowed too far below the over-hanging bank.

I could not see the flowing water, but as I glanced from the window, a wreath of white mist or spray floated up from it, stretched itself out before the wind, and disappeared after the fashion of a puff of steam. Probably there was at that point another fall (so I thought) churning the river into foam. But I had no time to waste in speculation, for we Larcombs adhere to the good ways of punctuality. I fastened a final hook and eye, and ran downstairs.

Captain Falkner came to dinner and made a fourth at table, but the fifth place which had been laid remained vacant. The two men were full of plans for the morrow, and there was to be an early setting out: Shepstow, the other moor, was some thirty miles away.

'I am afraid you will be dull, Mary,' Robert said to me in a sort of apology. 'I am forced to keep the car at Shepstow, as I am my own chauffeur. But you and Freda will have her cart to jog about in, so you will be able to look round the nearer country while I am away. You will have to put up with the old mare. I know you like spirit in a horse, but this quiet gee suits Freda, as she can drive her going alone. Then Vickers will look in on you most days. I do not know what is keeping him away tonight.'

Freda was in low spirits next morning, and she hung about Robert up to the time of his departure, in a way that I should have found supremely irritating had I been her husband. And I will not be sure that she did not beg him again not to leave her – to my tender mercies I supposed – though I did not hear the request. When the two men had set out with their guns and baggage, the cart was ordered round, and my sister-in-law took me for a drive. Robert had done well to prepare me for the 'quiet gee': a meek old creature named Grey Madam, that had whitened in the snows of many winters, and expected to progress at a walk whenever the road inclined uphill. And all the roads inclined uphill or down about Roscawen; I do not remember anywhere a level quarter of a mile. It was truly a dull progress, and Freda did not find much to say; perhaps she still was fretting after Robert. But the moors and the swelling hills were beautiful to look at in their crimson flush of heather. 'I think Roscawen is lovely,' I was prompted to exclaim; and when she agreed in my admiration I added: 'You liked it when you first came here, did you not?'

'Yes, I liked it when first I came,' she assented, repeating my words, but did not go on to say why she disliked Roscawen now.

She had an errand to discharge at one of the upland farms which supplied them with milk and butter. She drew rein at the gate, and was about to alight, but the woman of the house came forward, and so I heard what passed. Freda gave her order, and then made an enquiry. 'I hope you have found your young cow, Mrs Elliott? I was sorry to hear it had strayed.'

'We've found her, ma'am, but she was dead in the river, and a sad loss it has been to us. A fine young beast as ever we reared, and coming on with her second calf. My husband has been rarely put about, and I'll own I was fit to cry over her myself. This is the fifth loss we have had within the year – a sheep and two lambs in March, and the cart-foal in July.'

Freda expressed sympathy. 'You need better fences, is that it, to keep your cattle from the river?'

Mrs Elliott pursed up her lips and shook her head. 'I won't say, ma'am, but that our fences might be bettered if the landlord would give us material; as it is, we do our best. But when the creatures take that madness for the water, nought but deer-palings would keep them in. I've seen enough in my time here to be sure of that. What makes it come over them I don't take upon myself to say. They make up fine tales in the district about the white woman, but I know nothing of any white women. I only know that when the madness takes them they make for the river, and then they get swept into the deeps.'

When we were driving away, I asked Freda what the farmer's wife meant about a white woman and the drowning of her stock.

'I believe there is some story about a woman who was drowned, whose spirit calls the creatures to the river. If you ask Dr Vickers he will tell you. He makes a study of folklore and local superstitions, and

– and that sort of thing. Robert thinks it is all nonsense, and no doubt you will think it nonsense too.'

What her own opinion was, Freda did not say. She had a transparent complexion, and a trifling matter made her change colour; a blush rose unaccountably as she answered me, and for a full minute her cheek burned. Why should she blush about Roscawen superstitions and a drowned cow? Then the attention of both of us was suddenly diverted, because Grey Madam took it into her head to shy.

She had mended her pace appreciably since Freda turned her head towards home, trotting now without needing to be urged. We were close upon a crossroads where three ways met, a triangular green centred by a finger-post. There was in our direction a bank and hedge (hedges here and there replaced the stone walls of the district) and the right wheel went up that bank, giving the cart a dangerous tilt; it recovered balance, however, and went on. Freda, a timid driver, was holding on desperately to the reins.

'Does she often do this sort of thing?' I asked. 'I thought Robert said she was quiet.'

'So she is – so we thought her. I never knew her do it before,' gasped my sister-in-law, still out of breath with her fright.

'And I cannot think what made her shy. There was nothing – absolutely nothing; not even a heap of stones.'

Freda did not answer, but I was to hear more about that crossroads in the course of the day.

2

After lunch Freda did not seem willing to go out again, so, as I was there to companion her, we both settled down to needlework and a book for alternate reading aloud. The reading, however, languished; when it came to Freda's turn she tired quickly, lost her place twice and again, and seemed unable to fix her attention on the printed page. Was she listening, I wondered later. When silence fell between us, I became aware of a sound recurring at irregular intervals, the sound of water dripping. I looked up at the ceiling expecting to see a stain of wet, for the drip seemed to fall within the room, and close beside me.

'Do you hear that?' I asked. 'Has anything gone wrong in the bathroom, do you think?' For we were in Freda's snuggery, and the bathroom was overhead.

But my suggestion of overflowing taps and broken water-pipes left her cold.

'I don't think it is from the bathroom,' she replied. 'I hear it often. We cannot find out what it is.'

Directly she ceased speaking the drip fell again, apparently between us as we sat, and plump upon the carpet. I looked up at the ceiling again, but Freda did not raise her eyes from her embroidery.

'It is very odd,' I remarked, and this time she assented, repeating my words, and I saw a shiver pass over her. 'I shall go upstairs to the bathroom,' I said decidedly, putting down my work. 'I am sure those taps must be wrong.'

She did not object, or offer to accompany me, she only shivered again.

'Don't be long away, Mary,' she said, and I noticed she had grown pale.

There was nothing wrong with the bathroom, or with any part of the water supply; and when I returned to the snuggery the drip had ceased. The next event was a ring at the door bell, and again Freda changed colour, much as she had done when we were driving. In that quiet place, where comers and goers are few, a visitor is an event. But I think this visitor must have been expected. The servant announced Dr Vickers.

Freda gave him her hand, and made the necessary introduction. This was the friend Robert said would come often to see us, but he was not at all the stuffy old scientist my fancy had pictured. He was old certainly, if it is a sign of age to be grey-haired, and I dare say there were crows' feet about those piercing eyes of his; but when you met the eyes, the wrinkles were forgotten. They, at least, were full of youth and fire, and his figure was still upright and flat-shouldered.

We exchanged a few remarks; he asked me if I was familiar with that part of Scotland; and when I answered that I was making its acquaintance for the first time, he praised Roscawen and its neighbourhood. It suited him well, he said, when his object was to seek quiet; and I should find, as he did, that it possessed many attractions. Then he asked me if I was an Italian scholar, and showed a book in his hand, the *Vita Nuova*. Mrs Larcomb was forgetting her Italian, and he had promised to brush it up for her. So, if I did not find it too great a bore to sit by, he proposed to read aloud. And, should I not know the book, he would give me a sketch of its purport, so that I could follow.

I had, of course, heard of the *Vita Nuova* (who has not?), but my knowledge of the language in which it was written went no further than a few modern phrases, of use to a traveller. I disclaimed my ability to follow, and I imagine Dr Vickers was not ill-pleased to find me ignorant. He took his seat at one end of the Chesterfield sofa, Freda occupying the other, still with that flush on her cheek; and after an observation or two in Italian, he opened his book and began to read.

I imagine he read well. The crisp, flowing syllables sounded very foreign to my ear, and he gave his author the advantage of dramatic expression and emphasis. Now and then he remarked in English on some difficulty in the text, or slipped in a question in Italian which Freda answered, usually by a monosyllable. She kept her eyes fixed upon her work. It was as if she would not look at him, even when he was most impassioned; but I was watching them both, although I never thought – but of course I never thought!

Presently I remembered how time was passing, and the place where letters should be laid ready for the post-bag going out. I had left an unfinished one upstairs, so I slipped away to complete and seal. This done, I re-entered softly (the entrance was behind a screen) and found the Italian lesson over, and a conversation going on in English. Freda was speaking with some animation. 'It cannot any more be called my fancy, for Mary heard it too.'

'And you had not told her beforehand? There was no suggestion?'

'I had not said a word to her. Had I, Mary?' – appealing to me as I advanced into sight.

'About what?' I asked, for I had forgotten the water incident.

'About the drops falling. You remarked on them first: I had told you nothing. And you went to look at the taps.'

'No, certainly you had not told me. What is the matter? Is there any mystery?'

Dr Vickers answered: 'The mystery is that Mrs Larcomb heard these drippings when everyone else was deaf to them. It was supposed to be auto-suggestion on her part. You have disproved that, Miss Larcomb, as your ears are open to them too. That will go far to convince your brother; and now we must seriously seek for cause. This Roscawen district has many legends of strange happenings. We do not want to add one more to the list, and give this modern shooting-box the reputation of a haunted house.'

'And it would be an odd sort of ghost, would it not – the sound of dripping water! But – you speak of legends of the district; do you know anything of a white woman who is said to drown cattle? Mrs Elliott mentioned her this morning at the farm, when she told us she had lost her cow in the river.'

'Ay, I heard a cow had been found floating dead in the Pool. I am sorry it belonged to the Elliotts. Nobody lives here for long without hearing that story, and, though the wrath of Roscawen is roused against her, I cannot help being sorry for the white woman. She was young and beautiful once, and well-to-do, for she owned land in her own right, and flocks and herds. But she became very unhappy – '

He was speaking to me, but he looked at Freda. She had taken up her work again, but with inexpert hands, dropping first cotton, and then her thimble.

'She was unhappy, because her husband neglected her. He had – other things to attend to, and the charm she once possessed for him was lost and gone. He left her too much alone. She lost her health, they say, through fretting, and so fell into a melancholy way, spending her time in weeping, and in wandering up and down on the banks of Roscawen Water. She may have fallen in by accident, it was not exactly known; but her death was thought to be suicide, and she was buried at the crossroads.'

'That was where Grey Madam shied this morning,' Freda put in.

'And – people suppose – that on the other side of death, finding herself lonely (too guilty, perhaps, for Heaven, but at the same time too innocent for Hell) she wants companions to join her; wants sheep and cows and horses such as used to stock her farms. So she puts madness upon the creatures, and also upon some humans, so that they go down to the river. They see her, so it is said, or they receive a sign which in some way points to the manner of her death. If they see her, she comes for them once, twice, thrice, and the third time they are bound to follow.'

This was a gruesome story, I thought as I listened, though not of the sort I could believe. I hoped Freda did not believe it, but of this I was not sure.

'What does she look like?' I asked. 'If human beings see her as you say, do they give any account?'

'The story goes that they see foam rising from the water, floating away and dissolving, vaguely in form at first, but afterwards more like the woman she was once; and some say there is a hand that beckons. But I have never seen her, Miss Larcomb, nor spoken to one who has: first-hand evidence of this sort is rare, as I dare say you know. So I can tell you no more.'

And I was glad there was no more for me to hear, for the story was too tragic for my liking. The happenings of that afternoon left me discomforted – annoyed with Dr Vickers, which perhaps was unreasonable – with poor Freda, whose fancies had thus proved contagious – annoyed, and here more justly, with myself. Somehow, with such tales going about, Roscawen seemed a far from desirable residence for a nervous invalid; and I was also vaguely conscious of an undercurrent which I did not understand. It gave me the feeling you have when you stumble against something unexpected blindfold, or in the dark, and cannot define its shape.

Dr Vickers accepted a cup of tea when the tray was brought to us, and then he took his departure, which was as well seeing we had no gentleman at home to entertain him.

'So Larcomb is away again for a whole week? Is that so?' he said to Freda as he made his adieux.

There was no need for the question, I thought impatiently, as he must very well have known when he was required again to put up Captain Falkner.

'Yes, for a whole week,' Freda answered, again with that flush on her cheek; and as soon as we were alone she put up her hand, as if the hot colour burned.

3

I did not like Dr Vickers and his Italian lessons, and I had the impression Freda would have been better pleased by their intermission. On the third day she had a headache and charged me to make her excuses, so it fell on me to receive this friend of Robert's, who seemed quite unruffled by her absence. He took advantage of the opportunity to cross-examine me about the water-dripping: had I heard it again since that first occasion, and what explanation of the sounds appeared satisfactory to myself?

The fact was, I had heard it again, twice when I was alone in my room, and once more when sitting with Freda. Then we both sat listening – listening, such small nothings as we had to say to each other dying away, waiting to see which of us would first admit it to the other, and this went on for more than an hour. At last Freda broke out into hysterical crying, the result of over-strained nerves, and with her outburst the sounds ceased. I had been inclined to entertain a notion of the spiritist order, that they might be connected with her presence as medium; but I suppose that must be held disproved, as I also heard them when alone in my own room.

I admitted as little as possible to Dr Vickers, and was stout in asserting that natural causes would and must be found, if the explanation were diligently sought for. But I confess I was posed when confronted with the fact that these sounds heard by Freda were inaudible to her husband, also present – to Robert, who has excellent hearing, in common with all our family. Until I came, and was also an auditor, no-one in the house but Freda had noticed the dripping, so there was reason for assuming it to be hallucination. Yes, I was sorry for her trouble (answering a question pressed on me), but I maintained that, pending discovery, the best course was to take no notice of drops that wet nothing and left no stain, and did not proceed from overflowing cisterns or faulty pipes.

'They will leave off doing it if not noticed; is that what you think, Miss Larcomb?' And when I rashly assented – 'Now perhaps you will define for me what you mean by *they*? Is it the "natural cause"?'

Here again was a poser: I had formulated no idea that I cared to define. Probably the visitor divined the subject was unwelcome, for he turned to others, conversing agreeably enough for another quarter of an hour. Then he departed, leaving a message of concern for Freda's headache. He hoped it would have amended by next day, when he would call to enquire.

He did call on the following day, when the Italian lesson was mainly conversational, and I had again a feeling Freda was distressed by what was said, though I could only guess at what passed between them under the disguise of a foreign tongue. But at the end I recognised the words 'not tomorrow' as spoken by her, and when some protest appeared to follow, she dumbly shook her head.

Dr Vickers did not stay on for tea as before. Did Freda think she had offended him, for some time later I noticed she had been crying?

That night I had an odd dream that the Roscawen house was sliding down from its foundations into the river at the call of the white woman, and I woke suddenly with the fright.

The next day was the last of Robert's stay at Shepstow. In the evening he and Captain Falkner returned, and at once a different atmosphere seemed to pervade the house. Freda recovered her cheerfulness, I heard no more dripping water, and except at dinner on the second evening we saw nothing of Dr Vickers. But he sent an Italian book with many scored passages, and a note in it, also in Italian, which I saw her open and read, and then immediately tear up into the minutest pieces. I supposed he wished her to keep up her studies, though the lessons were for a while suspended; I heard him say at dinner that he was busy correcting proofs.

So passed four days out of the seven Robert should have spent at Roscawen. But on the fourth evening came a telegraphic summons: his presence was needed in London, at the office, and he was bound to go up to town by the early express next day. And the arrangement was that in returning he should go straight to Shepstow and join Captain Falkner there; this distant moor was to be reached from a station on another line.

Freda must have known that Robert could not help himself, but it was easy to see how her temporarily restored spirits fell again to zero. I hope I shall never be so dependent on another person's society as she seemed to be on Robert's. I got up to give him his early breakfast, but Freda did not appear; she had a headache, he said, and had passed a restless night. She would not rise till later: perhaps I would go up and see her by-and-by.

I did go later in the morning, to find her lying like a child that had sobbed itself to sleep, her eyelashes still wet, and a tear sliding down her cheek. So I took a book, and drew a chair to the bedside, waiting for her to wake.

It was a long waiting; she slept on, and slept heavily. And as I sat and watched, there began again the dripping of water, and, for the first time in my experience of them, the drips were wet.

I could find traces now on the carpet of where they fell, and on the spread linen of the sheet; were they made, I wondered fantastically, out of Freda's tears? But they had ceased before she woke, and I did not remark on them to her. Yes, she had a headache, she said, answering my question: it was better, but not gone: she would lie quietly where she was for the present. The servants might bring her a cup of tea when I had luncheon, and she would get up later in the afternoon.

So, as I was not needed, I went out after lunch for a solitary walk. Not being governed by Freda's choice of direction, I determined to explore the course of the river, and especially how it flowed under the steep bank below the house, where I saw the wreath of foam rise in the air on my first evening at Roscawen. I expected to find a fall at this spot, but there was only broken water and rapids, alternating with smoother reaches and deep pools, one of which, I concluded, had been the death-trap of the Elliotts' cow. It was a still, perfect autumn day, warm, but not with the oppression of summer heat, and I walked with enjoyment, following the stream upward to where it issued from the miniature lake among the hills, in which it slept for a while in mid-course. Then I turned homewards, and was within sight of our dwelling when I again beheld the phenomenon of the pillar of foam.

It rose above the rapids, as nearly as I could guess in the same spot as before; and as there was now little or no wind, it did not so quickly spread out and dissipate. I could imagine that at early morning, or in the dimness of evening, it might be taken for a figure of the ghostly sort, especially as, in dissolving, it seemed to move and beckon. I smiled to myself to think that, according to local superstition, I too had seen the white woman; but I felt no least inclination to rush to the river and precipitate myself into its depths. Nor would I gratify Dr Vickers by telling him what had been my experience, or confide in Freda lest she should tell again.

On reaching home, I turned into the snuggery to see if Freda was downstairs; it must, I thought, be nearly tea-time. She was there; and, as I pushed the door open and was still behind the screen, I heard Dr Vickers' voice. 'Mind,' he was saying in English, 'I do not press you to decide at once. Wait till you are convinced he does not care. To my thinking he has already made it plain.'

I stood arrested, not intending to play eavesdropper, but stricken with surprise. As I moved into sight, the two were standing face to face, and the doctor's figure hid Freda from me. I think his hands were on her shoulders, holding her before him, but of this I am not sure. He was quick of hearing as a cat, and he turned on me at once.

'Ah, how do you do, Miss Larcomb? I was just bidding adieu to your sister-in-law, for I do not think she is well enough today to take her lesson. In fact, I think she is very far from well. These headaches spell slow progress with our study, but we must put up with delay.'

He took up the slim book from the table and bestowed it in his pocket, bowed over my hand and was gone.

If Freda had been agitated she concealed any disturbance, and we talked as usual over tea, of my walk, and even of Robert's journey. But she surprised me later in the evening by an unexpected proposition.

'Do you think Mrs Larcomb would have me to stay at Aston Bury? It would be very kind of her if she would take me in while Robert has these shootings. I do not like Roscawen, and I am not well here. Will you ask her, Mary?'

I answered that I was sure mother would have her if she wished to come to us; but what would Robert say when he had asked me to companion her here? If Robert was willing, I would write – of course. Did he know what she proposed?

No, she said, and there would be no time to consult him. She would like to go as soon as tomorrow. Could we send a telegram, and set out in the morning, staying the night in York, to receive an answer there? That she was very much in earnest about this wish of hers there could be no doubt. She was trembling visibly, and a red fever-spot burned on her cheek.

I wish I had done as she asked. But my Larcomb commonsense was up in arms, and I required to know the reason why. Mother would think it strange if we rushed off to her so, and Robert would not like it; but, given time to make the arrangement, she could certainly pay the visit, and would be received as a welcome guest. I would write to mother on the morrow, and she could write to Robert and send the letter by Captain Falkner. Then I said: 'Are you nervous here, Freda? Is it because these water drippings are unexplained?' And when she made a sort of dumb assent, I went on: 'You ought not to dwell on anything so trivial; it isn't fair to Robert. It cannot be only this. Surely there is something more?'

The question seemed to increase her distress.

'I want to be a good wife to Robert; oh, I want that, Mary. I can do my duty if I go away; if you will keep me safe at Aston Bury for only a little while. Robert does not understand; he thinks me crazed with delusions. I tried to tell him – I did indeed; hard as it was to tell.' While this was spoken she was torn with sobs. 'I am terrified to be alone. What is compelling me is too strong. Oh Mary, take me away.'

I could get no fuller explanation than this of what was at the root of the trouble. We agreed at last that the two letters should be written and sent on the morrow, and we would hold ourselves in readiness to set out as soon as answers were received. It might be no more than an hysterical fancy on Freda's part, but I was not without suspicion of another sort. But she never mentioned their neighbour's name, and I could not insult her by the suggestion.

The letters were written early on that Thursday morrow, and then Grey Madam was brought round for Freda's drive. The direction chosen took us past the crossroads in the outward going, and also in return. I remember Freda talked more cheerfully and freely than usual, asking questions about Aston Bury, as if relieved at the prospect of taking refuge there with us. As we went, Grey Madam shied badly at the same spot as before, though there was no visible cause for her terror. I suggested we had better go home a different way; but this appeared impracticable, as the other direction involved an added distance of several miles, and the crossing of a bridge which was thought to be unsafe. In returning, the mare went unwillingly, and, though our pace had been a sober one and the day was not warm, I could see she had broken out into a lather of sweat. As we came to the crossroads for the second time, the poor creature again shied away from the invisible object which terrified her, and then, seizing the bit between her teeth, she set off at a furious gallop.

Freda was tugging at the reins, but it was beyond her power to stop that mad career, or even guide it; but the mare kept by instinct to the middle of the road. The home gate was open, and I expected she would turn in stablewards; but instead she dashed on to the open moor, making for the river.

We might possibly have jumped out, but there was no time even for thought before we were swaying on the edge of the steep bank. The next moment there was a plunge, a crash, and I remember no more.

The accident was witnessed from the further side – so I heard later. A man left his digging and ran, and it was he who dragged me out, stunned, but not suffocated by the immersion. I came to myself quickly on the bank, and my instant thought was of Freda, but she, entangled with the reins, had been swept down with the mare into the deeper pool. When I staggered up, dizzy and half-blind, begging she might be sought for, he ran on downstream, and there he and Dr Vickers and another man drew her from the water – lifeless it seemed at first, and it was long before any spark of animation repaid their utmost efforts.

That was a strange return to Roscawen house, she tenderly carried, I able to walk thither; both of us dripping water, real drops, of which the ghostly ones may have been some mysterious forecast, if that is not too fantastic for belief!

It was impossible to shut Dr Vickers out, and of course he accompanied us; for all my doubt of him, I welcomed the service of his skill when Freda's life was hanging in the balance, and she herself was too remote from this world to recognise who was beside her. But I would have preferred to owe that debt of service to any other; and the feeling I had against him deepened as I witnessed his anguished concern, and caught some unguarded expressions he let fall.

I wired to Robert to acquaint him with what had happened, and he replied 'I am coming.' And upon that I resolved to speak out, and tell him what I had guessed as the true cause of Freda's trouble, and why she must be removed, not so much from a haunted house, as from an overmastering influence which she dreaded.

Did the risk of loss – the peril barely surmounted, restore the old tenderness between these two? I think it did, at any rate for the time, when Robert found her lying white as a broken lily, and when her weak hands clung about his neck. Perhaps this made him more patient than he would have been otherwise with what I had to say.

He could hardly tax me with being fancy-ridden, but he was aghast – angry – incredulous, all in one. Vickers, of all people in the world; and Freda so worked upon as to be afraid to tell him – afraid to claim the protection that was hers by right. And now the situation was complicated by the fact that Vickers had saved her life, so that thanks were due to him as well as a kicking out of doors. And there was dignity to be thought of too: Freda's dignity as well as his own. Any open scandal must be avoided; she must neither be shamed nor pained.

I do not know what passed between him and Dr Vickers when they met, but the latter came no more to Roscawen, and after a while I heard incidentally that he had gone abroad. As soon as Freda could be moved, her wish was fulfilled, and I took her to Aston Bury. Mother was very gentle with her, and I think before the end a genuine affection grew up between the two.

The end was not long delayed; a few months passed, and then she faded out of life in a sort of decline; the shock to the system, so they said, had been greater than her vitality could repair. Robert was a free man again, war had been declared, and he was one of the earliest volunteers for service.

That service won distinction, as everybody knows; and now he is convalescent from his second wound, and here at Aston Bury on leave. And I think the wiser choice his sisters made for him in the first place is now likely to be his own. A much more suitable person than Frederica, and her name is quite a plain one – a real Larcomb name: it is Mary, like my own. I am glad; but in spite of all, poor Freda has a soft place in my memory and my heart. Whatever were her faults and failings, I believe she strove hard to be loyal. And I am sure that she loved Robert well.

The Lonely Road

'I am awfully sorry, Tom, I am indeed, and after all your kindness in coming down to see me about that tiresome business, but we can't drive you to the station this evening as I promised. The mare has been kicking in the stable again, and Summers has just discovered she is dead lame. You must really make up your mind to stay another night, and we will get a conveyance over from Ardkellar first thing tomorrow. If I write at once I shall catch the post: we haven't a telegraph office in the village, or I would wire. Summers has only just made the discovery, so he tells me. Now do be reasonable, and say you'll stay.'

'That is kind of you, Margaret.'

Tom Pulteney fixed again in his left eye the single eyeglass that was always dropping out. This so that he might look at his widowed cousin with the right expression, and she was good to look at, though no longer in her first youth.

'A few more hours here is a temptation; a greater one than I can say. But I'm positively bound to get back to Dublin tonight, and somehow or other I must contrive to catch the 8.50. I'm not such a weakling that I can't walk the distance. How far do you call it to the station?'

'It is eight miles good from here to Ardkellar. And it is a lonely road –'

'Well – I shan't need company for that short distance. I shall be too full of regrets after tearing myself away from you – to say nothing of Adelaide. Though you know very well that Adelaide does not count.'

'I don't know anything of the sort. But I hate you going – all that way on foot, and at such an hour.'

'Hate my going by all means – I'd wish nothing better. But for a different reason.'

'Oh, Tom, do be serious: but if you must go, take care. The road has had a bad character of late; there have been assaults and robberies. Of course you don't go about with a revolver – here. But do you carry a heavy stick?'

'I didn't bring one. But I've got my fists, and I know how to use them.'

'You must have a stick. I will lend you Laurence's; it is loaded at the head. I know you will some time let me have it back.'

'If it will make you easy about me – '

'It will make me easier. I am vexed about the mare – and not knowing till the last minute. I am afraid you will have to set off at once if that train is to be caught. And it is getting dusk even now.'

The farewells followed, which Tom Pulteney made as affectionate as he dared. It was something of a triumph to him that Margaret was really concerned about the possible risk he was running, on a lonely stretch of road where there had been at least one attempted murder; and he set out with that conviction kept warm at heart.

To him an eight mile walk was truly a light matter, but he happened to be burdened carrying a suitcase made heavy by expensive fittings, and before the end of the first half mile he began to wish he had slipped his pet razors into his pocket, and asked his cousin to send the case after him, which without doubt she would have done. And for a reason other than the weight: if thieves were abroad, and he was attacked by two, it would be easily snatched by a confederate while one of them knocked him on the head. And a good sound leather suitcase, all but new, is worth stealing nowadays apart from what it may contain. The contents of Tom's were also of value, things that he could ill spare – among other oddments a handsome finger-ring which he had brought from town, hoping he might find courage to offer it to Margaret as a *gage d'amour*. The parcel had not been opened: opportunity had not served, or else he had feared to damage his own cause by speaking too early in her widowhood. These articles would, he reflected, be safer if carried on his person, and then he could abandon the suitcase with less reluctance should there be need.

He was now far beyond Ballymacor, and the road before him was solitary. On a sudden impulse he deposited the case under the hedge, unsnapped the locks, and sought in the fast-fading light for his more treasured possessions. These he secured in innermost pockets, again shouldered his burden, and went on whistling under his breath, as might a man light-hearted and unafraid.

But was he unafraid? Was he not assuming the pretence of a boldness he did not possess? In the midst of that search into his luggage, a doubt beset him that the action there and then had been unwise; for at the same time he heard, or thought he heard, a rustle of movement behind the hedge. There was nothing for it then but to go on, and trust he had been mistaken, or the presence and movement wholly innocent. But presently he imagined – imagination first, but soon there was no doubt – that he heard footsteps following. He swung round twice and glanced behind him, but so far as he could see in the dusk the road was clear.

The sound went on, and now the footsteps approached nearer, quickening upon his, and he was already bracing every nerve, preparing for the encounter he expected.

At this critical moment a huge white dog leaped over the fence on the right.

'Why, Boris!' he exclaimed unthinking, and the creature came beside him with wagging tail: surely in the event of attack, here would be a formidable ally.

The dog was friendly, and appeared to answer to the name called. Margaret had had such a dog in her husband's lifetime, a Russian wolfhound of which she had been fond; Pulteney had often seen them together, the tall elegant woman followed by the noble hound. Surely this must be Boris; and yet he had a dim recollection of some mischance mentioned in a letter of Adelaide's, an accident in which the dog had been injured, and he thought killed. Certainly he had not seen Boris on any recent visit to Ballymacor. If only he could keep the dog beside him, he would, he thought, be safe. So he spoke to the creature by name, and spoke again; and each time Boris responded in dog fashion, pleased by the recognition, or so it seemed.

The footsteps still were following; and now, bolder because accompanied, he glanced over his shoulder. Yes, there were two men, and they were close behind, of villainous aspect in the dusk. The dog also looked round and growled, showing his teeth, formidable white fangs, set in a jaw like an alligator's; if the creature was strong enough and fierce enough to pull down a wolf, he would surely be a match for any man. But supposing the followers were armed, and their object murder and not mere robbery, what then?

The sky by this time was clearing, and behind the breaking clouds there came some shining of the moon, showing the way in front and the white hound beside him, and, as he remembered after, both their shadows. From time to time he spoke to his four-footed companion, and also put out his hand to pat the dog's neck; but somehow he never succeeded in touching him – the white rough coat seemed always just beyond reach, though there was no shrinking away to avoid contact.

Pulteney all the while was on the strain to listen, and though he still heard the following footsteps, double footsteps, it seemed to him that they were falling further behind. He could not now be far from Ardkellar, his destination; the railway-line here crossed the road high up on bridge and embankment, and a luggage train lumbered over before him, with gleaming lights and a long rattle of trucks. Not far beyond there was a crossroads, and here the footsteps stopped. Pulteney glanced again over his shoulder, and saw that the two men had halted there, and seemed to be consulting together.

He turned and went on, and now he heard no more the pursuing feet. He was close to the outskirts of the country town, and, he concluded, in comparative safety. He could still see the dog beside him, and was beginning to wonder how he could best dispose of his companion in safety, and contrive to let Margaret know; as Boris, who had befriended him, must certainly have strayed from Bally-macor. They had reached the first row of houses and the outpost of street lights, when he noticed that the form of the dog was altering, becoming shadowy in outline, instead of substantial as before. Still the creature kept step by step beside him, though a figure compacted of white mist growing more and more transparent, till at last, at the passing of the third lamp, this ghostly likeness of Boris faded into nothing and was gone. Tom Pulteney walked into the station of Ardkellar, grateful for his escape, but a bewildered man.

He wrote the history of that night's adventure to his cousin Margaret.

Upon my word of honour, this is the literal truth, though you will find it difficult to believe. I am sure the dog was yours, as he seemed to know me, and evidently would have shown fight had I been attacked. And I believe the men saw him just as I did, and were deterred from carrying out their plan. It is true I could not touch him, though I tried; but no-one could have been more astonished than I was when he dissolved into something like white smoke and then was gone. It was an experience I shall never forget.

To him, Margaret in reply:

I do believe your story, and to me it is altogether convincing, though so strange. My dear Boris died two years ago: there was an accident I cannot bear to think of, even now. He was caught by a touring car going at speed, and caring nothing for the life or safety of a dog. I had him shot in mercy; I never say destroyed. And what you saw that night is witness that under other conditions he is in existence still. He was so good, so faithful: I never called on him in vain, and he knew almost my thought before I spoke. I was thinking of him that evening. I said to Adelaide – she will tell you – how I wished I had had Boris here, for I would have sent him with you on that lonely walk, and then you would have been safe. For I was very anxious. I believe my thought, my wish, did send him, dear, dear fellow. But I cannot expect you to receive this as I do, or think that it explains.

Tom Pulteney to Margaret:

I am convinced, indeed. It was you who worked the miracle, and you worked it for me. Your letter, which explains so much, tells me one thing more: may I hope it is the one thing I would give the world to know? You were anxious – you cared what became of me. Could you care always – could you care enough? I pray that the post may bring me the answer I long for; but I am ever your devoted lover, however you reply.

A Girl in White

In telling the following story I give fictitious names. I do not wish the little house to be identified, nor would I do the owner of the property the slightest injury. It is, doubtless, a harmless place, where people have lived happily in the past, and will again in the future – ninety-nine people out of every hundred. That I happened to be the hundredth man who there underwent a notable experience, may have had nothing to do with local influence. I write this, but add a query: perhaps one wiser than I will answer, and unravel the mystery which I merely present. I do not pretend to explain.

I took Riverside Cottage for my mother and widowed sister, for three months of the summer of 1914 – mid-June to mid-September. They had both passed through a time of trial with which my story has nothing to do; quiet and change of scene became desirable, and mother wished to be within easy reach of London and of me. That was why I explored the Thames valley on their behalf, and was at once attracted to this house – a modern villa, with gay garden sloping to the water's edge, and boat moored at a small landing-stage overhung with trees: the stage and mooring-place shared, I may mention, with the villa next along the road, the garden of which joined with ours.

As soon as my mother and Lydia settled in, I ran down for the weekend. They were satisfied with the place, and indeed could not praise it sufficiently, or the wisdom of my choice. The quiet delighted them, the privacy, as well as the outlook over the broad stream, which seemed to exercise a tranquillising influence in its flow. Also the small house was sufficiently convenient; the two elderly servants were pleased, as well as the joint mistresses: what more could be desired?

Needless to say, I agreed with the encomiums and swallowed the reflected praise; but somehow there was a note which jarred. I was the discoverer of the cottage, its original admirer; but the very first night I slept under its roof, I began to wonder what attracted me to the place, and why I had thought it the right sort of nest for mother, who was old and tired, and Lydia, who was middle-aged and particular.

What was the jarring note? Did the 'softness' of the valley, the near neighbourhood of a vast body of moving water, depress my spirits? No, for when we sat out in the garden, bright with flowers, and when I rowed Lydia a mile or so upstream, for the sake of floating down in the cool evening, I felt as usual. It was the house which overpowered me with its influence (I use the word in a non-committal sense) – the house where I became oppressed and ill at ease.

It is just the place where a fellow would cut his throat: that was my reflection the next morning, after a night of broken rest and uneasy dreams. My mother remarked at breakfast that I was not looking well, and Lydia made some joke to the effect that it did not suit me to be off the pavements. I went to church with the two women; for, as a matter of course, the dear souls were punctual churchgoers, and expected me to be the same; returned to eat a light and digestible meal; and enjoyed a post-prandial nap in a basket-chair under the trees, which made up for the disturbed night. Where could be a passing of time more commonplace, and less likely to foster morbid fancies? Yet it was after this, while still broad daylight of a summer afternoon, that I had my first glimpse of the white girl.

The staircase came down into the square entrance hall, close to the door of the dining-room (it will be understood in the cottage there were no wide spaces; all was small and cramped). As I was descending the stairs, the figure of a girl in white passed quickly before me, from left to right, entering the dining-room. I felt a distinct shock of surprise, and, gaining the open doorway scarcely a minute later, paused to look into the room. There were no screens or recesses in which to hide, the room was plainly vacant, and here the bow-window did not open to the floor as in the other parlour. The latticed casements were set wide to admit the air, but they were narrow and high from the floor, and it would have needed a distinct effort for a grown person to squeeze through. I was still standing astonished in the doorway, when Lydia called to me from the garden. I was to make haste, for tea was ready; it had been carried out of doors.

Now the natural impulse would have been to tell out my uncanny experience, and enquire who was this girl in white who intruded upon us; but a curious reticence shackled my tongue and kept me mute. An inner voice might have been whispering – 'This is our secret, yours and mine, and you must reveal it to no other.' I did not consider then the scruple about alarming my mother; that developed later. As I took the seat placed for me under the tree, the servant emerged from the house carrying hot scones covered by a napkin; she wore the usual black gown and white apron, and I knew the other domestic was similarly attired. Lydia and my mother both wore black; it could have been no mistake for any lawful inmate; none of them were in the least like my white girl. I drank my tea and kept up an indifferent conversation, but all the while I was trying to reconstruct the picture of what I had seen.

It was not easy. As a rule, I pride myself on quick perception and ready memory, receiving clear imprints, which are correctly retained; but in this case it was as if the surprise of the vision had blurred its details. The slender figure of a girl in white, no touch of colour in her array, which seemed of ordinary modern fashion – quickly passing the foot of the stairs, and disappearing into the room beyond. I had seen no face, that must have been turned from me; but I thought I could recall fair hair, so fair as to be almost flaxen, swept up smoothly from the nape of the neck, into twists worn high upon the head.

Again at night I was ill at ease. The period of absolute darkness is brief at midsummer, and the first grey light was making lawn and flowerbeds visible when I drew away the screens from the window and looked out. There behind a rosebush, at the edge of the shrubbed border, was the same white figure. The girl might be stealing flowers before their owners were awake; I thought her action looked like it. Presently I saw her more distinctly, as she moved across the lawn to a heavy-topped standard, which had its own circle of root-room cut round it in the grass. She was welcome to our hired roses; but a desire beset me to accost her, and find out who she was, and whence she came. So I hurriedly flung on my clothes.

A last glance from the window showed her still in sight. I went down to the drawing-room, opened shutters and glass door, and stepped out into the garden; but, as will have been divined, in vain. There was no girl in white, nor did the lawn show any track of footsteps, though my own were plainly traceable in the morning dew.

I was glad that morning to get back to London and my work; and felt distinctly reluctant to view the approach of Saturday, when I was again pledged to spend the weekend at Riverside. But on this, my second visit, I experienced nothing more abnormal than the burden of melancholy and foreboding which the Cottage imposed on me before, weighing on my spirits and driving away sleep. I saw no white girl, and evidently my mother and Lydia had seen nothing, for they seemed wholly contented and at ease. For the third weekend I was engaged elsewhere; but the fourth, a Saturday late in July, found me again at the Cottage. Expectant attention is supposed by some people to account for psychical happenings. I went thither prepared to see the figure, and did see it, but under new conditions: no repetition of what occurred before.

My broken night repeated itself, though through the previous fortnight I had been sleeping well. I could get no rest in bed, and tossed there till I was almost in a fever. Plainly it was the house which affected me with this insomnia; and as soon as daylight began, I resolved to dress, take out a couple of cushions, and see if I could get to sleep lying in the boat. I crept softly downstairs, crossed the solitary garden, where all was wrapped in the Sabbath stillness of the early dawn, and, once in the boat, swinging to the silent flow of the great river, I slept delightfully and woke refreshed.

The servants were busy in the house when I went back, to bathe and shave and dress again, and doubtless they regarded me with wonder. To shave! I was presently at the glass, intent on chin-scraping – turned to moisten the lather – and, looking back, the face presented to me was not my own. Instead of the expected image, this was the countenance of a lovely girl, who looked at me with dark eyes full of sadness and appeal, whose lips moved as if to speak.

I cannot calculate how long the vision lasted; I only know it gave me full time to see – to note my own figure reflected behind her, shirt-sleeved and razor in hand, my head overtopping hers – to imprint on memory every feature of that face. Yes, I had been right; she was fair, the ghost girl, with hair so light as to be almost flaxen, which curled in rings on her forehead, while – an unusual combination – her eyes and eyebrows were of the darkest brown. My ghost was pale, but it was not the pallor of death; her lips were warmly red, and on the left cheek there was a dimple ready to deepen had she smiled. Her dress was white. So far I can describe her, though there is poverty about the written words. I stood frozen, gazing; and then the image melted into a haze of mist, which in its turn disappeared, and the mirror gave back nothing but my own swart reflection in the common way.

My hand shook, and I cut myself over the shaving which came after, which perhaps was not wonderful. The vision was not repeated, though several times that day I stood to gaze. And the second night was sleepless, like the first.

The experiment of the boat had answered well, so at dawn I betook myself thither as before. I fell asleep easily, but woke after the first hour, before the light was full. But it was sufficient to show plainly the slope of the garden, and there, wandering among the flower beds, was the white girl.

I did not spring up at once to confront her: something seemed to hold me paralysed and still. She came on towards me, walking uncertainly with spread hands, as I have seen the blind! On, till she stepped upon the wooden stage, and then, light as a feather, over the side into the boat.

It did not sway under the added burden. I lay in the stern, as I say, paralysed; and she went on to the bow, there turning to look back at me, and wringing her hands together as if in a passion of distress. Then – it all passed in a moment – she plunged into the river and was gone.

I was on my feet the instant after, but there was nothing to be seen. No swirling eddies, no bubbles coming to the surface, no human creature struggling and sinking in those dark depths. Then I remembered that I had heard no splash – all had passed in absolute silence – the boat had not swayed, as it must have done under a material weight. I was awake, I had not dreamed; but the being of my vision was not girl but ghost.

2

Close upon this last incident came the cataclysm we all remember, the outbreak of the war. I volunteered to rejoin my old regiment, was accepted, and in the hurry of preparation and equipment, my last days in England slipped rapidly away. But I found time to prosecute certain enquiries about the past history of the river cottage. I could not ascertain that it had ever been the scene of a tragedy, but people are not always candid in answering such questions put by a tenant. It was built some forty years ago, and the original owner died there, peacefully in her bed, and at an age exceeding the threescore years and ten. It was now the property of two middle-aged spinsters, who let it every year to cover the expenses of their autumn tour. All this was prosaic enough; the girl in white was not to be accounted for.

And, moreover, she seemed to have been visible to no-one else; the vision was to me alone.

Of my own fortunes during the following twelvemonth, I shall speak only briefly. I was in the great Retreat, and was twice wounded, but so slightly as to be able to return to duty after a brief sojourn in hospital. But in the early spring I received a third wound, which was a more serious matter, and sent me back to England for doubtful and difficult repair. My mother and Lydia came to London, where I was in hospital, occupying lodgings near me, and anxious, so soon as I should be pronounced convalescent, to have me handed over to their care. I was better, able to sit up, and discharge was well in sight, when my mother sprang upon me what she felt sure would be a pleasant surprise.

'Can you guess, Dick, where we are going so soon as you can be moved? We were so happy last year, Lydia and I, in the little house you found for us at G—, that I thought we could not do better than engage it again this summer, if it was still to be had.'

And here the dear soul paused, plainly expecting my expressions of delight. I could not spoil her pleasure by avowing I hated the place, the cottage and its surroundings, and of my free will would never have set foot in it again. So I swallowed down my distaste.

'And was it to let, mother?' I asked in my turn.

'Alas! no. Riverside Cottage had been snapped up before we enquired – and I don't wonder, it is so sweet a place. But I have taken the house next along the road, the one they call the Lodge, and I hope we shall like it as well. If you remember, the gardens join, and the landing-stage is shared between the two. The rooms are larger than at Riverside, and that will be an advantage when you are with us too.'

Not Riverside Cottage after all, but the house next door. That was something of a reprieve, for I did not know how, under invalid conditions, my jarred nerves would stand the reappearance of the girl in white. But it was not probable, at least I thought not, that two houses could be made uninhabitable by one ghost.

I did not leave the hospital so soon as was expected – complications arose, and healing was deferred. So I had time to receive a report, this time from my sister, of the neighbours at Riverside. The Tressidys were pleasant people, so I gathered; an old General who was subject to gout, and his maiden sister who kept house for him; also two unmarried daughters, both pretty and one charming, and the name of the charmer was Emily. The other daughter was, I gathered, something of an invalid; and Emily was the mainspring of the family, full of spirits and fun. Lydia so evidently intended me to fall captive to Emily, that the spirit of resistance quickened, and I was not sorry to hear, on my arrival, that Emily was away on a visit, and the introduction would be deferred.

The Lodge appeared cheerful and comfortable that first evening, and I was not visited with the depression of the year before; also, in my airy bedroom overlooking the river, I slept well and undisturbed. It was not until the second day that I was introduced to the Tressidy family. Lydia came to summon me from the small sitting-room which was styled the library. The General had called, especially on me, bringing with him his elderly sister, and the younger daughter, Grace. A pretty girl, Lydia said, preparing me, but not to be compared with Emily. So I was ushered into the room, halting with my stick.

There I was presented to a grizzled, choleric-looking old soldier, a meek elderly female, also grizzled; lastly to the girl. And how shall I describe my sensations, when from her seat in the background and the shadow, she turned on me the face of my ghost, and faintly smiled?

It was the very same face which had looked at me out of the glass at Riverside Cottage, the dark eyes and eyebrows, the almost flaxen hair, even the hinted dimple on the cheek, which became more evident with her smile. Was it wonderful that I felt myself stricken dumb in those first moments, and then that I answered with some odd misstatements in replying to General Tressidy, when he asked, as everybody does, about conditions at the Front, the service I had seen, and my wound. What the old man thought of my confusion I do not know; perhaps he concluded that the marring bullet had impaired, not body only, but also mind.

I had a chance to speak to Grace Tressidy later on when tea was served. The likeness persisted; it was no temporary hallucination. I wished she would have removed her hat, simple as it was, the ghost having been hatless; but in other ways she was dressed for the part, as her gown was white. She wished to relieve me of handing the cake, because I moved lamely, but this I would not allow; and when her wants were supplied, I sat down by her; the General was now talking to my mother. Did she like the river valley, I asked, and did she know it well? I wanted to ascertain if she had been in the neighbourhood last year, but could not put so bold a question. It was all new to her, she replied, and all delightful; and then she caught her breath, and looked at me with the dark eyes of the vision, eyes with a question in them on her side: was it possible she remembered me, as I recognised her?

'You will think me very silly,' she went on. 'Emily laughs at me. I have never been here before, and yet it seems as if this place was familiar – even the house where we are staying. I knew every nook of the garden, and every turn of the road. It is as if I had visited it in a dream.'

Was that in truth the explanation, and was my ghost nothing more than a perception of Grace Tressidy's dreams? I saw her several times in the days that followed, sometimes hatless, and twice I tried to draw the conversation again to this point, that I might ask her further, and perhaps confess; but each time she avoided it with timidity: had she taken herself to task for so un-guardedly speaking out to a stranger, or was she afraid of what I might have to tell? The charming Emily was still away, and I was told, among her other virtues and merits, that she had been a constant nurse and guardian to this younger sister during a period of ill health. My informant did not say the nature of Grace's illness, and she appeared now to have completely recovered. She walked and bicycled, and was as active as other girls; but the aunt would not let her go on the water, so the boat at the landing-stage was left to us.

I was disturbed by no ghost at River Lodge, but again I took to resting ill at night, though, up to now, mine had been the deep sleep of healthy convalescence. Perhaps I was thinking rather more of Grace Tressidy than was good for me, or would have pleased Lydia, who wished me to be attracted to her favourite, Emily. But, however caused, my insomnia returned, and the night it was at its worst; after tossing feverishly for a couple of hours, I re-collected how, the year before, I had been able to sleep in the boat. There it still was, moored to the landing-stage between the two gardens, and a longing beset me to try anew the experiment which succeeded before. So again I armed myself with cushions and went out, and, lying there in the stern, expected to find drowsy peace.

The summer was not so far advanced as when I slept out the previous year, and the early mornings were somewhat chill. It seemed to be the chill which waked me, and, raising myself for a change of position, I looked up the slope of garden to the Riverside house with its drawn blinds. And lo! there again was my vision, on the lawn among the rose bushes, recognised with a shock of heart which curdled through nerves and blood.

My white girl, who so strangely resembled Grace Tressidy; or was it this time Grace Tressidy herself? She moved away from the bushes, and came slowly towards me with her hands spread out, like a blind person feeling her way.

Was I dreaming or awake? The ghost had acted so; the figure was but repeating the scene of a year before. I lay as if spellbound, and could neither move nor speak. She came on, and as she crossed the stage I saw that her feet were bare. Then, as before, she stepped into the boat.

This time it rocked and swayed under a material weight. The spell was broken. I sprang up, but not soon enough to prevent what followed. The figure at the prow made the despairing gesture I well remembered, and then plunged into the water, now with a splash and scream.

The current in shore was slow, and what there was carried her past me. I seized her as she rose for the second time, and dragged her out drenched and gasping, but, thank heaven, alive.

'I was asleep,' she sobbed; and then, 'What will Emily say!' and she fell again to weeping.

I could seek no explanation then and there. My task was to hurry her back at once, and rouse the inmates of Riverside for those ministrations of which she stood in need – hot bath, dry rubbing, bed. I could see that the accident caused all that household deep dismay, but it was everything that the girl was saved.

When I went round later to enquire, I was told Miss Tressidy wished to see me: this was not Grace, but the aunt.

'We have no words to express our thanks, Captain Blake,' she began. 'I speak for the General too, for he is laid up in his room; the agitation has brought on a fit of gout. Our poor child would have been lost to us, but for you. It was just God's Providence that you happened to be there.'

Then followed her story. Grace was a somnambulist. She had walked in her sleep as a child, but the tendency seemed to be out-grown, till it returned after an illness early last year. Then it caused grave anxiety for a time, but the sister, Emily, was constantly at hand to watch, and so prevented harm. Grace was now well again as they believed; the trouble had not recurred for nearly a twelvemonth, so it was thought safe for Emily to leave.

The troubled period was, I gathered, in June and July of 1914, and so coincident with the appearance of my ghost, in a place unknown to Grace Tressidy, but where she was in the future to run so grave a risk to life.

Does this afford an explanation of the story I have told? It may, or it may not; but it is the only one I have to offer.

Some day I may tell the whole of my experience to Grace herself; but first there must be the telling of another tale I have in mind, and all will depend on whether she is disposed to listen. I think, I hope she will be favourable to a war-worn soldier, but I do not know. Then I shall perhaps discover correspondences closer than those of which I am aware, and divine how it came about that we were drawn together, I as her preserver, she to yield the life I saved, to my care for days to come.

A Perplexing Case

He opened his eyes; consciously opened them for the first time since the blow and roar of the explosion which had seemed to blot him out of life; and looked about him, wondering. He was lying on his back in a narrow hospital bed, next but one to the wall, and in the next bed somebody was groaning: that was the first sound received by his understanding ears. His right side appeared to be stiff with bandages, but felt benumbed rather than painful; he seemed to have no use in that arm. But his left arm lay out upon the covering, and he could move it without difficulty, and the fingers of the hand. And it was his hand which he was presently regarding with surprise.

If you had looked at the board hung over the head of the bed, you would have seen his name entered as Henri de Hochepied Latour, sous-lieutenant in a French regiment which cooperated with the British in a recent attack. His name as I have written it; his injury, wounds from shell-burst, and shock to brain – this a free translation of the surgical terms: and the date, five days before, on which he had been transferred from the dressing-station to this hospital behind the lines. Could the patient have lifted and turned himself to read, he might have challenged more than one item in this account; what these were will be apparent later. But for such an effort he had not the strength; he could only stare at his left hand, holding it before his face.

In this mischance that had befallen him, which he recognised as fortune of war, what had happened to alter that unwounded member? What he expected to see was a big brawny fist, with knotted joints and hard muscles; the hand of a working man, who, somewhat reluctantly and at the call of duty, had taken to shouldering a rifle. It might be whitened and attenuated by illness, but surely it still would be the same in form. What he did see was a hand delicately slender, olive in hue of skin, strong no doubt in a determined grip, but not with navvy's strength; the nails almond-shaped, daintily manicured and tended; in all these details unlike his own. How could such a change have come about? He opened and shut the hand before his face, staring stupidly at it in his surprise.

Presently a nurse, who had been attending to the moaning patient in the next bed, bent over him and noticed that consciousness had returned.

'I will bring you presently some tea, monsieur,' she said, to test whether he understood, speaking in slow careful French, the French of an Englishwoman.

The dark head moved on the pillow.

'Have you no English, Sister?'

This man had been in hospital before.

'Yes, of course I have. I am English. But I thought you would better understand my French, though I know it is not good.'

'Good or bad, it would be all the same to me. I can say *bon jour*, and ask for bread and cheese, and that's about all. What did you say to me?'

'Only that I would bring you tea as soon as it is ready.'

Sister Bennett glanced again at the board hung over the bed before she turned away. There must have been some mistake, for sous-lieutenant Henri Latour ought to speak his own language, and understand it when spoken, even by an Englishwoman. And he was a thorough Frenchman to look at, this wounded soldier, though he had an English tongue in his head, if not the most refined intonation of speech. But she made no comment in reporting to the doctor that Number Forty-nine had come to himself. If there had been a mistake, they would find it out soon enough without intervention of hers. And doctors and nurses were all closely engaged that night, as a fresh batch of wounded had come in.

But the next day there was further trouble. Number Forty-nine indignantly denied his identity with the French officer Henri Latour, declaring that he was one Richard Adams, lance-corporal, attached to the London Scottish. He persisted in this assertion with so much ruffled temper that the doctor gave direction that he should be humoured. Confusion was a common enough consequence of shell-shock, so said the man of experience; but, for all that, this was not quite a common case. It was an odd coincidence that Richard Adams of the London regiment was lying unconscious in that very hospital. He had been injured, so it was believed, at the same time as young Latour, and by the bursting of the self-same shell; and, though his wounds were not considered serious, he had not yet come to himself. Sous-lieutenant Latour would be all right in a day or two, so

Senhouse, the captain-doctor, forecasted. No doubt this young man had been in touch with Corporal Adams immediately before the catastrophe, and somehow – though how was unexplained – the impression of Adams' personality persisted in this condition of temporary aberration. That there could have been any actual mistake between the two was out of the question; the identification discs in each case furnished proof. And, beyond this, a friend of Latour's, visiting the hospital, had recognised him when he was carried unconscious from the ambulance.

Here was testimony enough, but further witness was forthcoming. The French lieutenant was presently enquired for by two ladies: Mademoiselle Ottilie Latour, his elder sister, and with her a charming girl whom she addressed as Julie, who was the young officer's betrothed. Might they be admitted to his bedside, such was Mademoiselle Latour's petition, just to look at him as he lay asleep, if they might do no more.

Senhouse the doctor was not hard-hearted enough to refuse. If the ladies could promise self-command, they could see the patient awake or asleep. His wounds were not serious, and recovery might certainly be hoped for. The shock of the explosion, however, had to a certain extent affected his mind. For this they must be prepared.

Mademoiselle Latour promised that neither she nor her companion would betray alarm or distress, and she held Julie's quivering hand fast in hers as they passed through the temporary ward, the eyes of broken men turning on them from their pillows of pain.

The young lieutenant was awake: he lay, staring at the ceiling, still with a puzzled frown upon his brow, though he had thrust the slender olive hand, which was not the hand of Richard Adams, away under the bed-coverings: he could not bear the sight of it, it perplexed him too much.

Senhouse paused by the bed as the two women came beside it, standing opposite, and he glanced up at them from the face on the pillow. Yes, there could be no doubt that this was Henri Latour, the likeness between brother and sister was so strong; the clear-cut distinguished features seemed to have been struck from the same die. This Henri might have been thought somewhat effeminate-looking when clean-shaven: now his chin was disfigured by an eight days' growth of beard: but there could be no doubt that Ottilie, the sister who resembled him, was beautiful, of the very type of womanhood that Captain Senhouse most fervently admired, noble-looking now in her calmness and her grief.

'He is awake,' she breathed in the lowest of whispers. 'May I speak to him?' Assent was signified.

'*Mon frère*,' she began, bending nearer, with the younger girl also pressing close and leaning on her arm. The face which was Latour's turned to regard them, but his air of sullen indifference did not alter or lighten into recognition. He looked coldly at the anxious sister, and the tremulous young beauty who was his betrothed, made a slight movement of negation, and closed his eyes.

'These ladies have come to see you. They are speaking: don't you hear them?' Thus the doctor, in English.

The man addressed replied in the same tongue. 'I am obliged to them, but I don't know them. And I speak no French.'

His manner suggested obstinacy as well as indifference. He did not know these people; he was annoyed by the emotion with which they seemed to regard him, and in his maimed state he was sensitive about pity: he wished they would go away. Ottilie Latour made another effort, naming the familiar home, the early interests they had shared; surely at such a hearing, the shattered memory would light up into renewed being, as might a smouldering fire! The younger lady fell on her knees, and her voice was broken by sobs.

'Ah, Henri – ah, Henri,' she cried. 'Don't you remember how we parted and what you said? Have you quite forgotten?'

The man opened his eyes again, but turned to Senhouse without notice of the appeal. He was fingering his chin, which showed a dark stubble of beard.

'Doctor,' he said, 'is there anybody here who can shave me? Nurse says I'm bound to ask you for the order. I hate to be like this.'

English again, and rough-toned English to boot.

'It is of no use at present,' Senhouse said to Mademoiselle Latour. 'You are only distressing yourselves needlessly. Better to come away.'

There were friends waiting who took the weeping Julie in charge, but the sister lingered behind.

'It is very strange,' she said to Senhouse. 'Do you often have such cases? Without doubt that is my brother, but it is not his voice. He would never speak like that; he is a cultivated gentleman. How is it that he forgets his native tongue? I could understand shock stripping off later acquirements for the time, but not what is the bedrock of nature.' Here she paused, her earnest gaze striving to read the doctor's countenance, on which was written deep concern. 'Do you think – really think – there is any hope?'

'We do not give up hope, we doctors, and you must not. The case is a peculiar one, that I grant; but others which have come under my notice have displayed equal confusion. Much may yet be done; we must have patience. Have you any knowledge of the man he seems to personate: one Richard Adams, a private soldier in the British army? Can you suggest any possible link between him and your brother in the past?'

Mademoiselle Latour shook her head, but she appeared to be considering. 'No, I recollect nothing. Of course Henri may have known him. He was in England two years ago, and made many acquaintances; but not army ones, so far as I am aware.'

'Oddly enough, a man of that name was wounded by the same shell-burst as Lieutenant Latour, and now lies in this hospital, also suffering from shock. Would it distress you too much – could you spare the time – to look at him? He is here, in this lower ward; the door on the right. You may recognise his face: if not likely, it is possible. I shall be greatly obliged.'

Senhouse had a special reason for this urgency, one he did not avow. There seemed little or no ground for supposing the inspection could be of use. Mademoiselle Latour, however, assented willingly. She was quite at leisure; she would do whatever was wished. So together they entered the second ward.

Richard Adams was conscious and very restless, the Sister in charge said when interrogated; he had been talking strangely all the afternoon, as if delirious. There seemed no sense in it, but what he jabbered was in French. She was glad the doctor had come. That was Adams, in the middle bed.

Adams was a herculean young fellow of the Saxon type, fair and blue-eyed, and in the eyes was a cloud of trouble. He was tossing restlessly on his narrow couch, as if no position could be easy; but when he caught sight of the lady-visitor, his countenance became radiant with joy.

'Ottilie! Ottilie!' he exclaimed, stretching out two eager hands burning with fever. 'This is good, to see someone from home. How did you come? Have you been anxious about me at Les Rochers? . . . Tell me, how is mother? And my Julie; how is she? You don't know what it is to lie here, and long to have word of them, if only a word. Now you are here, my dear sister, how long can you stay? Give me every moment you are able.'

For a brief instant the sister seemed on the verge of fainting, but she yielded her hands to the grasp of those others which were strange to her. The voice was familiar, and the questions: who could have questioned her so, but Henri only?

'Mademoiselle Latour cannot stay long,' said the doctor, bending down to him. 'No doubt she will come again. And now you must not excite yourself.'

'I want to hear of them all,' the man went on; this rough English private soldier. 'All of them – old François, and Madelon and Ninette: all, down to Ponto the dog. I dream of them at night, and I see them when I dream. Has mother been anxious about me? I feel sure she has.'

The sister at last recovered power of speech. 'Yes, yes – indeed – she has been anxious: she is. She talks of nothing but Henri. I am here to bring her news.'

'Tell her my last thought was of her. There was a blow which struck me – a great rushing, and a noise that stunned. The rush sent me spinning with it, as if I had been a bullet from a gun: spinning – spinning through space. I thought I was going to her – to Rochers la Vallière, and I cried out her name. But I did not get to la Vallière: I did not go so far. Everything went dark, and I remember no more. I woke in this place, and I cannot make them understand what I want. Take me with you, Ottilie; take me home. Are they well there? The invasion has not touched them? Is mother well?'

'They are all well, and safe, and hoping for news of – of you – of Henri.' As she spoke, she looked across at Senhouse in appeal: she knew not how much longer she could trust her self-command to keep up this farce: farce, was it, or fact and truth?

Not many more words were exchanged before the doctor asserted authority and led her away; and now she needed the support of his arm. Outside the ward she was thankful to sink into a chair, and drink the water he presently held to her lips.

'You did not know this Adams?'

'Not his face. But it was my brother speaking with his lips. My brother's body is in the other ward – his spirit here. *M. le docteur*, it is terrible. Body and soul apart! What can be done?'

'You must forgive me for exposing you to such an ordeal. I suspected what was the matter, but I wanted to be sure. I wanted to see if this Adams, as he is called, would recognise you. Plainly he did so: he spoke to you at once by name. It will be easier to treat, now that we understand. There may be need of long patience. But, to my thinking, there is no reason for despair.'

Mademoiselle Latour was gathering back her shaken self-control; she set down the glass of water.

'What can be done?' she repeated.

It was the question Senhouse had asked himself, and still he was groping in the dark after an answer. But he desired above all to reassure this noble-looking woman, who had been so sorely tried by his experiment. In replying, he assumed a confidence he was far from feeling, but hope was strong that it might be justified by the event.

'You will give me a free hand to do what I think best for M. Latour? There is a man, a Parisian doctor, who is great in these mysterious cases of – of brain-suspension, and confusion and all that. We will have him here in consultation, and he shall advise and treat the case. He has made some wonderful successes. You may be certain no pains will be spared by us to efface what now is wrong, and to restore the link of mind and body completely as before.'

Senhouse did not forget the apparent Latour's complaint about his sprouting beard, and he gave the required order that the lieutenant should be shaved – a simple matter, which had a somewhat unlooked-for result. The hospital orderly was sufficiently skilled to operate in this way upon the chins of the patients, and in due course of time he arrived with razor and lathering-bowl to shave the young French officer. He found the young French officer in sufficiently good spirits to be communicative . . . There was nothing, he averred, that did him so much good as a clean shave: it put him at once on right terms with himself and his world. And as (he hoped) his was a 'Blighty' case of wounding, it would never do for him to go back to England with so much bristle showing. Liz, his wife, as good an old girl as ever stepped, would in that case have nothing to say to him.

'You think of crossing over to England, sir?' questioned the orderly, mindful of necessary respect when he was shaving an officer. But this officer had an odd way of talking, Frenchman as he was.

'Why, of course I shall be sent to England, and I hope it will be to a London hospital. That will be convenient for Liz. She lives out Poplar way, and takes in fine sewing; and she has kept herself comfortable with that and the allowance – good old girl. And I know that, were it ever so, she'd never look at anyone but me; not like some of the fellows' wives one hears of. We've got a kid, too; eight months old he is, and so far I've never set eyes on him. Liz'll bring him to the hospital when she comes to see me, you bet she does, for she's as proud of him as – as – '

The illustration failed, as the razor was now operating round the lower lip, and silence was only prudent. But in another couple of minutes he would be released.

'There, sir, there's a clean shave for you. And, though I say it as shouldn't, one it would be hard to beat.'

The patient fingered his chin somewhat doubtfully, with the one hand he could move; the hand which had caused him so much disquietude when he came to himself.

'I've got a glass here,' said the soldier-barber. ' 'Tis but a little one, but if you look in it you can see for yourself. It has freshened you up above a bit, and you can't fail to be pleased.'

The small vanity-glass was produced, and held at the right angle. The patient looked, and, looking, gave a cry – a yell of horror which rang through the ward, so that all the heads on all the other pillows turned to gaze, and the sister in charge came hurrying to learn what was the matter. This Latour, usually quiet and biddable, was suddenly wrought up into a state of fierce excitement.

'What have they done to me,' he demanded wildly, 'to make me look like that? I never had that sort of f—— face. I'll have the law of the f—— doctors, f— me if I don't. If I go to England with that face, Liz'll never believe I'm her husband.' And so forth, in the teeth of regulations, and despite all persuasion, the protest garnished with sundry very forcible oaths which we omit, until excitement stilled away into exhaustion, and the sick man lost himself in sleep.

The Parisian doctor who had become the referee in shock cases which do not yield to ordinary treatment, we will call Despard for the purpose of this narrative; it is not his real name. It became known very shortly that he had been summoned to the perplexing case at the B— hospital, about which some rumour had gone abroad. Despard was supposed to pin his faith on hypnotism and suchlike uncanny nostrums, and in consequence his name stank in the nostrils of one half of the surgical staff. He was going to hypnotise the shock case, that was the assumption; and some surprise was evidenced when it crept out through certain preparations that Latour was to be treated by the more ordinary method of the transfusion of blood.

'I hope you've got a healthy subject to be donor,' said the C.M.O., meeting Senhouse on the stairs. 'And don't forget the saltwater admixture; for, whatever Despard says, I hold that to be essential.' And then the C.M.O. bethought him to ask: 'Who is the donor?'

'Well, sir, it is the other shock man, Adams. Despard has chosen him. He is healthy enough, I think, and a young Hercules for strength.'

'Tut-tut,' said the great man, who very plainly disapproved, and to whom the hypnotist and his methods were *anathema maranatha*. 'What! – two shock cases, and transfuse their blood! Never heard of such a proceeding in my life. What possibly can be gained by it but an aggravation of both their symptoms?' And so forth; and the C.M.O. may be written down as 'left objecting.'

The experiment was tried next day in the operating-room of the hospital, Senhouse acting as one of Despard's assistants, the other being a coadjutor who accompanied him. The door was of course barred against intrusion, and what took place within was never precisely known. The process was a long one, and once while it was in progress Senhouse managed to slip away, so as to convey a modicum of comfort to the room below, where Ottilie Latour had been allowed to wait. She looked up at his entrance, eagerly expectant. She was pale to the lips with anxiety, but as beautiful as ever – at least Senhouse thought so.

'Is it over?' she asked.

'Not yet, and will not be for another hour. But I thought you would be relieved to know all is going well, and Despard is quite hopeful. He says it is a simple case compared to some which have passed through his hands, and he expects complete success. They went off into trance without difficulty, both of them, and neither saw the other, as a screen was put up between them. And they will be moved into fresh quarters directly after, so that there will be nothing to revive former impressions. I am sorry you have so long to wait.'

'I do not mind how long; it is everything to be on the spot, and I thank you from my heart for getting me permission to wait here. I know you will bring me the earliest news.'

'I will come to you the instant certainty is assured. But I don't expect Despard will give leave for you to see your brother today. Don't let that disappoint you.'

Upon this, the messenger went back to his post at the theatre. There a certain amount of vital fluid was in process of interchange, and two spirits wrongly housed in their tenements of flesh were brought into touch by a force only partially recognised, though of existence coeval with human life.

After a while one of the patients began to stir and moan, and then to utter some querulous complaint.

'The young gentleman is coming round,' said the assistant, calling Despard's attention. '*And he is speaking French.*'

Despard gave a grunt of satisfaction.

'Ah,' he said, 'if that is so, we have done well.'

Some half hour later Senhouse went back to Ottilie.

'It is over, successfully over, and M. Despard confidently hopes the confusion will never be renewed. Your brother is in bed in the new ward, quite composed, and he remembers that you visited him. "When is my sister coming again: my sister Ottilie?" he asked me. I told him you had been here today, but the doctor thought it unwise to permit a visitor on the day of operation. He said: "Tell her to give my devotion to Julie and mother, and a message of remembrance to all at Rochers la Vallière." And then he turned his face away on the pillow and fell asleep. That was your brother in his true form, not as before. You understand?'

Yes, Ottilie Latour understood, and her eyes were full of grateful tears.

Four days after, the second shock case was entrained for Blighty. Another shave had smartened him sufficiently to appear as Liz would wish and expect; and now when the glass was presented he saw his own face in it – the face she would recognise and that he knew. And his hand was broad and muscular again, not the slim olive member the sight of which was his first perplexity. What had been the matter with him, he queried, and was told on the doctor's authority he had suffered from shellshock; and that to the victims of shock, confusion and dementia manifest themselves in many forms, including distorted vision, all owing to the temporary loss of balance by the brain.

Beyond the Pale

Without doubt the Hennikers' was a love-match. They had been married a couple of years, and it may fairly be said that neither party had found cause to repent. Rupert Henniker was sincerely attached to his wife, and she positively idolised him. The French proverb says that in all such unions there is one who kisses, and the other who permits the embrace. In this case Henniker was the one kissed, but he willingly yielded the cheek, and felt that Joan's adoration was well placed.

Joan began her married life with high ideals. She determined so to identify herself with her husband's pursuits, that she might everywhere be his unfailing companion; and to this young wife the nursery interests, which frequently alter such a programme, had not been vouchsafed by Providence. So when Henniker laid his plans for a season's shooting in the wilds of Western America, Joan, as a matter of course, expected to go too.

She did not claim to shoulder a rifle beside him; that was not her way: but she could keep the rough little mountain dwelling which had been placed at their disposal cosy and home-like for Rupert, and see that he missed no comfort that her care could supply. If on the spot, she could see that he changed into dry footwear when he came back of an evening; she could wash his socks and darn them, and contrive the best imitation possible of his favourite dishes over the stove, which there would be the sole substitute for an English kitchen-range. She had some practical knowledge of these matters, though it was slight and inadequate; but she determined it should be sufficient, and everything in the adventure before them was seen through the rose-coloured medium of romance. The separation which might have been had she held back was now no longer to be feared; and a prolonged tête-a-tête in the wilds would draw them together even nearer than before. Henniker had expressed himself as proud of his little woman's pluck, and she was determined to justify that pride and that praise.

Their solitude would not be absolute, as Arnott's ranch was distant only half a mile, which in that land of prairie wastes and wide distances seemed almost as close as next door. Arnott and Henniker had been boys together and schoolmates, and it was upon his suggestion they were going out. Arnott's wife was said to be a good sort, and on Joan's arrival she would equip her with all needful knowledge.

So young Mrs Henniker set out on her sea and land journey with a brave heart and bright anticipations, and her courage did not fail when at last they travelled on beyond railways and civilisation, into the great solitudes; climbing the spurs of the foot-hills, and looking up at the huge mountain wall and the high snows behind which the sun sank in the west. Perhaps the adobe hut when reached was something of a disillusion, though it was fairly commodious and not absolutely bare; the Arnotts had put in necessaries in the way of furniture, and had done their best to make it habitable. It would look more home-like when Joan had had time to unpack and arrange her possessions and his – other than the precious rifles, which were not for feminine handling: and about all this Joan would have the aid of a 'help' Mrs Arnott had engaged for her, to soften the edge of hardship in this strange new housekeeping in the wilds. Nita, the half-bred Indian girl, could at least manage the stove, and wash and scrub the place down, if she could do no more.

Mrs Arnott had of course her own establishment to look after, where a couple of pretty children added to the domestic cares and joys, so she could give Joan only occasional assistance; though a fount of practical advice was at her service whenever she cared to come up to the ranch. So the next day Joan was left alone with her wild-looking 'help' when Henniker went off to the hills.

Nita had a double tongue in her head, Spanish and Indian, on which a very little English had been grafted; and it was by the help of the very little English that she and her new mistress were to exchange ideas and commands. Joan would have scorned to confess that from the beginning she stood in some awe of her assistant, but it was so in fact. Nita's service was utterly unlike any to which she had been accustomed, and there was something disconcerting about the girl's sudden lithe movements, and the keen regard of her black eyes. At first mistress and maid were on good terms; and though Nita's ideas of necessary cleanliness were far from satisfying Joan, the young housekeeper hoped that admonition and instruction would have their due effect in time; and greater energy was displayed after the gift of a gay ribbon out of one of the Henniker travelling trunks.

But with the unpacking of these trunks came the development of an intense curiosity on the part of Nita concerning all kinds of civilised belongings, and, as Joan began uncomfortably to suspect, of a cupidity equally intense. The girl longed to deck herself out in imitation of her mistress, and pile on the few ornaments that were in evidence: Joan had, as a matter of course, left her jewel-case in the custody of an English bank.

Nita was nominally assisting arrangement upon shelves and drawers, and fingering the possessions that were laid away, when Joan first noticed the peculiar scar on her right wrist. Such a slender brown wrist it was, and at some time or other it must have been frightfully hurt. A deeply-seamed scar ran the whole way round the arm, or almost the whole way, as only about an inch of smooth skin was free from the ghastly indentation; and below this, nearer the hand, were a couple of lines of blue tattooing, twisted together at the back into a sort of device. Joan asked her how she had been hurt, but evidently Nita's English was not equal to the task of explanation; she frowned and drew back, pouring out a torrent of bastard Spanish, which left her mistress as wise as before.

Joan did not enquire further, but, thinking to please her, offered as a gift a string of coral beads which matched the ribbon. To her surprise Nita refused it, but snatched up a small miniature portrait taken from the trunk.

'Not those,' she said, 'I don't want those: I have beads enough. I will have this instead: give me this!'

The miniature was one of Joan's dead mother, and greatly valued by her; unluckily it was framed in a glittering oval of Paris paste. Joan was shocked at the greed and the demand, and wrenched the portrait out of those brown fingers which closed and clutched against her; there was indeed a struggle over it between the two.

'No, you cannot have that,' she said, trying to disguise her displeasure – for what was the use of being angry with this child of nature? 'You may have the corals if you care for them, but not this. It is the only portrait I have of my mother, and more than all the world.'

The girl looked sulky, but no more was said. Of course it was not the picture that she wanted, but the oval of shining mock gems. The attraction of this to one who had never before looked upon diamonds, real or imitation, was greater than Joan could divine. Yet civilised women have before now succumbed to such lures, so to covet possession may be reckoned less surprising in one beyond the pale. Joan was prudent enough again to lock the miniature in her travelling trunk, and when the key was turned she dismissed the matter from her mind. But it was by no means blotted out of Nita's by that closed lid and turned key.

Several days went by, full of small jarring discomforts which need not be enumerated here. One afternoon Joan went up to the ranch to take counsel with Mrs Arnott, and on her return she found the place deserted, her boxes broken open and ransacked, and, what specially moved her to wrath, the precious miniature was forced out of its frame and cracked across, while the glittering oval had altogether disappeared.

This was an outrage indeed. The actual thefts were of small account measured against this damage, the wrong of the disfiguring crack which split the beloved face in two. Joan cried out that the offender must be caught and punished, and Henniker was of the same mind; so he and Arnott, who was sheriff's delegate for that part of the district, rode up into the hills in search of Nita, making their errand known.

The girl was supposed to have her abode with the old Indian woman her grandmother, who received them with wrath and curses, and swore to Nita's innocence – as doubtless she would have sworn to any statement which suited her, having small regard for truth. Also she declared that she knew nothing of the grand-daughter's whereabouts, so the pursuing party returned baffled, after breathing forth vain threatenings.

Mrs Arnott was with Joan when her husband and his friend returned. 'Did you really beard old Rachel in her den?' she asked, and looked more than a little concerned.

'Why, of course we did. What else were we to do?' was his rejoinder.

'I suppose it was a matter of duty, but the old crone is what they call about here ill to cross, and likely to put ill luck upon you both. It was all very well for you to be out to catch a thief, but I wish you and Mr Henniker had left old Rachel alone. You must know,' she said, turning to Joan, 'deserved or not, this grandmother of Nita's has the reputation of being a witch.'

Of course they laughed at this as at an excellent joke, Joan and the two men, but there was an air about Mrs Arnott as if she more than half believed in Rachel's malignant powers.

'I am more sorry than I can say that I sent Nita to you,' she went on. 'But the girl seemed teachable and promised to do well. There is nobody else but old Mercy Clew, our herdsman's wife, and she is coming up to you tomorrow. She is a rough specimen, but I have always thought her honest, and I believe your possessions will be safe with her.'

The foregoing may be taken as the prologue to the drama, all of it commonplace enough, but needful to make clear what will follow.

Joan had spent a busy morning shepherding Mercy Clew – who was both deaf and obstinate – in the way of the help she required. It had been a strenuous time: a trial of patience as well as of physical strength in unaccustomed labours; and she had withdrawn into their living-room for a few minutes' breathing-space and rest, throwing herself into the one cushioned chair with a gasp of relief. Her eyes were closed, her muscles all relaxed, when tap-tap came behind her – the rapping of impatient fingers on the glass. Mrs Arnott sometimes tapped like that on her way to the entrance door; and Joan started round to face the window, feeling rather aggrieved by the intrusion. But Mrs Arnott was not there. The tapping came again, and now she saw something where the glass was struck; only a shadow, but the shadow of a hand.

A hand reaching down from above. If the shadow was of any real substance, the intruder must be crouched upon the roof; the hut had, of course, no storey above the ground floor. It must be Nita; that was her instant conviction: Nita playing some annoying trick: but with a warrant out against her it was surprising that she dared. Joan ran outside to see. No, there was no-one on the roof, either above the smitten window or behind – no-one hiding round the chimney-stack, no-one within sight; but, passing it on her return, she discovered that the smitten glass retained the print of a hand.

The hand had been pressed flat against the pane, palm and out-spread fingers, and it seemed to have been dipped in something viscous and sticky, faintly streaked with blood. She looked at it from time to time during the day, and watched the gradual drying off of the mark in the keen hill air; but it was still faintly visible when Henniker returned, and his attention was called to it.

'Yes,' he said, 'whoever made that mark must have stretched down to do it from the roof. A daring trick, and likely enough to be Nita's, unless indeed she has an accomplice. We shall catch her at it if she is foolhardy enough to come again.'

There was no more tapping on the glass that night, to call attention to what was going forward; but when they got up the next morning a second window was marked. This one lighted the bedroom and looked to the other side of the house. Here there was no roof-slope above it but a gable, so it would have been more difficult, well-nigh impossible, to reach down to the glass from above. The print of the hand, however, was made precisely as before, wrist upwards and fingers downwards, a sticky impression streaked with blood. It was Henniker this time who discovered it when he drew aside the window screen to shave; he called to his wife, who was kindling a fire in the stove, and they both regarded it together.

'Somebody is trying to take a rise out of us' – such was Henniker's ultimatum. 'No doubt it is supposed we shall be scared by these cursings of the witch. I'd like to get to the bottom of it before anything is known, so do not let us appear to take notice. I shall not say anything to Jack Arnott – yet, and do not you to his wife.'

It was all very well to resolve on this course of action – or inaction, and easy to take no notice of a sticky mark on the outside of a window, which was presently effaced with a wet cloth. But the next demonstration, if it can be so called, was of a different nature and less possible to ignore. Mercy Clew came rushing in from her wash-bucket to where Joan was stirring a saucepan over the stove. 'Come you out here, Mis' Henniker. I cannot go on in the yard. They have been throwing stones at me this half hour!'

The woman had an air of passionate indignation, but together with the anger there was fear. Mrs Clew's command of English was super-ior to Nita's, but Joan found her almost as difficult to understand.

'Do you mean that somebody is throwing stones, and at you? Who would dare to do such a thing? It must be a mistake.'

'Come you out and see' – taking hold of Joan by the arm. 'I wouldn't like to have you hurt, but I want you to believe. And if it is the doing of old madam, like enough she'll stone you too.'

It was true that stones and pieces of rock were scattered over the beaten earth of the yard; but, for all Joan knew, they might have been there since the beginning of time. The woman showed the spot where she was standing, and the direction from which they struck her; and, the moment after, another stone fell plump into the water-bucket, and a second bruised Joan on the shoulder. Nobody was in sight.

'It is horrible of them. What have we done that we should be so persecuted! We must find out who is doing this.'

She was angry rather than dismayed, and eager in searching round the dwelling-house and outbuildings. Except for these possible screens, Hunter's End stood in the open, away from trees and rocks. There seemed no possible cover to conceal the thrower of the stones, and yet again, immediately on their return, one was tossed into the yard.

'Bring your pail indoors into the kitchen,' Joan commanded. 'We shall be safe there.'

But safe they were not, though shut in by walls and doors. The stones still struck them both, and fell within on the floor. The elderly 'help' reached for her shawl and bonnet, which were hanging on the pegs.

'I'm sorry to leave you, marm, but stay I can't where there are such goings on. It's all through the old madam that your place has got bewitched. And, if I'm not mistaken, you'll have no more peace here, day nor night.'

'Who is this old madam, and what do you mean about bewitching?' Joan held her back, almost by force, till she answered.

Mercy Clew dropped her voice to a whisper. ' 'Tis not well to say the name of her, but she is kin to the girl you had here, her you sent after with a sheriff's warrant. It is well known that madam puts spells upon people, and has laid a spell upon the girl herself, if what one hears is true. She's an awful woman when she is angered, and you will have to get quit of her one way or another, or there will be no peace for this house. Mis' Arnott, she knows something of what has been done elsewhere, enough to pass her word to you that I am telling truth. And until madam's quit of you, I can tell you this. Not a soul about will come nigh the place, or drive their beasts past it. I'm sorry from my heart for what's before you, but you'll have to fend for yourselves.'

And the Hennikers had in fact to 'fend for themselves' in the days that followed. The witch, if truly a witch was in fault, had contrived to put upon them a boycott as stringent as any that existed in Ireland. And it was not only that the report of the stone-throwing had gone abroad, and the superstitious were afraid to venture into the bewitched quarter – animals, who could not be affected by hearsay, were also a prey to terror. Arnott's dog, who was used to accompany him in visiting Hunter's End, on the first occasion after these events began, hesitated when within twenty yards of the door, and appeared to scent danger: he then turned tail and fled for home, despite the calls of his master. And one of the ranch horses, drawing a load of logs for the Hennikers' use and led by Arnott, jibbed determinedly at about the same distance, and neither blows nor coaxing could induce it to approach nearer. It was impossible to get help for Joan, other than what Mrs Arnott could occasionally give; and Henniker did not like to leave her uncompanioned in the midst of such eerie happenings, so the guns were idle in their rack, except for the shooting of some rock pigeons and conies in the near neighbourhood of the hut.

Henniker's opinion had altered from the scornful disbelief professed in the beginning, to a mood of unwilling and annoyed conviction. The stone-throwing against old Mercy in the yard he had dismissed as nothing more than a spiteful trick; the tapping on the glass fell into the same category, and the impression of a human hand in an impossible position might even have been made by a dummy pressed against the pane. But when it came to later experiences which he shared, occurrences when he and Joan were alone, in the house, stone-throwing within shut doors which went on at intervals, the affair assumed a different complexion. Stones – it is true they were small ones – were thrown when the two were sitting at supper, first from one side of the room and then from the other; and a good-sized pebble was dropped from above into his coffee-cup, breaking the cup and spilling the contents. Even at night they were allowed no peace; articles left in the kitchen were brought through the shut door into their room and hurled upon the beds; the coverlets were grasped and dragged by something which remained invisible; fingers rapped a tattoo against the window; and, what seemed more extraordinary than all, running footsteps passed backwards and forwards overhead, where was nothing but the sloping roof.

Henniker started out again and again, gun in hand, but there was no target for his shot. Joan kept her courage wonderfully through those harassed days and nights; but when at last her husband accorded her a well-deserved meed of praise, she broke down and shed tears.

'I don't mind – that is, I can bear it so long as it is only what we hear and feel. But if it should come to seeing anything dreadful, I am sure I could not go on being brave.'

It was after this avowal that Henniker asked advice of Arnott, who had come down to see how they were faring; and it may be noted here that this friend had now been taken into the full confidence which was at first withheld.

'What would you do in my place? It's beyond endurance that we should be driven out by sheer devilry – for devilry it must be; but how can I stay on here when it is killing my wife? She won't leave me, or I would send her away, and stay and brave it out by myself.'

'What would I do? Why, I'd be inclined to try what the half-breeds resort to in similar cases. Rank superstition you will say, and so do I; but it is possible there may be something in it as they say that it succeeds. They pit one witch against another, and let the two of them battle it out. There's a man up the river who goes by the name of the witch-doctor. If I were you I'd have him over, and pay the dollars of his fee. I understand it is a big one.'

'If we can be freed from this, I don't mind what I pay, or what absurdity I have to put up with.'

'You will have to put up with absurdity, if his rites are of the sort I imagine. I have heard of them of course, living here, but I have never seen the thing done. I may as well say this is Cora's advice as well as mine.' (Cora was his wife.) 'Very well, as you are willing, I will send Clew with the buggy at dawn tomorrow to fetch down Hill-of-the-Raven, and you must be prepared to receive him here.'

Hill-of-the-Raven professed himself willing to undertake the job, and soon after midday Arnott brought him to Hunter's End. He was a very lean, very tall old Indian, who looked inappropriately garbed in European dress instead of his native paint and feathers. Arnott acted as interpreter, as his English was of the smallest; and he also mounted guard over the old man's bag of conjuring tools while Hill-of-the-Raven made first the outer round of the house, and then entered every room, standing and snuffing the air as a stag might who perceives a taint to windward, all the while muttering incantations to himself. Finally he confabulated again with Arnott, who looked distinctly annoyed.

'Hill-of-the-Raven wants more money,' he informed Henniker. 'The old rascal says it is a worse job than he expected, and of a different sort: "plenty magic here, and bad magic". He was to have cleared you out for ten dollars, but now he says he must have five and twenty.'

For answer, Henniker counted the bills into his friend's hand.

'No doubt he is scoundrel enough for anything, but I will not stint the money. Tell him to go ahead with what he has to do.'

'And he says the *señora* must help him. There is a woman in it, and there must be a woman against. Will Mrs Henniker mind?'

Joan raised no objection, and the preparations went forward. The man stripped himself to the waist, wearing only his leather breeches. He then laid a sheet of iron on the wooden top of their table, and produced an odd-looking bowl of beaten metal, which he required Joan to fill with spring water, dipping into it the forefinger of each of her hands, first one and then the other, and stirring the water from left to right. He gazed into the bowl for a few minutes in silence, and then spoke rapidly to Arnott, who translated.

'He is enumerating the articles you have lost and wish restored. Some blouse-waists and a skirt, a belt and buckle, a scarf, and a circle of stones that glitter. That is right, is it not? But nothing more than he could have learnt from Clew.'

This seemed only the preliminary. The witch-doctor now built up with great care four little pyramids of some stuff which looked like dried herbs, one at each corner of the iron sheet, the water bowl still occupying the centre. He took a hot coal from the fire and lighted these pyramids, one after another. As they smouldered he began to speak, as if in conversation with some person invisible, upbraiding, commanding, threatening; and now the sweat stood in beads on his brow and rained from him with the effort he was making, though it appeared to be mental rather than bodily. At intervals he sprinkled water round him in the room, finally snatching up the bowl and emptying it by tossing the whole contents upwards into the air. This in itself was a conjuror's marvel, as the water totally disappeared and nothing was wetted by it; but this crowning action had a result which astonished the three spectators. A material object fell from the ceiling and dropped upon the iron sheet. A woman's hand.

They all looked in amaze at this product of Hill-of-the-Raven's incantation.

'I have succeeded,' the witch-doctor announced to Arnott. 'The *señor* and *señora* will have no more trouble. But they must fold the hand in a fair white cloth, and bury it at sundown under the nearest tree. The *señora* will receive again what she has lost, but she will be asked to give back something in return. And that something she would do unwisely to refuse.'

The Hennikers were by no means anxious to detain Hill-of-the-Raven, and he departed with Arnott to set out on his return journey in the buggy. Joan and her husband were left possessors of the strange Thing which had fallen from the ceiling: could it really have been this slight small hand, now lying limp and dead, which had caused all the disturbance and trouble. A human hand, of natural flesh at least, though drained of blood; and – wonder the more, as Joan presently cried out in recognition – it was Nita's hand. It bore the double line of blue tattooing twisted into a knot, which she well remembered on the girl's wrist; and the hand appeared to have been severed exactly where Nita bore on her forearm that deeply indented scar. That the hand should have been hers, seemed to make the whole thing more horrible even than before. Joan shuddered away from the touch of it.

'Let us do what the man said: let us bury it out of sight.'

'Yes, but not till sundown,' replied her husband. 'We had better keep to the letter of the instructions, absurd as they may seem. Find the white cloth he spoke of, and have it wrapped in readiness, and I will go and dig the hole under the tree.'

So the burial of the small limp hand took place exactly as Hill-of-the-Raven had enjoined, hastily and almost furtively conducted, at least to the consciousness of these two people; they felt almost as if they had been concerned in a murder, and were now hiding away the corpse. There was something solemn, too, in that still evening in which hardly a breath of air stirred, with sunset flush still lingering behind the mountain peaks, and a few faint stars beginning to look forth.

Henniker smoothed over the disturbed ground, and then shouldered his spade. 'That ends the trouble, we will hope,' he said.

Joan had kept her courage well in hand through the long strain upon it, but the events of that day had overtaxed her nerves.

'I am ready to hate *out west*,' she sobbed. 'When we have turned our backs on it, and are again in safe England, shall we ever believe that these things really happened, and were not from beginning to end an evil dream?'

A quiet night followed for the inhabiters of Hunter's End; there were no more tapping fingers, nor scampering feet above upon the roof. The next morning Mercy Clew came back to work, unafraid of further peltings, as she had full confidence in the witch-doctor's power of exorcism, and belief that all would now be well. And, more notable still, Arnott's horses driven by no longer held back and sweated in terror, nor did the dog refuse to accompany his master. Whatever it was that had scared them from the place was plainly removed and gone; and, now Joan had the companionship of Mrs Clew, Henniker was released to carry his gun to the hills. This seems like the end of the story, but it is not. There is one more episode to be related, stranger than all.

Six days had gone by, and the seventh had dawned. It had been an undisturbed week, and the first vivid impressions of the witch *diablerie* were beginning to fade.

The first change that came was in the weather, which recently had been oppressive, heavy with heat, and scarcely a breath of air fanning down into the valley from blue heights and distant snows. The cup of it had doubtless been charged to the brim for a crisis of electrical disturbance. Never had Joan in her English experience witnessed such lightning or heard such thunder: the jagged flashes seemed to leap from peak to peak, and the thunder was caught up by the mountain echoes and doubled and redoubled, rolling like a cannon-ade among the hills. Then followed torrential rain, driving and pitiless, scourging all before it, and creating, as it seemed in a moment, streams and rivulets where all had been as dry as dust. In the midst of this downpour a hail came from without: a buggy and pair of mules had halted at the gate, and two people were craving shelter, a boon that could hardly be denied.

Henniker opened the door, and a man staggered in supporting a woman wrapped in a hooded cloak, who seemed to be ill or faint. He placed her in a chair, and cleared the wet, lank hair out of his own eyes; he was a good-looking young half-breed, about twenty years of age, and he had some broken English.

'This Hunter's End?' he asked, looking round. 'And your name Henniker? My sister here is ill, having lost her hand. She has come to claim it again from you. And she has brought back the things she took away.'

The fainting woman in the chair was Nita. The man opened a bundle on the table, and there, crumpled and soiled, were Joan's possessions, and rolled within them the oval frame of paste. As he took the bundle from her knee, the cloak that covered her fell apart, and showed that her right arm ended in a stump, about which a linen bandage was twisted, and the bandage was stained with blood.

'My sister's hand?' he continued, looking from Joan to Henniker, and back again to Joan. 'You have it here. I bring you these in exchange: you have no claim to keep. If you do not restore her hand, she will die.'

Joan whispered hurriedly to her husband. 'This was what Hill-of-the-Raven meant. *The thing* we were to give back if it was demanded of us. You will have to dig it up.'

'Are your afraid – to be left with them?' he queried.

She shook her head, so he shouldered his spade and went forth to the tree-root to open again that small and uncanny grave, which was dug and filled in seven days before. He brought back the parcel in its folds of fair linen, from which he had shaken the dry earth; the rain which still fell without had not penetrated so deep.

The hand when unrolled from the cloth appeared to be unchanged, corruption had not set in. All this time Nita sat with closed eyes, leaning back in the chair, as if barely conscious of what was taking place. Now she moved when her brother addressed her in their native tongue, and held out the maimed stump of her right arm, from which he unwound the binding cloth, exposing the raw wound. He then united the severed parts, and Joan used afterwards to aver that she heard the bones grate together as they met. And when the bandage was re-wound (a couple of pieces of bark folded in it to keep straight the wrist), she saw the dead fingers move, and the hue of life suffuse them once again.

This was the last of madam Rachel's magic, and of the uncanny events at Hunter's End. The brother lifted Nita to her feet, and half carried, half supported her to the waiting buggy, where his mules were hitched to the post. Both of them were apparently indifferent to the still falling sheets of rain, through which they presently disappeared in the direction of the hills.

The Pipers of Mallory

While my last letter was flying out to you in India, dear Margaret, and your reply flying back to me, a great deal has been happening.

My last letter was all about Jack, wasn't it? – How we met and fell in love and how he was under orders for the war, and so we had to be married in a desperate hurry – such a hurry that it shocked Aunt Winifred, glad as she was to get rid of me.

I told you what I was going to wear, and Jack says I made rather a nice-looking bride (he put it more strongly than that). He was, of course, in khaki, and looked dearer than ever, and half an hour or less turned me into Mrs Frazer. We had only nine days for our honeymoon instead of the three weeks we hoped for, but they were nine lovely days. Then there was the dreadful going away; but, before that came about, the question had to be settled – the question you ask, my dear cousin – what was to become of me while Jack was away in France fighting those horrible Huns?

It was over this Jack and I had our first difference – not a serious difference, for we kissed and made it up at once – when I found out what he wanted me to do. He actually wished me to make my home with his mother in Scotland – fancy that! – to bury myself for months and months in the wilds with a woman I did not know, who would be worse than Aunt Winifred twice over. I had never been free in my life, but always in leading-strings, and I made up my mind I would be free now, quite on my own, to make up for what I should suffer through Jack being away.

I didn't tell Jack that – about wanting to be emancipated. He would not have understood. I told him what was quite true – that I wanted to make my V.A.D. training of use, and do war work of sorts in a London hospital, like Violet Power. And my plan was that Violet and I should take a flat together, a tiny flat, which would cost next to nothing (I thought), near enough to her hospital to be convenient, a hospital which needed helpers, and would find work for me, too.

Jack did not like it. Dear fellow! He is one of the old-fashioned sort who thinks women should be hedged about and protected, and give themselves up to looking after their household concerns; but he gave in when he saw I was determined.

That was nearly at the end of our time together – our lovely time. He had planned to take me up to Mallory, to say goodbye at the end of his leave, but having to go off suddenly altered that. However, he made me promise I would go there alone as soon as he left, to pay my mother-in-law a long visit before I settled down with Violet in the flat. Over that I was obliged to yield (with some private reservation about the *long*), for, as you will understand, I could not say 'No' to him just then.

Well, we parted, and it was a hard parting. He put me in the night train for the North, before he left to cross over to France. Peters, his mother's servant, was to meet me in Edinburgh and take care of me from there; you see, I could not get away from the 'take care'.

Now you will know from my letter, the 'Jack' letter, that I had never seen Lady Heron. She is always more or less of an invalid, and bronchitis, or something like that, prevented her taking the long journey to be present at our wedding. Fancy having attacks of bronchitis, and yet living up there in the North! She has been a widow for many years, and Jack is her only son; there is a son by a former marriage, Jack's half-brother, who is now Lord Heron. The Frazers are poor in these days, but Jack's mother has an income of her own, though I do not think it is a large one. Mallory is the old family place – mind you pronounce it right – *Mal*-lory, and not the other way. I suppose Lady Heron would not live there if Heron married, but he is still a bachelor, and with the regiment somewhere in France. Jack does not say much about his half-brother. I fancy the two are not very good friends.

Peters was waiting for me on the Edinburgh station, and by that time I was feeling rather better, and able to take an interest in what was new. Breakfast was ready for me at an hotel, with no bill for it, as Peters paid everything. I was 'her leddyship's guest', he said, and it was by Lady Heron's orders; he seemed quite hurt when I offered. A very good breakfast it was, and I was hungry, for I had been far too wretched to eat any dinner the night before. Then, after rest and refreshment, I had to sally forth again to a different station, Peters carrying my hand-luggage. And when we gained the street – that wonderful street with the Castle opposite, standing up grey against the morning sky – there was a skirl of wild music coming towards us, with the tramp of marching feet.

A skirl. That is the right word for bagpipes, as perhaps you know. I dare say you have heard them in India, as there are Scottish regiments there, but I had never heard them before. Their music may be barbaric – people say so; but there is something about it that fires the blood – that fired my blood, though I am only a Scotswoman married and not born. I could understand how it put spirit into the tired feet which were following, muddy from a long route march, as they kept time to the swing and beat of the brave tune. Jack belongs to a Highland regiment, of course, the same that Heron is in. And at that moment I felt prouder than ever to be Jack's wife.

'I suppose Lady Heron has a piper at Mallory, has she not?'

It was the first question I had put to Peters. I had the notion that a piper must be a necessary appendage to every Highland family of importance; Lady Heron would not of course detain a young man, but she might so employ some old retainer, past the age to be of service in the war. But the servant shook his head. He, too, is quite elderly – did I say? – and speaks broad Scotch, though his name might as well be English.

'No, mem,' he answered, 'we her no piper at Mallory. Her leddyship does not like the pipes.'

Not like the pipes! How odd of her, I thought. And upon this scrap of information the latent opposition which I had felt towards Jack's mother from the beginning swelled and took shape. How strange of a woman who had soldier sons – a son and a stepson – and who wrote as if she were proud of them and their calling; and of one who I knew from Jack was Highland bred to the backbone!

Throughout the journey north-west, now great hills looming up through mist, now by the side of rushing streams, I was thinking of my mother-in-law, and how much easier it would have been to meet her for the first time if Jack had gone with me to Mallory. I was afraid of her, to tell the truth, and that made me brace myself beforehand to be defiant, picturing a great lady who would stand on her dignity, and think Jack might have done better for himself than in marrying me, an Englishwoman of no particular family and small fortune. She would condemn, she would dictate, she would want to interfere.

The day wore on; the train was not a fast one, and there were frequent stoppages, and every hour Peters would come to the window to know whether I wanted anything. But at last there came the station where we alighted for Mallory.

There was a car to meet us, and in less than half an hour Mallory came into view. Not the fine place I had been picturing to myself, only a moderate-sized country-house, but possessing a tower with corner-turrets in the Scottish fashion, which gives it some distinction. The rest of the house is low, with thick walls of undoubted antiquity. The windows are small, but beyond them there are lovely views.

It was only a confused impression I derived from that first entrance – of a hall warm with firelight, decorated with heads of beasts, and skins and weapons, of a room beyond, also warm, and of a frail little lady rising from her chair at the window, and coming lamely across to greet me with an embrace and a kiss.

Such a frail little lady to be the mother of a great, strong man like Jack! She, like the house, was not what I expected, but I was right in two particulars. She is *grande dame* to the fingertips, and I am certain she views me critically.

2

On further acquaintance I like Lady Heron better than I expected, and I have been able to express myself somewhat enthusiastically in writing to Jack; this will please him. I would give a good deal to know what her letter – the long letter I saw her writing – said to him about me. She is kind to me, painstakingly kind, but still we are strangers to each other, and I think it likely we shall be strangers to the end. That she is fond of Jack ought to knit a bond between us, but somehow I strongly suspect it is the very thing which holds us apart.

She is always testing and appraising me, though not in the way I expected; she tells me little anecdotes of Jack's youth, and watches to see if I receive them with the enthusiasm I ought; she shows me some cherished pictures – stupid, old-fashioned photographs of Jack as a baby, Jack as a toddler learning to walk, and upwards at various stages of his boyhood. It is plainly my duty to care about these, but I don't particularly; they seem too far removed from the Jack I know. The pictures bore me, and I shudder inwardly when a new anecdote is presented. And, sitting here in the chair of truth, I must confess it – I find Mallory dull.

My chief amusement is going out for rambles by myself, rambles Lady Heron is too lame to share; she can only walk up and down the terrace with her stick by way of exercise, and that at the sunniest time of the day. The surroundings here are certainly beautiful, and the

Highland people interest me. I talk to them when I have a chance, and try to get accustomed to their way of speech. It was from one of these Highlanders I found out the reason why Lady Heron does not like the pipes.

I never put the question to her. I do not know why not, as it would have been a simple thing to ask, but whenever it came into my head, something happened to divert the thought and keep the words unspoken. But that thrilling pibroch heard in Edinburgh seemed to haunt me here at Mallory, though not always the same tune. I dreamt of it the first night I was here; it waked me from sleep as a real thing might have done; but when I listened in the deep, country stillness and the darkness of the unfamiliar room, there was not a sound. And each time I walked in the direction of Glen Fruin I heard it with my waking ears, very faint and far in the distance, but I could be certain it was there.

I went some way up the Glen on the third occasion, hoping to get nearer to the sound, but it seemed to recede as I approached; the preliminary skirl, and two or three bars of a tune, as if the musician were practising, and then a fault and silence. Presently my watch warned me I should return, for Mallory is a punctual household, and Lady Heron would be waiting tea. I was well on my way home when I met an old shepherd I had spoken to before, and, as I still heard the music at intervals, I bethought myself to ask him: 'Who is it about here who plays the pipes? Somebody is practising away there in the Glen.'

Highland fashion, he met my question by another, and his shaggy brows drew together. 'You be the leddy Frazer, be you not?'

I was Mrs Frazer, I told him.

'Eh, weel, ye are Frazer married, and so have a fight to bear. 'Tisn't lucky for the Frazers when the pipes are sounding in Glen Fruin, but the Lord be thankit that they don't come lower down! I do not look to hear them mysel', being nobbut Steenson that was once Macgregor.'

This was pretty well Greek to me.

'Why isn't it good for the Frazers?' I demanded.

'Ye've never heard the legend? Mebbe 'tis not for the likes of me to tell ye, but seeing as ye ask – Time gone by the chief of the Frazers had his pipers equal with the best, always seven of them in his tail, and callants growing up to take the place – and a proud place it was – of them as were short-winded or old. Glen Fruin was full of folk in those days, where there's nought now but a wheen ruins, or a square in the green to mark where walls have been. And custom was that Frazer's pipers should be chosen from the Glen Fruin folk.

'That was a time of battles, same as now, and the Frazers were up in arms. I don't mind the name of the battle, no, nor how long ago, but there was a great slaughter, and the Frazers fell to a man, and the pipers with their chief. It is said there was none to fill their places, for the callants had not been instructed, and the head of the clan was nobbut a wailing bairn. And since that day the Frazers have had no pipers – the Frazers of Mallory. Mebbe that is why the dead men are not content, and when a Frazer is about to die they are heard piping in Glen Fruin.'

I am putting down the old man's words as nearly as I remember them, but I dare say I spell them wrong. As I listened a cold shiver went down my spine and crept among the roots of my hair; if my hair had been undone I think it would have stood up with fright.

'Why, you don't mean to say,' I stammered, 'you don't mean to tell me that what I have been hearing is a ghost? A ghost in broad daylight and in the open air! And who is it who is going to die?'

'You needn't be afeared, my leddy, for him as is your own. There's a many Frazers at the war besides, and the pipers pipe the same for a death in bed. There's John Frazer near his end at the Mill, and mebbe 'tis for him. He has a son fighting, and Donald Frazer, farmer, has two more. Ye need na fear for the heads of the clan, or for their womenfolk, unless the pipers come right down to Mallory, and go round the house.'

'Do they come as close as that?' I asked, shuddering.

'Ay, my leddy, that they do. And they are heard by all of the Frazer name, and sometimes by them as are not so called, but I never heard tell of their being seen. It is just a sound and no more, sometimes a lament on the pipes, sometimes a fine march for them as fall. And they go once round for a woman, and twice for the heir, and three times for the head of the clan. They went three times round the house when the late lord died, and there was many who heard them, together with my Leddy Heron hersel'. And ever since then she hasna been able to bear the pipes, the real pipes, and they are warned not to come nigh.'

After that I wondered no more at what Peters had told me in Edinburgh. The faint, far-off skirling, which had sounded even while old Steenson was speaking, ceased as I hurried back, but Mallory looked a dark blot in the prospect, dismal as it had never seemed before. Was it because of this superstition that Lady Heron had grown old and grey before her time? It would be awful, I thought, to live here year in and year out, eternally listening for those notes of doom. What should I do, I, a married Frazer, if I heard them circling round the house, and if it meant that Jack – ?

I tell you frankly what was my first impression; afterwards some healthy scepticism came to my relief. An old man's story of impossible ghosts – where was the need to credit it?

Through that day and the next everything moved on velvet – the quiet, regular hours, the careful service, the slightly formal ways with an old-world atmosphere about them, which I found piquant and attractive when not in one of my impatient moods. And I was perhaps more patient, more inclined to be appreciative, because the weeks of my visit had nearly run out; very soon now I should be setting out to establish myself with Violet at the flat, in the midst of London and life.

I was softened, too, because Lady Heron appeared to recognise my right of choice as to what I would do in Jack's absence. All she said was: 'Your home is here, my dear, when you care to have it so. When you wish to come back to Mallory you have only to let me know.'

Then I heard her sigh softly to herself, perhaps because she recognised that I did not care. I thanked her and said I would write, and she replied: 'I think I shall know without telling.' An odd thing to say.

On the next evening, which was the last but one, we were sitting together in the half-light with the windows open, for although it was late October the weather was still warm. I was holding wool for Lady Heron to wind, and was so close in front of her and could clearly see her face, when, in the distance, and a mere thread of sound, but perfectly distinct, I heard the skirl of the pipes.

I do not think my hands trembled, held out stiffly with the skein, but hers did in the effort to wind. The thin, faint music came near, nearer, and then seemed to turn away. Not to the house; for all my cherished unbelief. I was thankful that it was not coming to the house.

Lady Heron had dropped her ball of wool, and now stooped to regain it.

'We will not wind any more now, my dear,' she said. 'I am obliged to you, but I shall have enough.' And then she crossed the room and rang the bell, a hanging bell-pull, old-fashioned like all else at Mallory. Peters came quickly; was it only my fancy that he looked disturbed?

'We will have the windows closed now and the lamp lit.' Such was her commonplace order. I heard no more of the pipes that night, but next morning came the news that John Frazer, the tenant of the Mill, had passed away.

It was no doubt a coincidence, nothing more, but we may put it down as an odd one. That was the day before yesterday. I left early yesterday morning, Peters going with me as far as Edinburgh, and I have been busy writing, writing, all these hours in the train. What a packet you will have to wade through!

3

You have been good, dear Margaret, in liking my letters about the hospital work, although while I was so busy they could only be scraps. (And, what was worse, I am afraid my letters to poor old Jack in the trenches were scrappy too. Ungrateful, perhaps, for I have lived all this while on his scraps to me.)

But to go back to the hospital. You will be surprised to hear that I have had to give up my work there, which is a great disappointment. But everything has been horrid of late. I am alone in the flat. The beginning of the upset was that Violet turned horrid; wasn't it nasty of her, when we had been such chums? I told you about Captain Bridgwater, who used to come to see us after he left the hospital; he was cousin to some of Violet's people, and an old schoolfellow of Jack's. It seemed right and natural to be friends, as that was so; I liked him in the beginning – really I liked him very much, and was pleased when he showed that he liked me. But Violet liked him in a different way, and expected a flirtation they had begun years before to have a serious meaning; she declares it would have meant something serious if it had not been for me. So we had a quarrel, and she said dreadful things, and I was indignant, as I had a right to be, and was not sorry when she packed her boxes and gave up her share of the flat, leaving me alone.

I was not sorry, but I was shaken by it, and it so happened that when Captain Bridgwater came in he found me crying. Then he was horrid, too, and said things – things that at first I did not understand, and that he had no business to say to Jack's wife, he who had been Jack's friend. I shall never speak to him again, you may be sure.

After this I went to the hospital, to my work as usual, but I did not feel a bit like myself. I had a fainting fit for the first time in my life, and they were a long while in bringing me to. Afterwards the doctor told me I should have to give up V.A.D.-ing. I am not strong enough.

I am wondering what I ought to do. Jack would not like me being here by myself. He only consented to the plan because Violet was joining me, and I do not know of anybody else. But nothing on earth will induce me to go back to Aunt Winifred.

I was interrupted there, and now where do you think I am continuing my letter? I am writing in the train, the Scotch express, and I am on my way to Mallory. There is a surprise for you, and a surprise for me, but I begin to think it is the best solution of the difficulty that could have been found. Lady Heron sent for me, and the queer thing is how she could have known or guessed. I begin to think my mother-in-law must be a bit of a witch.

Where I broke off above was when the servant came in to say a man named Peters had called and had brought a letter. It was a kind letter, so kind a letter that it made me cry, though that is saying little, as tears have been close to my eyes of late. The rigours of winter were past, Lady Heron wrote; the days were already lengthening into spring; a visit would give her the utmost pleasure, and she fancied it might now suit me to come to her again. Peters was her messenger instead of the post, and if I were willing Peters would arrange my journey, and spare me all trouble about it, as indeed he has done. And it was not necessary for me to write. Peters would send her a wire, and a warm welcome would await me.

So here I am travelling North. And I think you will agree it has been a wise decision, and one that will please Jack as things are. I shall post this to you in Edinburgh, my dear, and write again from Mallory.

4

Really, Margaret, I am happy to be here, much happier than I was before. Lady Heron is so kind, and I think we understand each other better than we did. I have a lovely room on the south side of the house, and the air is far milder than you would suppose. We never say anything about the pipes, but I fancy they must have been heard twice at least while I was in London, because two more of the Frazers have fallen; sons of the people at the farm; and another of the clan name died in hospital the week before my return.

Alas! we have heard the pipes again, and I will tell you how. They came at the edge of dusk, not what they call here the murk of the night, but while there was still light enough to see, had there been bodily presence to be seen.

Lady Heron likes me to play to her, and I was sitting at the piano, recollecting old airs, and sometimes crooning a bit of song half to myself, when it seemed as if my music had an echo outside the house. My fingers fell from the keys, and in another moment I was sure what it was, and where.

It came with a sweep, swiftly, devouring space, heard afar, and then immediately close, passing our window, which looked out upon nothing – nothing, not a shadow even, nor the print of a foot. The wild pibroch passed by, but it went circling round the house, and, oh, it was coming back! We both sprang up and met in a close clasp together, each of us calling the other by name. 'Mother!' I cried to her – the first time I have called her so, but it seemed rent from me without thought. It passed the second time, and now there was a cry with it, like a human voice in pain, and again it went circling through the air which had been still, but was rising with a gust of storm.

Twice for the heir! That was what the old man Steenson said, and, oh, me! Jack was the heir. There was a pause of seconds, and then it passed for the third time, the pibroch and the shriek. Afterwards there was a great silence. The wind which had swept with it fell also – if it were wind indeed; and we two women drew apart and looked at each other. Her face was ghastly, and I expect mine was no better.

'Cecily,' she said, 'you know!' And then, 'Who told you?'

Soon afterwards Peters came in to light the lamps, and the old servant's hands so trembled as he performed his task that the glasses clashed and clattered – he who was usually noiseless. He, too, had heard; of that I made no doubt; he had heard even as we.

It was the sign for the head of the house. Lady Heron heard it just so before her husband died. There was some small comfort to us both in the belief that it came for Heron and not Jack. But that comfort did not last. The telegram from the War Office came two days after – 'WOUNDED AND MISSING, BELIEVED KILLED' – the intimation to Lady Heron about both her sons, Lieut-Colonel Lord Heron, and Captain the Hon. John Frazer; not one alone, but both.

I cannot write about that time. A chink was left to us through which hope came, but one could hardly look at it in face of the awful doubt. And the sign for the head of the house would stand also for Jack, provided Heron had been the first to fall.

5

Looking back I cannot think how we endured the suspense. Counted by days the measure of it was not long, but it seemed as if ages went by. We tried to comfort each other; Lady Heron was an angel to me through all her own pain; but for her I would have died.

I cannot write about it; you must take it for granted, and I hurry on to the end. We were sitting together, we two alone, as we were when the sign came. Lady Heron was knitting, feverishly knitting at those socks for Jack which she would not lay aside, little as either of us believed they would be worn. We were together, as I said, when Peters rushed into the room with another telegram on his silver tray. (I wonder he remembered the tray.) Lady Heron tore it open; it was addressed to her. 'HOME SLIGHTLY WOUNDED. WITH YOU AND CECILY TOMORROW – JACK.'

My mind takes a leap from that moment to another when he stood at the door. Lady Heron would not let me go to the station because I had fainted again, and as I might not, she would not either; she said it would be unfair to take the advantage. Jack at the door, a figure in soiled khaki, very pale, with his head bandaged and his arm in a sling; Jack himself, alive and still to live. My Jack; and I do not mind now, as once I did, that he is his mother's Jack as well.

He had been through dreadful things. Heron fell – poor Heron – and was left in No Man's Land, and Jack went after him. At the utmost risk to himself he dragged out his brother from under a pile of dead, and into the shelter of a shell-crater. There they existed for three days under incessant fire, all hope of them being abandoned; existed by a miracle, for it was death to move. Heron was fearfully wounded, but Jack, wounded himself, managed so to bandage him that the bleeding stopped; and then he found some emergency rations on which they sustained life. If there ever were a coldness between the brothers, as I thought, it must have melted away in those dreadful hours.

On the fourth day our troops attacked again on the farther side of the wood, which diverted attention, and then Jack began the task – the difficult and painful task – of half-carrying, half-dragging Heron to where he could be helped, as his only chance of life. All this time Jack was wounded himself, in the head and on the shoulder and side, but the burst of shrapnel which shattered his arm did not happen till they were close to our own lines. By this Heron was wounded again, but in any case Jack thinks he could not have survived; the doctor at the dressing-station said so. Heron died there, but not till some hours later, and Jack was with him to the last.

So the pipers were right and not wrong when they bewailed the head of the house who had fallen. What it meant to Jack I did not consider then, and it came on me with a shock of surprise when Peters, some time later, addressed him as 'my lord'.

But I think more – much more – of the fact that he has been recommended for the Cross.

The Whispering Wall

My story begins before the war, though not long before. We were a party of light-hearted undergraduates in Jack Lovell's rooms at Cambridge, and we had been laughing uproariously over some story of psychical marvels. Jack was the only one of us who took the matter seriously.

After the others had gone, I said to him: 'Surely you didn't believe that farrago of nonsense Smith was telling, did you? I was surprised to hear you argue that it might be true.'

'Only that it might be true, not that it was. I saw no impossibility; that was all.'

'Why, old man, you do surprise me! You are the last fellow I should have thought likely to give in to spooks.'

Jack was smoking; he knocked out his pipe before he answered, and began to fill it with deliberation.

'And you would have been right, when the evidence was hearsay. But the position alters to one who has heard and seen.'

'Why, you don't mean to say that you have – '

Jack had his pipe between his teeth again, so he merely nodded. But the nod was enough.

'My dear old Jack! But you haven't reflected what cheats these mediums are. They are past masters as conjurers – have to be, and all their spooks are faked. I know a fellow who is a Psychical Researcher, and he says – '

'I have not been to mediums. My people live in a house up north which has a queer reputation. The old wing is practically shut up, because of what you call spooks: a ghost that is heard rather frequently, and sometimes seen.'

'And you do not suspect anyone of playing tricks?'

'What, for a hundred and fifty years on end?' Jack seemed to consider the question, and then he shook his head. 'There is no trick about it. No.'

'Before I believed, I should have to hear and see for myself, and investigate a lot to make sure. I would rather like to try.'

'Then come down to Marchmore with me next week. We go down then, as you know. You will be very welcome. You are not fixed anywhere else?'

I had no fixtures, and I accepted the invitation then and there. I received the welcome he promised me, and Jack did not proclaim me a ghost-hunter, or give me away.

Marchmore was a larger house than I expected: Jack was not one who said much about his family. It was built on three sides of a quadrangle, of which the iron gates supplied the fourth, and surrounded by a stretch of parkland. The centre was the family dwelling, with an older wing on your left as you faced the entrance, and a quite modern one on the right, which contained the servants' quarters. The guest-chamber allotted to me was in the centre building, but Jack's rooms, bedroom and sitting-room together, were on the first floor of the old wing, which was supposed to be the habitat of the ghost.

I went off to smoke with Jack when we retired for the night, and found him pleasantly established, with cheerful light and fire, lounge-chairs, and every comfort. I suppose I was impatient, for I said as soon as we were alone: 'When is the entertainment going to begin, and where is it to be held?'

I do not think Jack quite liked his spooks taken in that spirit. 'I told you I could not answer for it, and you might be disappointed,' he returned with some sharpness in his voice. 'It may happen at any moment, or you may have to wait for it – days, or even weeks. But as to where it happens, I can show you now. Come upstairs with me.'

He took up the lamp, and led the way out to the landing, where he unlocked a door which shut in an enclosed staircase leading to the attic floor.

'Come up here whenever you like,' he said; 'you will have a better chance alone.'

The stairs were uncarpeted, with a window behind them at the top, which lighted a narrow passage under the pitch of the high tiled roof. A closed door faced us at the end, and there were also doors to right and left.

'You can look into all these rooms,' Jack said. 'You will find them empty, as we do not use them, even for lumber. But it is here in the passage that you must listen for the voice.'

The place was grim enough. I confess I did not care for it, but I was not going to show the white feather.

'You haven't told me yet what I should hear.'

'It is a sort of whispering which travels along the wall on the left, beginning quite away at the end; and as it draws near and passes you it gets distinct.' He touched the side wall of the passage as he spoke.

'Hum – some acoustic peculiarity?' I suggested.

'Very likely! I have often thought that, but the sound shapes itself into words, and sometimes – not always – they have meaning. Probably they differ to each hearer. I cannot say how they would come to you.'

We stood in silence for a while, and nothing happened; the place was close and oppressive with its one window closed – indeed, there seemed to be some unnatural deadness about the air. Jack moved first.

'It will not come tonight, so we had better go down,' and he led the way with his lamp. At the foot of the staircase he locked the inclosing door, but left the key standing; and I confess to a certain relief when we were back in his pleasant sitting-room, and the ghost hunt was over for the night.

Marchmore had other attractions, but I tore myself away from them next morning on the pretext of letters to write in Jack's room. I did write one or two, that there might be some correspondence of mine in the letter bag as a result; but these epistles were of the briefest. Then I sought the attic staircase, closing the door after me to prevent surprise from below. The narrow passage, with its blank surroundings of shut doors, lighted only from the window behind me, was hardly more cheerful on a daylight view. I did not believe in the thing; I was determined not to believe in it; but, despite my scepticism, I experienced a creeping thrill about the spine, and an odd sensation in my ears, which were strained to listen.

The silence, however, was absolute. Of course, I said to myself, this happened to be a still day, and no doubt the phenomenon depended on the wind whistling round the caves and crannies of the old house. Then I turned my attention to the five shut doors.

Those on the right and left opened into four narrow garrets, empty as described to me; two of them lighted with small dormer windows, the other two by oblongs of thick glass let into the slope of the roof; dismal chambers, which, apart from the ill reputation of this upper floor, would hardly be chosen for occupation.

The fifth door at the end of the passage opened into a much larger and more cheerful room, which had the advantage of a broad, low window, nearly the width of the front gable, and also of a rusty fireplace at the side. Probably at some distant date children had used it for a playroom; it was empty of furniture, but in one corner was a dilapidated rocking-horse, and a lidless box half-full of broken toys.

I wondered who were the children who had once played here unafraid; and then as I turned away from the toy-box, as if caused by its suggestion, I had the brief illusion that one of them stood beside me: a little fair-haired lad in a belted pinafore. Of course, it was a trick of the imagination, and I quickly saw how it was caused. This room also had a glazed pane let into the roof, and sunshine through the parting clouds had thrown down, on to the floor below, a shaft of light.

After that I went downstairs, but I resolved not to mention that odd fancy of mine to Jack, as he might attach to it some psychical meaning. He had described to me no visible ghost; he had spoken only of the whispers, and these I had not heard.

I was in Jack's room the third evening of my stay, and we had been discussing quite other matters. I had not even the ghost in mind, when there was a patter of footsteps overhead, quick small footsteps, like a child's. They seemed to run across the large attic and along the passage, and presently back again over the uncarpeted floors.

'What is that?' I exclaimed.

Jack did not give a direct answer. 'It often comes before the whispers,' he said. 'If you come upstairs now, I believe you will hear.'

He took the lamp and led the way. I noticed that he needed to unlock the door shutting in the staircase. His light showed the passage empty and doors shut, and the pattering footsteps had ceased.

We stood as before, facing the wall on the left; and presently, at the far end, the whispering began. However caused, it was undistinguishable from a human voice, and, as the whisperer approached, the vague sounds formed themselves into spoken words, but words without meaning. '*Ah Mont*,' and again '*Ah – Mont*,' and then, with a sort of sighing gasp, it added, '*Year*.'

The voice died away to our left, above the hollow of the stairs; and then, after the interval of a couple of minutes, began again by the shut door. The same words were repeated as it approached us the second time, and after that the stillness was unbroken. Jack, still holding up his lamp, opened the five doors one after another, and showed the rooms empty.

Then we went down into the smoking-room, locking in the ghost as before. 'Well,' he said, 'can you account for it?'

'No,' I answered.

After we had settled back in our respective chairs and relit our pipes, Jack asked: 'Did you distinguish words?'

'Yes,' I replied, and told him what I had heard. 'Is it always the same?'

'I heard it just as you did, and the phrase was new. I have no idea what it means. The words sometimes are: "Come and play" – as if a child spoke them.'

The impression was too recent and vivid to allow of jesting, as I might have jested once. I enquired if there were any legend which explained the haunting.

'No legend. But there is a saying that if one of us Lovells sees the child, he will not live to have children of his own.'

I heard no more while I was at Marchmore, and, the day but one after, my visit came to an end.

That fateful summer of 1914 brought many changes. Jack Lovell and I ceased to be students at the University. We both joined the Army, and went out immediately after the retreat, so we were in the November fighting, half-forgotten now amidst all that had come after, but it was mentioned in the dispatches as 'heavy'.

A village was held by our regiment against stubborn assaults, repulsed with the bayonet. Jack Lovell was wounded, how severely we others did not know, for there was much confusion.

He was sent down to the base hospital; and two days after that I got a shrapnel tear on the shoulder – a surface affair, but it began to look angry, and so I too was ordered down. I asked at once for Jack, and was deeply distressed to be told his hurt was serious, and he was not expected to live.

I was allowed to see him, and presently was at his bedside, with his hand in mine. His face looked grey and pinched; it was hardly the face I knew.

'You'll be going back to England, Eccles, lucky fellow!' he said presently, and he smiled – such a wan smile it was.

He would come too, I answered; he mustn't lose heart about himself; you know the sort of thing one says, even when it is a lie.

'Yes, but not the way you will,' he answered. 'The child at Marchmore wants me; he was always whispering for me to come and play. And you know what you heard at the wall: what we both heard there. I've been thinking about it tonight. You know the place where we were fighting? Tell me the name of it – Eccles – tell me!'

Was he wandering? I thought so. But, of course, I answered him. 'It was near Armentières.'

'Wasn't that what the voice whispered? You heard it too. *Ah-mont-year*. Why, of course it was! I know what he was driving at, though I did not understand it then. It's all as it should be.'

And then again he smiled, and, turning his face from me, appeared to fall asleep.

I went home for my wound to heal, but he remained behind. That is, what was mortal of him; for I left the best pal I ever had laid in a soldier's grave in France.